Praise for *The Last Voyage of the Marigold*

"A talented new voice in crime fiction, a story of murder, revenge and greed set on the high seas, written by a former nuclear submarine captain. You really don't want to miss this one."

—Mike Lawson, Edgar Award Nominated author of the Joe DeMarco series

"Dan Moore knows his way around ships and the sea. He takes the reader on a suspense-filled ride halfway around the world to places most have neither seen nor heard of. Captain Johnny O'Scanlon's fortunes are made and lost as readers follow a rollercoaster ride of conspiracy, betrayal, and a greedy hunt for gold. His literary descriptions of places and characters draw the reader deep within a tale of twists to the very last page."

—C.R. Bell, Vice Admiral USN (ret.)

"Johnny O'Scanlon loves the sea but bridles at his grandfather's advice to end the family's shipping company, scrap their last freighter, and start a new career. Help seemingly comes when Dillon O'Connor, a shadowy figure from his grandfather's Irish IRA past, offers a tempting deal.

"Underwritten by O'Connor, Johnny sails *Marigold* one last time. He is served by an unknown crew and must follow a rigid schedule to reach the west African coast on time to transport O'Connor's lucrative cargo. Misfortune, treachery, and greed plague *Marigold*'s every sea mile and foreign port call. Johnny faces financial ruin, or worse, unless he can decipher his grandfather's cryptic hints of ill-gotten gold. Journey with author Dan Moore through a story of mystery, thrill, and seaworthy adventure."

—Mary Davidsaver, author of *Clouds Over Bishop Hill* and *Shadows Over Bishop Hill*

Other Titles by Pearl City Press

Married, Living in Italy by Misty Urban

Books by Writers on the Avenue

Winter Holidays in the City of Pearls

Climbing the Hill of Life

From River to River

Everything Old is New Again: 30 Years of WOTA

The Last Voyage of the Marigold

DAN MOORE

Muscatine, Iowa

Published in the United States by Pearl City Press
An imprint of Writers on the Avenue

This is a work of fiction. All characters, incidents, and events are products of the author's imagination or are used fictitiously with no relation to actual persons or events.

For permission to reproduce selections from this book, contact Pearl City Press pearlcitypress@writersontheavenue.org

ISBN-13: 978-1-7369498-2-5

DEDICATION

To my grandsons:
Hayden, Boone, Wesley, and Landon

THE LAST VOYAGE
OF THE *MARIGOLD*

CALCUTTA • • CHITTAGONG

•
DIEGO GARCIA

• MAHAJANGA

ACKNOWLEDGEMENTS

The quote on page 59 comes from Rocco Fiammetta's *The Miraculous Fever-Tree: Malaria and the Quest for a Cure that Changed the World* (HarperCollins, 2003), p. 156.

Contents

The
Last Voyage
of the
Marigold

Chapter 1

FROM MY WINDOW overlooking the Dublin docks, I saw my ship, *Marigold*, riding easily at the pier. Her transom nameplate showed dull black against her light blue hull. Smaller letters beneath read *Dublin*.

A few rust streaks from the deck scuppers ran down her sides, but overall, she was in good shape—good enough to earn money still, if I could just get the bookings. Lately, these were harder and harder to come by.

Behind me, the toilet flushed.

"You okay, Pop?"

"Yeah, yeah, I can still wipe my own arse, thank you very much."

The door to the bathroom opened. My grandfather, stooped and holding on with both hands, shuffled his walker across the floor, turning the light off behind him.

"You need a new roll, laddie."

He plopped down in the captain's chair, in my opinion the most comfortable chair anywhere in the world, though it had no cushion. The old furniture makers knew best how to form fit hardwood to the human anatomy, much better than modern upholsterers ever did. I could sit for hours in that chair, and I had. I only tired of it when I had the need to go to sea.

"When are you going to change the name on the door, Johnny?" my grandfather asked. "It's been your business now for near half a decade. You should name it O'Scanlon's, not TC Miriam."

1

His comment caught me off guard. My grandfather and grandmother, Miriam, had raised me since I was four, when both my mother and father died. That was thirty-one years ago. When I was in my teens, Grandfather introduced me to the sea by taking me on cargo deliveries across the Channel and as far away as the Baltic. Once I finished my university degree, I earned my merchant mariner's license and served as an officer, beginning as first mate and, for the last five years, as captain of the *Marigold*.

"You know, Pop, Grandmother's name brought you luck for a long time. I think we should stick with it at least a little longer."

"She's smiling down on you, Johnny, me lad. I guess there's no harm in the name staying up there a little longer. But sooner or later you'll have to admit the facts. You no longer have five ships working for ya'. You're down to just the *Marigold*."

"But we're still making a little, Pop."

"And that's because I man the phones and run the office while you're at sea. I've said it before, Johnny. You need to sell the works while you can. It's time.

"You're doing a grand job 'cause you know your business. It's just that business in small lot, bulk sea cargo is getting harder to find. I watch you working hard at it all the time—drumming up clients and keeping the crews happy between runs. I'd hate to see you spending the rest of your young years in a failing enterprise when you could be starting something with more promise. Don't stick with this because you think you owe me or your grandmother something, God rest her soul. The sea has always been part of my life; that doesn't mean it has to be in yours. Sell out! Get some money to fund a head start on your future."

As much as it hurt my pride, I knew he was right. Customers were still gratified at hearing the gruff voice they'd grown accustomed to when calling to book cargos. But that wasn't enough to make ends meet. TC Miriam was no longer a profitable proposition.

Grandfather had put me in charge five years ago when the clutches of old age told him he couldn't go to sea anymore. The business was still good then, not like it was now.

Work as I might, the orders for coastal sea cargo just weren't that plentiful. The long-haul freight giants could stuff a thousand times the deadweight we could into their neat containers and keep efficient track of it all with computers. Shipping small lots of bulk cargo, like we did, was almost a thing of the past. And clients were more than willing to pay the extra tare for air freight, just for the convenience of speed. With my one tired old coastal freighter, I couldn't keep up with them. I knew it, but my pride wouldn't admit it.

"Sell! You can't be serious. How will we pay the bills?"

His urging, no matter how well-reasoned, didn't sit well with me. I'd always been able to do what I set my mind to. If I worked hard, I could bring TC Miriam around to being profitable.

Grandfather wouldn't hear any of my protests. "I didn't get you on with Tommy Corrigan as an apprentice on the longshoreman docks for nothing. He made you a dock manager in a heartbeat. I even made sure you got time at the university so you could learn modern business to help run the company.

"And don't forget, that two-year apprenticeship with Captain Pavel Gorik in Riga got you plenty of experience with handling those big ships he runs out of Estonia up and down the Baltic. There's nothing wrong with your seamanship skills. You could be master on one of those big ships without thinking twice. I say sell out and don't end up like me, just fighting to stay afloat."

"That's your pride talking, Pop, not your common sense. One thing I learned from you was to work hard. I needn't point out there's a big difference between a 690-ton *Marigold* and one of those Maersk 150,000-ton behemoths. I think we can still make a go of it here. So quit complaining about how you can't keep up. That's your frustration reminding you of your bum hip and the diabetes that are keeping you from getting around like you used to."

"Used to! I can't get around at all! And my days of drumming up phone business with longtime clients are getting bleaker. I book a client whenever I can, but it's tough to find paying cargo returning to Dublin to cover the roundtrip costs. When we had five ships running freight from Dublin to West Anglia, Normandy, and maybe past Calais to Jutland, we had a lot of options. Now, not so much."

The hurt welled in his eyes. He wasn't getting to the office as much he used to, having to spend more time in the private nursing home I'd set him up in at the edge of town. This made for a long bus ride from his beloved docks. His robust life at sea was a waning reminder of former times.

And with his wife Miriam gone now for three years, it was all that much harder. Though I loved the stories he told when he reminisced, I needed to get his mind off Miriam and onto something that didn't remind either him, or me for that matter, of our current state of financial stress.

"Okay, Pop. Want to get a drink at the Temple Swan? I know you like a Black and Tan with a Jameson at the end of a day."

His eyes twinkled even as he grunted to stand up from enjoying his panoramic view of the harbor's comings and goings to join me for the two-block walk up the hill to his favorite pub.

"Can we get a meat pie to go with my B&T and chaser?"

"I will if you can maneuver that walker you keep abusing to get your old bones there."

The complications of diabetes and the need for a new hip weighed on his mind, as well as hampering his physical abilities. Maybe he was right. Seeing him struggle like this just to get around, on top of the worsening prospects of an already declining income, forced me to at least consider his advice to sell the enterprise. He and TC Miriam were the only tangible things in my life. Cutting loose of the business might be the only way I could save what I held most dear.

"Come on, old man, get a move on. I know how you like the Temple Swan."

AS WE MADE our way to the pub , I thought of those times I spent with Captain Gorik plying the stormy Baltic waters off Scandinavia, the low countries, Germany, and Poland. He taught me how to sail in heavy weather, pick a crew, and minimize times in port when off-loading and lading cargo because time not at sea meant lost business opportunities. Most of all, I loved seeing the rest of the world. Foreign places fascinated me and satisfied my desire to pursue unknown things: different languages, cultures, and cities. I even bought a camera so I could revisit my travels when I was home in Dublin.

I knew Grandfather was being practical. He didn't want me spending good money after bad. But I didn't want to let him down and was determined to show him I could turn TC Miriam around. I was going to make a name for myself in the shipping business, just as he had.

"I'd swear you're getting taller and handsomer every day, Johnny," the barmaid said, handing me two Black and Tans with a Jameson's back.

"Thanks, Sheila, and you haven't changed a bit." She puffed a lock of hair off her face and whisked me on my way with a flip of her bar rag.

I took the drinks with a smile, happy to be among old friends. The sight of his favorite drink lit up Grandfather's face. He took a long swig and wiped the foam from his mouth with a sleeve. But his respite was short lived as he forced the discussion back to TC Miriam's problems.

"You're wasting time with this firm. You know that, don't you, Johnny? You can't sustain it."

I followed his lead with a swig of my own. It tasted good. I wanted him to relax and not worry, but I didn't know how to make that happen. Then, as was his way, he said something on an entirely different tack.

"Johnny, you should be enjoying life more. Get yourself a girl."

"I've time enough for that later, Pop. Right now, I've got you and the business to worry about."

"Bah! I can take care of myself. And a business is just that...business. But a girl, she'll last forever."

This wasn't the first time he'd floated this argument. "I know, Pop, 'and give you the grandchildren you deserve,' right?"

"And what's wrong with that?"

He started to motion for another round, but I stopped him.

"Pop, you know I love you, but I couldn't give enough of myself to someone else right now, much less take care of a child."

"Just the same, you need to have something in your life besides a worthless enterprise. The cost of running *Marigold* will keep going up even if you're not sailing her. Barnacles grow whether she's sitting alongside the pier or running with a bone in her teeth passing Cape Verde." He gazed at his glass, lost in momentary thought.

His comment caught me off guard. I hadn't heard this story before.

"Cape Verde? *Marigold's* 'na been there."

"Beg to differ, laddie."

He took another swig and followed it with the shot of Jameson. "There's a lot you don't know about me and that ship." He motioned to the keep for another B&T, but this time I made no attempt to stop him. "I did a few things back in the day I'm not too proud of."

"You, Pop? What could you have possibly done that would raise my eyebrows?" I took another swig of my B&T, but only a sip of the Jameson's this time. I'd learned years ago not to attempt to keep up with him during his favorite pastime.

"Running stuff for the IRA was one of them."

He said it matter of factly, as if everyone had done it and it was common knowledge.

"I'm no illusionist or politic fanatic, but it paid the bills. In fact, I made enough to buy the *Marigold*, which at that time improved my profit margin. She was bigger than my other four ships. That gave her a greater range and almost three more knots of speed. Back then, even a half full hold of consignments from Liberia or Angola brought in enough to keep the roof over your and Miriam's heads during those lean years."

Africa? Why was he telling me this now? Was he using a sea story to teach me a lesson—the lesson that I shouldn't be so foolish as to keep this enterprise afloat? As he went on, I searched my mind for what cargo he could have transported from Ireland to a jungle nation. Surely it wasn't fine Irish linens or cut lead crystal.

A noticeable crack entered his voice and a tear drew down his cheek as he paused at the mention of his dear Miriam's name. I couldn't tell if it was the B&T or the Jameson's taking hold or some unsaid memory. I gave him time to regain his composure, which gave me the opportunity to think of a way to find out what he was referring to. Nothing I'd learned growing up ever hinted that he wasn't completely honest and forthright. It was hard to think of a circumstance where he would have had dealings with the likes of the IRA.

"Wasn't that dangerous?"

His voice regained its strength. "Aye, but danger is relative. Not eating is dangerous, too."

"How'd you avoid the Royal Navy? I can't imagine they took kindly to what you were doing."

"A man I knew in Wexford, Dillon O'Connor..."

8

He paused and pursed his lips, as if remembering something unpleasant.

"Was he a partner of yours?"

"Partner, ha!" Then he mulled a thought before saying, "I guess, in a way, he was. Dillon O'Connor did up official dummy manifests that could've fooled the Queen's Privy Council. He could forge any document, passport, or identity papers the IRA told him to."

The first half of his second B&T disappeared.

"This Dillon O'Connor fellow, he was your mate?"

Grandfather looked askance at me. "Mate! He was no mate of mine, or anyone else's, for that matter. However, he had the knack of getting a few of us cargos which paid very well in a day when coastal shippers were going out of business everywhere.

"The first few runs I made were for him. He set them up and hired me, and a few other captains, to deliver the cargos he contracted. After a year or so, he asked if I wanted to earn some extra. He told me I was doing a lot better at making the deliveries than the other skippers— getting in and out of the ports with no questions asked.

"He offered me an extra twenty percent. That made us partners of sorts. The cargos got bigger and I had to travel further. Only a few went to Africa, but the majority were headed from Yugoslavia and Poland to the west coast of Ireland—always in the dead of night.

"I'll say this about O'Connor—get your money and count it twice to make sure he isn't pulling a fast one on you. And never turn your back on him. There was many a time I knew he was overbilling clients, but I didn't say anything 'cause what came to me kept TC Miriam afloat."

"So, he was skimming people?"

"That's a nice way to put it, laddie. Me and the other skippers didn't have to front our own money to fuel and provision our own ships on trips he chartered for us. O'Connor covered everything, and paid us our consignment fees, although not always as timely as we would've liked.

"And that was a rub, because we could all see there was plenty of money sloshing around. I'll admit, I had my own rainy day stash, but I hid it so no one, especially O'Connor, could find it if they went looking. I wasn't proud of it, but I didn't trust O'Connor after seeing what he did to the clients and the IRA bankrollers. I was careful to take the money out of his provisioning funds, never from the cargo funds of the clients, mind you, but..."

I was intrigued, and at the same time found it upsetting that my grandfather had associated with such a person. If it were true, however, and he did hide something for a rainy day, where had he put it?

"The IRA paid for everything in gold—Krugerrands, to be specific. D'you ever see a pile of gold coins? It's impressive. Since they were pure gold, a little bit was worth a king's lot. Prices of the goods we carried were listed by weight, which cut down on conversations with inspectors and the need for interpreters. It was an efficient system—efficient for the IRA, O'Connor, and me."

He stopped to tug on his B&T. "Haaaa!" He smacked his lips. "When it comes to hiding things, the smaller it is, the easier it is to hide."

"Weren't the people who hired you afraid you'd cheat them?"

"The clients weren't the type you'd ever think to cheat, not by a long shot. The penalty for doing that was too dear. I remember when the Senegalese discovered a mate of mine double crossing them, they sliced off his testicles, split his tongue, and gave him a permanent grin by cutting off part of his lower lip."

"Jesus, Mother Mary, and Joseph!" The mental image alone put perspiration on my brow. I had the answer to my question about the people this Dillon O'Connor dealt with, but still knew nothing about the man himself .

If these revelations weren't surprising enough, he continued.

"Being partners with Dillon O'Connor was like partnering with a spider—he built the web and promised to share what he caught, but be careful when it came time to collect. I learned in short order to take care of my own profits because he always paid me late. After almost two years, however, he suspected I wasn't handing over all the payoffs he figured he should be making, and we had a falling out."

"How's that?'

"Like I said, us skippers learned to take our profits where we could. Because Dillon got in the habit of paying us our cuts late, we were short-changing payments before turning the profit over to Dillon. When he suspected he wasn't getting his full share from the clients, he came looking. But not knowing which of us were holding out on him, he became belligerent and harder to deal with. I started looking for a reason to get out of the business. That's when we had a falling out.

"We exchanged words in the office and I told him to get out, that I was done. Your grandmother Miriam was working our books in the office and overheard. After he walked out, she told me we didn't need his kind of help."

"Grandmother didn't like him?"

Pop didn't answer right away. He eyed his B&T then said, "No, she hated him, in spite of the money coming in from his extra deals he set up. She'd never forgiven O'Connor for getting your mom and dad involved in one of his IRA schemes."

"My folks?"

"I never told you about it because you were too young to understand. Dillon needed a courier to take some paperwork to a meeting on the border with Northern Ireland. The regular one wasn't available, he said. The meeting went bad and they were killed by British soldiers."

He took a long pull on his beer. "In any case, she blamed O'Connor for getting them killed. Now you understand why she and I never talked about it. I kept working for him for almost a year so I could steal more gold from him. He owed me and it was the only way I figured I could make him pay. I never told your grandmother about taking the gold, 'cause I wanted to be the only one who knew in case O'Connor started poking

"So how much gold are you talking about?"

"Let's just say it was a good bit. I hid it where neither he, nor anyone else who might choose to look for it, could find it."

"Don't you think now would be a good time to dig it up, to save TC Miriam?"

Grandfather downed the rest of his B&T, then eyed me. "Johnny, as long as Dillon O'Connor is alive, I'll not show my hand with a sudden windfall to bring him nosing around, nor giving him the satisfaction that his suspicions about me were true.

12

"But, that's beside the point. I'm telling you again; you need to cut the losses right now and get a fresh start. Sell *Marigold* and fold the business. You'll be better off in the long run."

"But what if something happened to you and got killed? What good would that gold do anyone if none of us knew where it was?"

Grandfather gave me a look. I couldn't tell if he thought I had an ulterior motive, or if it was a valid question. Then he said. "Don't you worry, Johnny. That will be your nest egg, as soon as Dillon O'Connor finds his rightful place in the afterlife. In any case, I have the location documented in my will on file with our barrister for safekeeping. It will be yours one day. I just can't have that bastard O'Connor finding it as long as he's alive."

As strange as these revelations were, I couldn't imagine that Dillon O'Connor could still keep a grudge alive and behave the same way he had when he was with the IRA. After all, the secession conflict of Northern Ireland ended years ago and amnesty had buried any lingering stigma to the contrary.

FIVE MONTHS LATER, I sat in the office going over the company books. I had to admit Grandfather was right. Business was showing no signs of hope for picking up. The mail contained a tax due notice on the *Marigold*, plus the annual property tax bill on my modest home and office space.

Compounding this was the marginal increase in the monthly private nursing home bill. Pop's physical condition was worsening, and diabetes was taking his eyesight. It wouldn't be long before he would be totally dependent on others for his care—care that was more expensive than I could afford.

Without a better source of income, I'd have to move Grandfather to the state-run facility over fifty miles away. Not being near family would be the end of him if I couldn't see to his proper care on a daily basis.

Additionally, fatigue was taxing his abilities to sustain conversations for long, the conversations I enjoyed so much. If my shipping volume didn't pick up soon, I was going to have to consider finding a partner with the resources to keep me afloat, or worse yet, selling the business outright.

Neither of these appealed to me in the slightest.

When Grandfather arrived on one of his increasingly rare visits to the office later that morning, he saw the opened bills on my desk and the worry on my face. He immediately resurfaced the issue of selling *Marigold*.

"Take her to the Bristol breakers. They'll pay you £200 a ton clear after breaking costs. That should cover the tax bill. Don't worry about me. These doctors don't have much hope for me. I'll be gone before you know it and they'll have to gouge some other poor soul for my bed."

"Come on, Pop, that's a defeatist attitude. I'm not ready to give up yet, and neither should you."

He was rambling. I knew only too well I wouldn't abandon him to his plight. But his comment about selling *Marigold* for scrap finally spurred me to action.

FOR A FEW weeks I tried to find a business partner willing to inject the capital necessary to keep TC Miriam afloat, but the few leads who gave my business proposal any serious consideration couldn't see their way clear to invest after performing their due diligence. About the time I figured all my options were up, I got the most interesting phone call—from Dillon O'Connor.

When I answered the phone, the name didn't click at first. Then I recalled Grandfather's revelations that night at the Temple Swan.

Dillon O'Connor quickly got to the point. "I want you to partner with me in the shipping business."

I was stunned, but managed to say, "Mr. O'Connor, how did you know I was looking for a partner?"

"Let me just say I have a great many contacts in the shipping business. I heard from some colleagues you had contacted."

"Then you know that not one of them saw fit to make me an offer. In retrospect, Mr. O'Connor, I've been doing some serious thinking and I'm not sure continuing with TC Miriam is such a good business idea."

What I told him was true enough. And when I coupled that with my grandfather's comments about the questionable deals between the two of them, leading to their falling out, I determined that to continue talking with him was fruitless.

"Hold on, Johnny. I'm sure with my backing, you and *Marigold* will fit nicely in my company's plans."

He sounded very sure of himself, I had to give him that. "And just exactly what is it you do?"

"I book high-value, small-lot bulk cargos, which clients see as a priority to send, but which other carriers find not worth the risks involved."

"Risks?"

"I'm talking about small bulk that has to be delivered to parts of the world that can't take the deep draft ships like Maersk or Evergreen have. They would have to drop shipment at an intermediate port, one big enough to handle their vessels, and then transship the consignments via rail or truck, adding delays to the process and considerably greater expense."

He stopped talking, but I didn't reply.

"Are you still there, Johnny?"

After a moment's wait, I said, "Mr. O'Connor, I don't know how to say this, but I've made up my mind to sell my ship for scrap."

There was a pause on his end. Then he said, "And where are you going to scrap your ship?"

I realized he was challenging what I'd said about scrapping *Marigold*. He was testing to see if I had a plan.

"There are companies in Great Britain that break ships," I said. "But the Bristol prices for the scrap iron don't compare to the companies in Turkey or Bangladesh that don't have to contend with the same safety or environmental laws."

Cutting up ships, especially those built decades ago, is nasty business with all the asbestos insulation and lead paint. Evidently third world countries didn't have laws mitigating the impact of spreading contaminants to the surroundings. I didn't tell him, but I had figured the difference in what I'd make by sailing 12,000 miles to scrap *Marigold* in Bangladesh, rather than Bristol, was well worth it.

My problem still remained, however. I needed funds to make the journey possible.

"I can tell you've put some thought into this," O'Connor said. "But tell me, Johnny, if you can't afford to run your one remaining vessel, how do you expect to be able to sail her half way around the world to collect the salvage scrap value?"

Dillon O'Connor had all but read my mind. I had a plan but none of the means to carry it out.

"Johnny, are you still with me?"

"Uh, yes, I'm here. I was just thinking."

"I have a suggestion. Why don't you come visit me in Wexford and we can talk about it? I might just have a solution that will satisfy the both of us."

I vaguely heard myself reply, "All right, how about the first of next week?"

"Fine. I look forward to your visit."

I hung up the phone and began rationalizing why I was going to do this, Grandfather's warnings notwithstanding. I could at least listen to his approach to resolve my financial problems. Maybe Dillon O'Connor had mellowed with age. The IRA was defunct, thanks to making peace with Her Majesty's government almost two decades earlier, and now he had legitimate connections with a client base I could work with.

But, for my grandfather's peace of mind, I thought it best not to confide my plan in him.

Chapter 2

EARLY THE NEXT week, I made the trip in my aging Morris Minor down the coast from Dublin to Dillon O'Connor's Wexford address. I worried he might have called the office in an effort to talk to Grandfather. I wasn't ready for Pop to learn I'd been looking for a partner or I was considering a deal with O'Connor. Most of all, I wasn't ready for one of his lectures on the subject.

The village of Wexford hugged the sea port with tree-lined lanes radiating from the waterfront's harbor road. The address I was searching for was set on a side street in a neighborhood of single-family and row houses. A gated fence, overgrown by an arborvitae hedge, bordered the small yard of Dillon O'Connor's home.

I parked a few doors down, thinking this might obscure my arrival should he be watching from a window. I don't know why I needed this small subterfuge, perhaps because I was apprehensive of the outcome of my venture.

When I knocked on the door, I was surprised when a rugged man, robust in stature, answered the door. At first he only opened the door halfway and stared at me with a stern face under a full head of salt and pepper hair. But when I mentioned my name, his face softened. He opened the door and motioned me in.

"Ah, Larry Shaughnessy's grandson. Come in, son. I'm glad you made the trip. I assure you, you'll be glad, too."

He showed me to a living room with a sofa and a single overstuffed, well-worn armchair. Antimacassars,

19

stained from years of use, covered the arms and the backs of each chair. A coffee table, centered in front of the sofa, held a teapot and two cups, and the two end tables had table lamps with shades now yellowed with age. I would have figured his dwelling to be much more elaborately furnished, based on the Pop's stories of O'Connor's high value IRA dealings. For someone who supposedly conducted business dealings in gold, I thought he might have a grander home.

"Tea, Johnny?"

"No, thank you, Mr. O'Connor. If it's all right, I'd like to hear what you had in mind to help me with my plan regarding my ship, *Marigold*."

"Not help you, Johnny, join with you. Now tell me, are you resolved to sell the remaining asset you have? I can assure you, between the two of us, we can make a go of TC Miriam with the connections I have."

With Pop's Dillon O'Connor stories foremost in my mind, I was leery about embarking on a one-time business deal with him, much less an ongoing relationship. "I appreciate that, Mr. O'Connor, but my mind's made up."

He raised his eyebrows and stirred his tea slowly. "And what does your grandfather think of your decision?"

I didn't want to reveal to this man that I hadn't told him of our meeting. So I simply stated, "He's the one who's been trying to get me out of the shipping business."

His eyebrows raised ever so slightly and I barely caught what he said under his breath. "Hmm, I'm sure he has."

"I'm sorry, what was that?"

"Nothing, Johnny, just thinking out loud. Do you know where you want to go to break her up?"

"Yes, I do. I've done the research. What I'm having trouble with is, how do I afford the cost of the trip to reach the breaking yards?"

He eyed me closely and then spoke. "Johnny, I'm not in the charity business. If it's help you want, you'll have to earn it."

The tone in his voice was ominous, devoid of the pleasantries he used before.

I quickly offered, "If it's hard work you're suggesting, I'm no stranger to that. But what is it exactly you're saying I'd have to do?"

"Do? Why, carry cargo, of course. What did you think?"

I wasn't all that sure. I distinctly thought he was playing with me. "Well, I was...I don't want to get involved in something that..."

"That will interfere with your plans to scrap your ship?"

"Uh, yes." I was going to say I didn't want to be involved in anything illegal, but he'd interrupted.

"Johnny, I have several partners throughout the world. Are you up for making the long trip down the Atlantic coast of Africa and around the Cape of Good Hope?"

I hesitated, neither expecting nor being prepared to make a decision that quickly. "Well, I guess..."

"Guess? I thought you wanted to do business."

His constant counterpoint to my comments was dragging me down. Worried that I was looking too unsure, I said, "I do, I just don't know how to hire a crew for a one-way trip halfway around the world."

"Then take your bloody ship to Bristol and get what you can."

His abruptness caused me to lean back slightly. "That doesn't solve my problem. It's not about me. I've got my grandfather's future to consider, not just the dissolution of a faltering business enterprise. I need enough to pay the tax lien and insure for his well-being until I can get a new career started."

I sounded desperate, but I knew he and Grandfather had worked together in the old days to make ends meet. Perhaps a nostalgic appeal might sway him.

"Grandfather told me that years ago you were able to keep TC Miriam and other local shippers going with your IRA connections. I just need to earn enough to make the long trip to the breaking yard. The proceeds from the sale of *Marigold* will secure Grandfather's future."

"Son, I donae know what you've been told, but Mr. Gerry Adams gave up the Cause in 1998, when Sinn Féin retired from the fight by signing the Good Friday Belfast Agreement. We've all given in to more honest livings since then."

Dillon O'Connor paused and looked me over carefully. I knew he was considering something, but what, I wasn't sure.

He continued. "Johnny, I know you're in a hard spot, but I've a business to run. You must understand that the past is the past. Men do what they have to feed their families and keep them safe.

"I'll tell you what. I'm thinking that if I look hard enough for a few days, I can come up with a client with a shipping need you can handle that's valuable enough to pay for your whole trip, perhaps even give you a few thousand Euro profit. No promises, mind you, but I'll check.

"You're a fighter, I can tell. And you're the grandson of Larry Shaughnessy, which tells me a lot. I guess it's the least I can do. You know, I remember your grandfather and his son-in-law, Ben. That would be your father, I take it?"

"Yes, sir."

"It's a shame about your parents. They were good people."

Where was he going with this? I didn't have any personal recollection of my father or mother. Grandmother had told me a few anecdotes over the years, about my mother growing up and meeting my father, but she never mentioned his part in the business.

And from what Pop had told me in the Temple Swan, I knew Grandmother was bitter about my parents' deaths until the day she died and that she blamed Grandfather for getting them involved with Dillon O'Connor in the first place.

O'Connor shook his head. "Ah, I remember when your mom and dad were killed. Your grandmother never accepted their deaths. Even though I explained how I'd also lost my own son in the cause we were fighting for, she remained bitter.

"Anyway, the game today has changed. Now there's legitimate money to be made in supplying the sides that donae have good sponsors—mostly A-rabs."

He pronounced the word with strong emphasis on the A. "At any one time there's three or four different A-rab factions fighting some other A-rab rabble. All of them, A-rabs on both sides, have lots of oil money...and profit is what business is all about. So, they can buy anything they have a mind to. That means I can get you the kind of commission you're needing, Johnny. There's always someone wanting to buy something that pays well to ship."

What he said made business sense to me. There were lots of legitimate materials these oil-rich nations needed, which Europe, Ireland in particular, could supply: machine parts, construction and agricultural equipment—hard goods.

"Mr. O'Connor, I'm an honest man looking for a fair cargo."

I looked directly into O'Connor's eyes; they didn't waver or dart to one side. He didn't blink. His stare froze me and all I could think was that this was the man my grandfather had described as an IRA paymaster. But if he was willing to help me, I could at least wait the next few days to see what he offered.

He broke the impasse and said, almost as if he were family, "Trust me, son, it'll be on the up-and-up. However, I wouldn't go mentioning this to Larry Shaughnessy just yet. Sit tight for a day or two. I'll send a message around to you. I'm still not too keen on using cell phones and such."

My grandfather's warning about never turning my back on Dillon O'Connor flooded back to me. Perhaps his scoundrel days were behind him, perhaps they weren't. As I looked at this aging man in his pedestrian home, I told myself I had been forewarned, but knew I was sharp enough to ensure he couldn't do me any harm.

*

TWO MORNINGS LATER, there was a knock on my door at the boarding cottage where I'd spent some of my dwindling funds for a room and to await word from Dillon. It was the landlady.

"A gentleman dropped this letter off for you, sir." She spoke without a tinge of curiosity or any overt interest, as if she were used to being a messenger.

I thanked her and opened the note. It simply read, "Harbor overlook statue, 11:45 today."

As I headed out just before lunch time, almost as an afterthought I grabbed my camera, figuring I might as well look like a tourist. It was only a five minute walk to the harbor overlook, a semicircular concrete pad with a waist-high railing affording a reasonable view of Wexford harbor. Two people read a plaque beneath a statue of a long-deceased native son, while a few others took in the harbor view.

A teenage boy and girl finished at the railing and backed up to leave when the girl bumped into me.

"Oh, I'm so sorry," she said.

"Quite all right, Miss." By the time I had gotten the words out, she had put a flyer for a local rock concert into my hand and walked away with her boyfriend without comment. About ready to drop the flyer into the public waste can, I noticed there was something handwritten on the reverse side. It read, "The Morrow 10 minutes."

I knew of The Morrow. It was a pub on the other side of the town center. I'd been in there the day before for a beer while killing time awaiting contact from Dillon. It was nondescript and only marginally more entertaining than sitting in my room watching reruns of "Downton Abbey" on the telly.

The short walk from the overlook gave me little time to ponder why all the cloak and dagger. Perhaps secrecy was simply one of O'Connor's quirks. All I really cared about, however, was the chance to get out of my financial bind, and to get on with life for me and Grandfather. I could put up with a few of this man's idiosyncrasies for now.

The inside of The Morrow was dim compared to the morning sunshine. My eyes were still adjusting when a waitress got my attention.

"Follow me, sir." She led me to a booth at the back of the establishment. "Here you are, sir. Please have a seat. Your waiter will be here shortly."

I remained standing for a few seconds to check out my surroundings. The day's lunch crowd was arriving, creating a rising murmur of conviviality as friends greeted and took their seats at tables. A pervasive pub smell of stale beer mixed with the savory odor of the day's luncheon special, both on the verge of being served to a hungry group.

A familiar voice came from the seat deep inside the booth. "Have a seat, Johnny."

Still trying to gain my bearings, I hesitated.

"Sit down, lad, before you attract attention." It was Dillon.

"I thought—"

"From now on, donae think. Just do exactly as you're told. The first thing you're going to do is take this pint, drink a least half of it, and act like you're with a chum you have known since school."

Something was different in O'Connor's voice. It was demanding, not the helpful tone I remembered when we

26

last met. I sat as he instructed and took a large swig from the pint on the table, startling myself at not being able to suppress the ensuing belch.

"Good, lad. Guinness will do that to you." He pushed across a backpack. "Take it, but donae open it here. Inside is a key to a strongbox being placed in your cottage room as we speak. That strongbox contains €7.8M.

"When you get home, deposit it into your account, making sure you can issue drafts on it from overseas if need be. There is also a written web address for a travel company—agents who book tours in Africa. You will go to an internet café in Dublin by midnight tonight and log onto that website. Go to the Contact Us part of the web homepage. There you'll find an address and phone number in Cotonou, Benin. You must be at that address by noon on the twenty-first of next month."

Cotonou? Where the hell was that? I'd never heard of it.

"Someone will greet you upon arrival at the port facilities in Cotonou. A port official will give you information on how to contact him. But if they don't, go to that address and ask for Mr. M'Nasi. He is the man you will be doing business with. When you meet Mr. M'Nasi, you will identify yourself by telling him the name of your ship—"

Everything he described—clandestine meetings, places and people I'd never heard of—was raising red flags in my mind. I knew he saw the doubt in my eyes because he changed tone.

"Johnny, this is a legitimate enterprise. The building supplies you'll be picking up are critically needed on the other end to help refugees. Are you still with me, lad?"

I was torn. I needed this man and the business he was offering. In a call to Pop the night before, I learned the doctors were putting him on a new medicine, one which would strain our budget even further. Additionally, he had received a letter from the city that the wharfage fees for water and sanitation connections were being raised. I simply had to push aside my concerns about O'Connor's circuitous description for obtaining funds and the mysterious person I'd have to locate in the heart of Africa.

I abandoned my lingering doubts and gave in to the intrigue. However I thought of it, O'Connor presented the only practical solution I knew of to resolve my financial problems.

He'd stopped talking and was giving me a look of impatience. "Sorry, yes I'm with you. You were saying I should tell this man the name of my ship...*Marigold*."

"Unless you have bought a new vessel in the last two days, in which case, I would surmise that this entire endeavor is no longer required."

His sarcasm disarmed me. All I could say was, "Does this man speak English?"

We both remained silent for a long moment. I realized he might be reconsidering if I were too naïve to do business with me. But I was the one asking him a favor. He needed a shipper and I needed the job.

Finally, he spoke. "You don't need to concern yourself with Mr. M'Nasi. I've dealt with him many times, and yes, he speaks English. In fact, he speaks it quite well—with a Liverpool accent he gained growing up and attending school there.

"Once you've identified yourself, negotiate with Mr. M'Nasi for a consignment of hardwood logs, eight-hundred-gallon storage bladders, and bundled shake shingles from Niamey, Niger. How much you pay for them is up to you, but you only have €4.1M in that envelope for that. If you make the purchase for oh, say, €3.7M, then you pocket the rest. The other €3.7M are for the final fitting out: diesel fuel, food, and crew's salary. I'm providing a crew for you. If you spend less, you keep it."

My eyebrows went up. I stood the chance to make more than enough to resolve my financial bind and ease my sensibilities. With that much capital, I'd have enough to make the journey and still have a good bit to begin a new career and take care of Grandfather. Besides, shingles, municipal water bladders, and logs seemed innocuous enough.

"But where are these building supplies going? It seems that's a lot of money for—"

He dismissed my question by handing me a piece of paper with the name Chamberlain's, Ship's Chandler, Dublin, with a phone number. This was the first time any part of this conversation had been committed to paper.

I read it. "I've never heard of it, and I've lived in Dublin all my life."

"I assure you it exists…as long as you contact them within the next five days. Any longer and you will not make your contact in Cotonou in time. Chamberlain's will have a suitable crew available and ready to embark."

"I can't just push off on a five-thousand mile trip to Africa with a bunch of blokes who—"

"Trust me, these men will have the skills you're looking for, as well as some skills you may not have thought useful."

"So, what do I do with these logs, buckets, and roofing parts?"

"I'm getting to that." His exasperation with me was evident as his brow furrowed. "You will take them south to the mouth of the Congo River, then up river to Brazzaville, Congo. Don't make the mistake of making port calls on the southern bank of the river. That's the Democratic Republic of Congo, a place where you won't receive a very warm reception—or perhaps I should say, too warm.

"When you reach the river barge complex just downstream of Brazzaville, you will meet your contact from Portland Exports, Liverpool and Manchester. The customs necessities will be handled by a UN representative who is in charge of the barge complex. The shipping agent you will be dealing with is Leonard Ótubé."

"Does Leonard run a hardware or building supply business?"

"Stop asking questions; you'll be better off. Leonard Ótubé's business is not your concern. Within the backpack you have on the table are the trade and customs documents you will present to the UN representative for this transaction.

"They certify you as a jobber for a civil project construction company out of Marseilles. Your goods are bound for a United Nations housing development project in the interior of Congo. You are to negotiate a price with Mr. Ótubé not to be less than €27M in a single lot. No partial payments. If you can get more, then more power to you. It's yours to keep. But, of that €27M, you must wire transfer me €5M and send €22M to Ontotoupolos

Shipping, Thessaloniki, Greece, attention Arman Byassian."

"Whoa. Write this shit down, will you. I can't—"

"You can remember and you will." He was unequivocal without raising his voice. "I will give you time to memorize it before you leave this booth, Johnny. It's important that you can do this. My business reputation and your ability to fulfill the contract, and earn the fee to help your grandfather, depend on it."

I nodded. He was right. It was a daunting challenge, but I was an experienced captain and knew I could do this. It was evident, however, that my outburst concerned him.

He grasped my arm with a grip of astonishing strength considering his age. The timber of his voice dropped. "Are you motivated? Son, this isn't charity; it's business. I'll not hide the fact that your grandfather and I didn't always see eye to eye. That was then, but this is now, a new reality.

"You do as I've told you on this trip and you'll come out with your reward. I promise you that. But this deal is between you and me and no one else. If you fail, or if you cross me, you will regret it. Do you understand?"

His eyes bored into me.

When I didn't immediately answer, he said, "Are you having second thoughts, lad? Did you all of a sudden find a leprechaun's pot o'gold?"

His retort hurt. Was I overthinking this? It was just a pickup and a delivery, something I'd done hundreds of times. And the fees I'd earn would solve everything.

"Sure. I just didn't realize construction materials cost that much. Excuse me, I need the loo before we continue."

What I really needed, however, was a moment to think of the dozens of questions I should be asking. As I slid from the booth, I could see Dillon O'Connor was amused as he drained the last of his Guinness. He banged the empty pint glass on the table and called after me.

"Go on, son, you better, before you piss your pants." Then he laughed.

As I walked to the back of The Morrow, I wondered, what I had bargained for? And who was I bargaining with?

When I returned, he was gone and the bar tab lay on the table...unpaid. I put €7 down and made my way out, still pondering my two questions. I might not know who Dillon O'Connor was, but at least I could be alert for whatever the downside could possibly be. I'd mustered resolve in my moment away from him. I'd do what he asked, get paid, and be done with him.

Back at my boarding cottage, I found the strong box and verified its contents were as he described. Quickly, I gathered my things and settled my account with the landlady, who didn't ask any questions as to why I was leaving with an unused night still left on my rent.

ON THE RETURN drive to Dublin from Wexford, I had time to think. Grandfather's caution to not trust Dillon O'Connor still poked at me. I trusted Grandfather's judgment; he'd never let me down. Now he was firing up my conscience with his advice. Even my not-so-Catholic upbringing told me to beware of this man. Grandfather, Captain Gorik from the Baltic, and Tommy Corrigan on the Dublin docks had taught me to stand for myself and had given me the confidence to make my own account.

The logic played out in my head. I needed money to close this deal with *Marigold*. O'Connor was offering me more than enough to solve that problem and get me started on something new as well. There was no way I could explain any of this to Grandfather's satisfaction, and I didn't want to listen to his arguments. I knew the risks and could succeed without allowing any of O'Connor's tarnished past to rub off on me. I was resolved.

When I arrived home, my consternation over whether or not to tell Pop of my dealings with Dillon O'Connor was eating at me. Everything I'd become, whatever successes I'd achieved I owed to him. Even though TC Miriam was dying, it wasn't due to any lack of effort or skill I possessed, or failing on his part. In good conscience, I couldn't keep what I'd done from him, regardless of what O'Connor had advised. I owed Pop too much.

With this debt in mind, I decided to share my decision with him, including the part Dillon O'Connor would play in the dissolution of what had been a viable a concern of ours for almost four decades. The only part I would hold back would be mentioning the amount of the money involved.

We sat at a table in the Temple Swan that evening and shared a bottle of Jameson Black Barrel with the evening special: shepherd's pie, mash, and peas.

"Pop, I've decided to take *Marigold* to the breaking yards in Bangladesh. Try as I could, no buyers or partners showed any interest in rescuing her."

To my surprise, his eyes brightened and his face lit up in a big grin. "So you've come to your senses. Good on you, laddie. I know you did your best, but sometimes the stars that guide us just don't align." He raised his glass and we clinked them in a toast.

"I wasn't sure you'd take the news so well, Pop."

"Well, it took you long enough, but there's no surprise on my part. I raised you too well not to make the right decision.

"All your hard work learning to be a ship's master was time well spent. Your term with Tommy Corrigan as an apprentice longshoreman on the docks taught you the value of hard work as well as gave you a solid foundation in the unglamorous side of manhandling cargo. That two-years with Captain Pavel Gorik in Riga got you plenty of experience in handling big ships running out of Estonia throughout the Baltic. And for the last twelve years, I've seen you sailing *Marigold*, manning crews, and hustling for consignments with the best of them. So here's to you."

As he raised his glass his eyes glazed, betraying his hard-earned, weathered demeanor. He started to speak, but emotion wouldn't let him. To hide his embarrassment, I said. "To *Marigold*."

He nodded and we tossed back a shot.

Our food arrived and I let the conversation drift to other matters. He told me his hip wasn't bothering him near as much as was the inconvenience of taking his daily insulin shot.

"I hope dinner tonight doesn't mess with your diet."

In a stage whisper, Pop partially shielded his mouth with one hand and said, "Not as much as this eighteen year old Jameson does."

We both laughed.But I still hadn't told him who I was dealing with and I knew I had to. "Pop, I just want you to know, I got a call a few days ago from Dillon O'Connor."

His fork paused part way to his mouth. He didn't look up.

"He'd read my appeal in the trade papers looking for a partner."

He took a bite. "Yeah, and wha'd you say to that bastard?" Then he chewed, still not looking at me.

"Actually, I went to see him."

"In Wexford?"

"Aye. I turned down his offer of a partnership."

"Hmm."

"But he did offer me a consignment of building materials to deliver to a UN mission in Brazzaville, Congo, which will get me near halfway to Bangladesh. With what I'll make from that I can pay for the whole trip and then some. And with the proceeds from scrapping *Marigold*, you'll be set up for good in the nursing home. I can clear our remaining debts and get a head start on a new career."

I waited for a reaction, but he kept eating. Finally, he looked up. "Is he going with you on the *Marigold*?"

No warning or remonstration, just a simple question.

Only slightly relieved, I said, "No, he's simply the broker. When I make the delivery, I'll wire him his portion of the proceeds and bank the rest."

Pop wiped his mouth and folded his napkin neatly beside it.

"Laddie, I'm glad you've made the decision to put an end to our business, as much as that reality hurts me to say. All I'll add is don't let him step foot on *Marigold*. As far as I'm concerned, she's hallowed ground." Then he recharged our glasses with the last of the Jameson's and said, "To *Marigold*."

ON THE MORNING I was to go to Chamberlain's, I stopped by the TC Miriam office to pick up my log book, *Marigold's* registry documents, and my professional papers. I knew Grandfather wouldn't be there till later in the day, so I wrote a goodbye note for him.

I found Chamberlain's easily enough shortly after 8 a.m. It consisted of a nicely appointed office just a dozen or so yards up from the main wharf. Inside, the on-duty outfitting agent greeted me warmly. When I told him why I was there, he asked me to have a seat, explaining he would have to call the purser, who didn't normally arrive before 9:30 or 10:00.

While I waited, I noticed an atlas on the table by my chair. It was a photoessay book about European colonial trade with Africa in the late eighteenth and nineteenth centuries. As I thumbed through the first few pages, I became absorbed by the narrative, maps, and etchings depicting those early days of Europe's commerce with the sub-Saharan regions. The more I read, the more my mind was taken off the bittersweet reason for having to come to Chamberlain's in the first place.

In magnificent detail, the book described life in the mangrove swamps of the coastal lagoons, mudflats, and river deltas. This life was made treacherous by snakes, scorpions, lions, hippos, and crocodiles—hazards for natives and interlopers alike. One of the book's more chilling revelations was that if a trader survived these, then the rough lifestyle that played out on the waterfront docks presented equally perilous outcomes from robbery, injury, or both.

One passage proclaimed that if a man were lucky, he left Africa with more riches than he could have ever imagined; if he were not—and most who tried were not—he never left at all. Sailors transporting these fortune hunters fared no better odds. In the age of sail, they had to overcome becalmed seas in the fetid reality of the doldrums before a wisp of breeze should take them away from an unforgiving shore that abounded with malaria, yellow, and dengue fevers. While enduring stagnation or light winds, tars lucky enough to survive the insects succumbed to scurvy, or worse, they were afflicted by exposure to the relentless equatorial sun.

Turning a page, I read with fascination 'an ancient seafaring chanty of the traders of the day:'

Greed is the king in Grand Benin
Where there's naught but swamp and lagoon,
And blue mangrove birds and elephant herds,
Survive the hottest month in June.

Equatorial swelter is a lifeblood melter;
The best you can do is perspire.
Where the locals are greedy, everyone is needy,
And every man's skill is for hire.

It is godforsaken with fever shakin',
Where you're lucky to save your life.
Naught Mohammad nor Christ about it were nice;
You'll have mosquitoes and snakes for a wife.

Your only friend is the high tide at ten,
Which in fact is your only way out.
If you're stuck there at night, you're in for a fright.
It does no one any good to shout.

There's muck and mire and lots of quagmire,
That will suck away your life blood.
You can take precaution, but stick to the ocean;
Going ashore will be worse than the Flood.

There's a fever swamp where the crocodiles romp,
In the stagnant crush of fauna.
There are monstrous bats and baobab rats,
And the heat is the world's worst sauna.

Send in only porters to be cargo sorters,
While you safely avoid the miasma.
Seek a hasty retreat or you'll suffer defeat,
For missing your chance at diasp'ra.

The cheats will rob you, and your friends far and few,
Though some shills will offer you gold,
Then pull it all back with a stab in the back,
And take everything includin' your soul.

Greed is the king in Grand Benin
Where there's naught but swamp and lagoon,
And blue mangrove birds and elephant herds,
Survive the hottest month in June.

If that weren't chilling enough, the next chapter described the pirate trade that plagued the coastal region. Knowing the waters better than any merchant sailor, seafaring denizens reportedly used agents ashore to tell them when a laden ship, lucky enough to have escaped all other hazards, headed to sea. Sailing well-gunned, light ships with abundant sail, pirates overtook, boarded, and stripped bare like locusts all but the most heavily armed wallowing merchants before they could clear the coastal currents. Avarice drove these men to take the risks: pirate, entrepreneur, and sea captain alike.

I was broken from my educational perusal when a man asked, "May I help you? My name is Griswold. I am the purser here at Chamberlain's."

I put down the book and rose to shake his hand. We talked for a few minutes as I explained the nature of my business.

"Of course, Captain, I've been expecting you. I will have your provisions ready to load aboard *Marigold* tomorrow, sir. If you please, have MV *Marigold* at pier nine, starboard side to, no later than 1030 in the morning. Your crew will have you fueled, equipment checked out, victuals loaded, and ready to depart the harbor by 1830 that evening. And O'Scanlon, would you want to pick up a few extra quid along the way?"

"Depends on what's involved," I said, not willing to commit to anything that would jeopardize the contract I had with O'Connor. I was too close to my not-necessarily-planned retirement from the sea service to put anything at risk.

But a little bit extra could always come in handy. It was going to be a long trip and a lot could happen.

"I fashion you'll have to make a stop somewhere between here and Africa to top off fuel. I've got two con-boxes full of Irish crystal, woolens, and dry goods destined for the tourist traders of Madeira. I figure you can carry them topside on your fantail, no problem. It should bring you something a bit over expenses, as well give you a nice reserve, if you will."

His offer was reasonable and safe. "Load it up. I'll take anything extra I can get."

We haggled over the price for the consignment cargo and agreed to a sum that would give me over a thousand Euro profit upon conclusion of the deal in Madeira. That would be enough to cover my fuel and provisioning expenses to Benin, as well as cover the leg up the Congo River to Brazzaville.

The sentimental doldrums I'd harbored of my home situation lifted from my shoulders. I was on track to gain financial freedom from the fear of taxes, medical costs, and Grandfather's living expenses while looking for a new career. Eased too was my initial apprehension of what O'Conner might be up to.

He was measuring up to be an opportunist in a capitalistic system. The rough edges I had feared seemed to have smoothed over. Those tales of IRA intrigue were definitely a thing of the past. And, if I was ever going to get the true story of what happened to my parents some thirty years ago, he was perhaps the only person on the planet who could fill me in. All in all, this endeavor was sizing up to be much to my liking.

Chapter 3

AT PRECISELY 10:30 A.M., Mr. Griswold arrived at the pier escorting the people I suspected were my nine-man crew. In actuality it was eight men and one woman. The men were a mix of the modern merchant marine sailors, representing many nationalities. As for the woman, I wasn't certain.

"Ah, good morning, Captain O'Scanlon," the Chamberlain representative greeted me.

"Aye, good morning, sir."

He handed me the crew's papers, which after a quick check proved to be in order. Inwardly, however, I harbored some misgivings of this group for several reasons.

First, I wasn't used to sailing with a crew I'd never previously been with at sea. There was nothing like observing a crew turnabout during actual sailing rigors to gain their measure. Second, by the sheer nature of the job, being ship's captain was a lonely occupation. I had no one with whom I could confide concerns, to compare ideas in times of uncertainty. The relationship of captain to crew wasn't the sort that produced confidantes.

The reality I now faced was that I had an entire crew with whom I shared no professional history whatsoever. I had nothing but their résumés, documents offered by the ship's chandler, another person who was also a perfect stranger—a crew provided by someone other than me.

A quick glance at the roster told me I had one man from Africa and seven others from the Indian subcontinent. The lone woman was of Mediterranean origin. Three of the men, the African and two of the Indians, stood on the pier as if they knew each other. They were similarly dressed in dark baggy trousers, well-worn work boots, and light blue chambray shirts. The remaining five men and the woman stood apart from them and displayed no association with one another.

I looked up from the résumé files the chandler had given me. "Mr. Griswold, I see one fellow has his first mate's license in order. That's good." Looking at the group, I asked, "Which one of you is Andjou?"

The Black man stepped forward, but made no attempt to shake hands or offer any form of greeting.

Griswold interrupted the awkward moment. "Captain, this man's name is Osaze Andjou."

I was struck not only by his appearance, but also by his uncommunicative manner. His skin was darker than a Channel run on a stormy night in contrast to the flint white around dark pupils. His piercing stare unsettled me. His eyes had a self-contained brightness that couldn't be ignored. Around one wrist he wore two amulets: one made of bright, multi-colored braided cords, and the other was a metal cuff bracelet.

Clumsily lowering my unaccepted hand, I asked, "Yes, uh, Andjou, do you speak English?"

"Yes I do, Captain. I speak it quite well."

His facial expression remained unchanged. His accented English was French colonial, well-spoken with a confident tone. But his body language was reserved. He had keloid welts, small raised scars, at several spots on his face and neck. The tips of three rather large scars inched above his shirt collar at the side of his neck. These aroused my curiosity, but instinct cautioned me not to inquire as to their origin.

"Nice to meet you, Andjou. Your papers seem to be in order. I see you carry a first mate's license."

"Yes, Captain."

He wasn't helping me with any forthcoming information, much less pleasantries. Rather than force a conversation with an unwilling participant, since that appeared to be what he was about, I figured it time to get to other business.

"Well, since your papers are in order, you will be my first mate. Please separate the crew by discipline. Have the operators stand here and the engineers over there."

Andjou barked rapid fire orders and the crew formed two groups as he directed.

The woman—I had momentarily forgotten about her with the distraction of my first mate's aloofness— remained where she stood. She was taller than all but two of the men. Her complexion was light olive with the smooth, pleasant features of southern Mediterranean stock. She had large, dark eyes and long black hair that reached her shoulders. She was no youngster directly out of school; I guessed she was in her early thirties. Svelte would not have been a good description; robust was a better word, I thought as I stepped towards her.

"And you are Ms.—?"

She smiled and said, "Occhipinti, yes, Capitáno, Miranda Occhipinti from Lipari, an island north of Sicily. I will be your cook." She extended a slender hand and shook mine firmly.

"Well, welcome, Ms. Occhi—"

"Please, Capitáno, call me Miranda."

"All right, welcome, Miranda. I look forward to your service."

I don't know why I worded my response the way I did. For the moment, I was at a loss for anything less formal to say. Perhaps her friendly nature, in contrast to my new first mate's demeanor, was refreshing. I had the sensation I was a schoolboy meeting his neighbor's older sister.

I turned to Andjou, who stood with the two operators. Neither of these men stood as close to him as did the two engineers when I had arrived. The men introduced themselves as Daniru Malik and Chenal Patel. I exchanged pleasantries with the two and learned both men were from Sri Lanka and were veteran operators with years of merchant marine service on a variety of vessels, but hadn't previously served together.

The two seemed amiable enough and spoke accented English well. My first impression was they would do well as bridge officers on this trip. Though the exchange was brief, Andjou chose to remain at a distance, socially as well as physically, an oddity I'd have to contend with.

Surprisingly, when I turned next to the five engineers, Andjou dropped his aloof stance and took the lead, introducing me to the two men who had been with him on the pier.

"Captain, meet Radeep Rajman and Pradesh Wahral. Both men are from India and I can vouch for their expertise in the engine room."

I shook hands, glad to see that Andjou was warming at the chance to communicate. However, the change in his personality towards conviviality gave me pause that his sudden pleasantness wasn't sincere. Maybe it was the set of his eyes or the crisper inflection in his voice. I didn't know for certain, but something was different—different to the extent that my instincts were put on alert.

My caution was further reinforced when he introduced the other engineers. He had to revert to the Chamberlain outfitter's personnel files to remember their names. Clearly, he was not familiar with these three men at all.

I shook hands with Waajid Prankiop, Kaamil Tengazy, and Rajip Tasmoon-Shamlyn. I made the effort to repeat each name as I shook hands, but pronouncing their names was an awkward mouthful for me. I only hoped I would do better at our next meeting.

After posing a few questions to each of them, I learned that all five engineers were experienced men, having sailed the North and South Atlantic coasts of Europe and Africa for years. Since I had never been to Africa, I welcomed this information. The three men unfamiliar to Andjou appeared to be happy having again signed an employment contract. I took this as a good sign.

Their reactions to my few questions were in contrast, however, to the expressions on Rajman's and Wahral's faces. Apparent acquaintances of Andjou's, they showed neither pleasantness nor concern. I was certain they were taking body language cues from Andjou. The three of them displayed indifference, almost resentment at having to associate with the other crew members. I would have to ensure they didn't form their own clique, that is, if they hadn't already done so.

I turned to Griswold, who I hoped could shed some light on the nature of the relationships I observed among my new crew. Drawing him to one side, out of earshot from the crew, I asked, "Griswold, do you know anything about the backgrounds of these folks?"

"I'm afraid I don't, Captain. Why, is there a problem?"

Since a crew at sea is something I had to trust completely, I probed further. "No, it's just that First Mate Andjou and two of the engineers seem to have some familiarity amongst themselves, while the others have never sailed with one another. I was hoping you knew more of their backgrounds, which aren't forthcoming from the dossiers you provided."

"Captain, all I know is their merchant marine licenses are current and they have excellent ratings. Where they've been recently and with whom, I would have no way of knowing."

I tried a different tack. "Your office was recommended by a Mr. Dillon O'Connor. I wonder if he offered more information on them when he contracted your services?"

"I'm afraid I wouldn't know him, sir. The contract orders come via telex from our home office. I've never heard of the gentleman you mentioned. His name wasn't on the personnel service order."

I thought this was odd. I'd have suspected that the shipping agencies were more close-knit with their personnel service providers.

First impressions have always been important to me. My initial assessments of people have usually proven to be correct in my years at sea. I would have to watch this group's dynamics closely to insure they worked well together. For now, however, I would have to rely on the face value of their maritime papers being in order, with due regard to my instincts. Molding a crew to work together was a challenge I hadn't anticipated. I hoped this wouldn't hinder my efforts to sail *Marigold* to the breaking yards halfway around the world.

Chapter 4

I GOT *MARIGOLD* underway from the pier late that afternoon, not wanting to remain in port longer than necessary. This journey wasn't something I looked forward to. I never fashioned myself as being sentimental, but it was just starting to hit me. I was in for some big changes in my life—changes for which I wasn't fully prepared. I would never be sailing my own vessel into my Irish home waters again. But I was resigned, and now anxious to get it over. All I had to learn was patience.

It took me seven hours to clear the Irish Sea, leave Land's End astern, and head *Marigold* into the Atlantic. Daniru Malik was on the bridge for that first evening watch. He seemed to be a good enough seaman and well understood the formal routine required of a proper bridge watch. His seamanship was excellent in that he avoided potentially embarrassing traffic and kept strictly to the course I had plotted.

As night took hold after dusk, I finished up my night star sightings with the sextant and then set about reducing the star-sight angles to a usable navigational fix. It wasn't necessary for me to perform this schoolhouse exercise; I had a GPS repeater on the bridge. But I found solace in being able to navigate the way I'd been taught by my grandfather when I first ventured onto the high seas. I wanted to be self-sufficient, just in case I ever lost electrical power. Who was I kidding? Who lost power in this modern day and age? I was simply being stubborn about changing my ways.

While I went about my calculations and referencing the nautical almanac, I heard the cook, Miranda, talking to Malik behind me.

"I brought you sweet biscuits from the batch I made for tomorrow's breakfast. I thought you might like a treat after such a busy day." She held the plate out for Malik, who thanked her. She then held it for me.

I spoke without looking up. "Thank you, Ms. Occhipinti. I'll have one in a minute. Please put the plate on the plotting table. First I have to complete the calculations for our position."

"Certainly, Capitáno."

From the corner of my eye, I saw her set down the plate. Momentarily, I stopped fidgeting with my pencil. The ensuing silence was as brief as it was awkward. I turned my head enough to notice she was looking into the darkness at the waves. I returned my attention to my calculations.

I wasn't sure what she'd done to instill this reaction in me, but I was flustered. My goodness, had it been that long since a good-looking woman had done anything for me?

It's just a biscuit, you fool. I chastised myself for letting the thought intrude into my work.

And work I did, continuing with the tedious navigation calculations in the glow of the bridge's red lights. It wasn't until I had finished my busy work that I again acknowledged Miranda's presence. When I finally spoke, it disrupted the quiet on the bridge.

"Oh, I'm sorry, Miranda, but I lost track of what was going on around me. Let me try that biscuit. You weren't waiting to talk to me about something, were you?"

Her closeness continued to unnerve me. I was absorbed in self-critical thought, that if spoken out loud, would have been unengaging at best and regretful at worst. *Think of something, Johnny. After all, you're the captain of the* Marigold.

Miranda rescued me from my awkwardness. "That is quite alright, Capitáno. I was enjoying the peace and quiet of the ocean. Don't you think it looks peaceful tonight?"

"Mmm, yes it does." I damn near choked on the bite of biscuit in my mouth as I tried swallowing it to reply. "The forecast for the next few days should be much the same. By the time we get to Madeira, the temperature should be at least ten degrees warmer. Maybe by then you can take your evening walk out on the main deck instead of the bridge enclosure."

"That would be welcome, Capitáno. And maybe by then you can join me." She said this with a twinkle in her eye. "Now, if I may be excused, I must finish cleaning the galley and get some rest. Breakfast for the morning watch will come much too soon."

Malik cocked an eyebrow, but said nothing until she had left the bridge. "Captain, I agree with you. I can feel it in my bones. We are in for a good spell of weather."

We both knew, however, that that wasn't what either of us was thinking. Then he reached into his trouser pocket and pulled out a short, fat cheroot. Not the stub of a half-smoked cigar, but one made for at least forty minutes of solid smoking enjoyment.

"I have two, Captain. Would you like one?"

I briefly thought of replying with his first name, but years in command had ingrained in me the need to remain formal.

49

"No thanks, Mr. Malik. If I start one, I would be obliged to stay up here and finish it, and I'm too tired for that right now. I think I'll turn in. We still have 1,315 miles to go before we reach Funchal. Keep a good watch tonight for you and your relief at midnight. Call me if you have any questions."

"Aye aye, sir."

I left the bridge for my sea cabin thinking Malik was going to be a good shipmate indeed.

I AWOKE A LITTLE after five a.m. Within minutes I dressed and made my way to the bridge. Patel had relieved Malik as the bridge watch.

"Good morning, Captain. Coffee?" He pointed to a pot on a hot plate next to the piloting chart. "Miranda brought it up ten minutes ago. By the smell coming through the ventilation duct, she has a great breakfast for us. I'm guessing the bacon, eggs, and biscuits are ready."

"Let me get my eyes open first, Mr. Patel. Then I'll go check it out."

I took a sip. The satisfaction of that first taste of coffee in the morning is hard to describe to someone not so addicted. Over my twenty some years at sea, it was a potent and essential part of my morning routine. Thus fortified, I satisfied myself we were where the chart said we were and everything was as it should be. Normally, I wouldn't have been so intrusive in double checking the bridge watch's skills. That was the mate's job. But I had to satisfy myself with their expertise.

As I started down the ladder from the bridge, I said, "Mr. Patel, I think I'll verify your suspicions and check the accuracy of your prediction about breakfast."

Miranda had a plate of bacon rashers on the mess table, as well as a platter of biscuits. "How would you like your eggs, Capitáno?"

"Two scrambled would be fine, Miranda. Thank you."

My first mate, Andjou, was already seated and eating his breakfast. Taking a seat opposite him I asked, "May I join you, Mr. Andjou?"

Being captain, this was a needless request, but I'd been brought up to treat everyone with the civility and courtesy I liked to receive in return, regardless of social convention.

The roped muscles of his wrist caught my eye, as did the multi-colored band and amulet which were stretched all the more tightly by the strength with which he gripped his fork. But before I could ask about his bracelets he said, "Most certainly, Captain. Have you been to the bridge yet?"

Another good sign. His was no idle question to inquire about the weather. He was testing my thoroughness as captain.

"I was just there, thank you. The weather is clear and you should have an uneventful watch."

"That is good, sir. I for one don't like surprises."

He hesitated taking his next bite. "Have you ever been to Funchal?

"A few times, but it was never a regular run for me."

"How about Cotonou, Captain? Have you been there?"

"I can't say that I have—neither for business nor for pleasure."

"Aha, Captain, when it comes to the Bight of Benin, there is no pleasure. Or maybe it is all pleasure, depending on Fate and your personal nature."

51

I was glad to see that his aloof nature had disappeared and he had decided to engage in conversation. "You make it sound mysterious, Mr. Andjou. Is that a riddle?"

"I should hope so. Benin is the birthplace of Voodoo and Cotonou is auspiciously situated at the mouth of the River of Death, Captain. What could be more mysterious than that?"

There was a devilish pleasure in his eyes as he waited intently for my reaction.

Taken unawares by his comment, I let my curiosity take its hold of me. "Voodoo—do you believe in that, Mr. Andjou?"

"Why of course, Captain, and you should too."

His tone was ominous, as was the intensity in his eyes, which bored straight into my soul. I wavered, thinking perhaps he was threatening me by the way he said it.

I shook it off. I didn't know him well; maybe he was testing me somehow. That look in his eyes, even though he had resumed eating, told me I should not make light of the subject. I decided on a more neutral response.

"Tell me, Mr. Andjou, what is Voodoo? The way you refer to it, you make it sound religious."

"And just what is religion, Captain, except a belief in something that is greater than either of us? Voodoo is a belief in the power of natural forces that course through all living things. There is one supreme being who is the creator and controller of life."

I felt comfortable with this response. "That's not too much different than Christianity, or Judaism, or even Islam."

"No, no, no, Captain." If possible, the grip on his fork grew tighter. He stopped eating and looked straight at me, his eyes dark and hard, like obsidian. "Voodoo deals in many gods. There are lesser gods to the supreme one who aid in the controlling of life. Each lesser god has its own job to do."

"Well, that sounds like they could be the saints or angels of the Roman Church."

"If only it were that simple, Captain." He stopped speaking and rested both hands on the table, still holding his fork. He looked directly at me, the whites of eyes in stark contrast to the darkness of his skin. "People speak to the lesser gods through sacrifice and rituals. It is these lesser gods who communicate their thoughts, then, with the supreme being."

He relaxed and resumed his breakfast, giving me time to digest his words.

Somehow, I replied.

"It may be a little different, but I know many Catholics who pray to Saint This or Saint That, asking for something, like they were intermediaries between man and God."

"That may be true, Captain, but you believe saints are sacred—that is, divine. In Voodoo, everything in the universe is part of the whole, linked to everything else. There is no distinction between sacred and non-sacred. Neither humans nor lesser gods are perfect. Suffering, sickness, and death, all of these are part of the cycle of life. Lesser sins can be amended through rituals and sacrifice. Humans can only be delivered, however, through punishment for sins men have committed which offended the gods."

I managed to say, "If you change that to the singular, then again, it is not unlike Christianity. However, I can't speak to the other great religions of the world. Maybe some of what you say is like Buddhism or Hinduism. I don't know."

"Yes, Captain, most true. But the nature of each offense we commit requires appeasement to a different god. We, the living creatures, cannot help but make offense with all of our inherent flaws."

My attempt to steer his lessons in life towards a less ominous topic had failed. It was clear he was no longer speaking in generalities. He was becoming personal. But I couldn't disengage.

"Flaws?"

He squinted one eye. The other, fully open, sharply fixed on me.

"Captain, even in your exalted position as master of this vessel, you have flaws. Tell me you have never lusted after a woman whom you shouldn't have, or craved something beyond your means, or hoarded gold to keep from the roaming eyes of others."

My reaction was one of insult, which I am sure he saw on my face. Yet I didn't respond directly to his statement. Instead I replied, "I grant you there is no perfect man. But perhaps the flaws of the majority who are honorable don't rise to the status of being sinful or criminal in nature."

His face beamed. "Ah, yes, Captain, exactly so. All life, including the unborn and the dead, is communal—that is all beings, animals and plants, are part of the living community, and the living must interact with the spirit world to keep the dead and unborn happy."

Where was he going with this? "I didn't say or imply that there was no inherent responsibility. But I think you must recognize I'm talking about the real world, not some fantasy." My voice was getting louder. My Catholic up-bringing was urging me on. He had bested me and I was frustrated.

"Aha, but magic, too, is part of this community because of its unworldliness. It is essential that we beg for protection or forgiveness. Voodoo uses ritual magic aided by amulets and charms for their inherent magical powers."

"Magic! You can't be serious."

In a different setting, I might have thought Andjou was proselytizing, and I was unprepared for a debate of religious tenets. However, here on a ship at sea bound eventually for the home of the beliefs he espoused, I could only conclude he was sending me a warning. I needed to subtly lighten the mood. But he beat me to it.

"Amen, as you would say, Captain. Let us hope that you stay very busy in Cotonou and have nothing to hide."

His eyes refocused and his countenance relaxed. For the first time since he began describing Voodoo rites, I could tell he was looking elsewhere than directly into my soul. Then he picked up a slice of bacon, put it whole into his mouth, and chewed.

It was difficult to discern if he was cautioning me, blessing me, or absolving me—of what, I didn't know. I needed to say something, if nothing else than to reassure myself I was not persuaded as to the veracity of what he had said. But I could no more ignore the dark side of his message—a warning, almost—than I could abandon my cargo in Benin.

"In any case, we will only be in Cotonou long enough to on-load cargo. Then we're off to Congo. I am sure that nothing will go wrong."

"Ah, you are right, Captain. What could go wrong?"

I looked at my first mate. What was he saying to me?

IT TOOK US just under five days to reach Funchal, Madeira's main port. The previous few times I'd been here were with my grandfather. We had taken on loads of the world-famous Madeira wine and fine linen products to bring back to Ireland and the UK. My work then was below decks, which deprived me of the beautiful spectacle I now enjoyed from the bridge as *Marigold* entered the harbor.

The sun was bright and the sky was high, dotted with sparse cirrus clouds. On a southeast prominence of the island, the harbor was semi-circular with the elevation rising gently from the harbor's edge to a high ridge and single mountain a few miles distant. The town and its red-tile buildings crowded right up to the street abutting the wharfs and spread steadily inland, riding the slope until finally reaching the steeper flanks of the mountain.

Hundreds of ocean going sailing boats, all for pleasure cruising by wealthy patrons, rocked gently at a series of piers tucked away to the harbor's far side, their single naked masts swaying gently, like slow motion fencing swords in action. Opposite *Marigold*'s pier was a much larger pier, which jutted several hundred feet to seaward. A passenger cruise liner was busy discharging eager passengers for a day stop of fun and shopping.

As Patel made the entry into port and moored *Marigold* to the customs wharf, I took pictures of the picturesque harbor from my supervisory perch on the bridge wing. I watched two of the engineers, Pravesh Wahral and Rajip Tasmoon-Shamlyn, work with the stevedores to position the large overhead crane for off-loading the con-box cargo.

Someone called for my attention from the bridge house. It was Miranda escorting a chubby, jovial customs inspector, presumably here to oversee the cargo transaction. He was huffing and puffing from climbing the ladders from the main deck.

"Thank you, Ms. Occhipinti."

Miranda flinched at the formality of my greeting, but I had no time to follow up, since the out of breath official spoke first.

"Good morning, Captain." The inspector held up his credential card. "If you please..." He bent slightly at the waist to ease his breathing. "...what have you got to declare coming into port today?"

I read his name tag as he straightened: Luis Albreggo.

"Good morning, Senhor Albreggo. I just have two con-boxes of Irish goods destined for your merchants engaged in the tourist trade. Here are the manifests." I handed them to the smiling, if not fit man, whose pallor and composure were slowly returning to normal.

"Ahh, Irish crystal—don't go telling my wife, senhor. I have enough of this in my house already." He let out a laugh while continuing to read the manifest in a self-absorbed, if not professional manner. After he finished the last page, he looked up. "Do you have any other transactions, sir?"

"No, Inspector, I will leave as soon as I offload this cargo, top off fuel tanks, and Ms. Occhipinti takes on fresh stores." I gave Miranda a curt smile as a way of indicating she should get on with whatever business she had left to do. She curtsied and left the bridge without a word.

Albreggo gave an admiring glance at her as she departed. "That is one good-looking woman."

Ignoring his comment, I said, "If we could, sir, I have a tight schedule if I'm to reach my next port call on time."

"And where would that be, senhor?"

"Cotonou, Benin. I must reach there by the nineteenth of the month." I stated my arrival as two days earlier than need be. I figured if I said it often enough, I would ensure I reached my destination at least on time.

His smile faded. "I see. Perhaps you and I could take a walk somewhere private, perhaps about your decks, senhor. It's just routine. I like to spot check the cargo being transshipped through Funchal."

Though I had nothing to hide, I was concerned by the odd change in his demeanor, along with his sudden interest in examining what I might or might not be carrying. But I readily agreed.

"Mr. Patel, I will be with the inspector on the main deck. Continue fueling the ship. Ask Ms. Occhipinti on the pier to notify you as soon as she has completed taking on fresh stores."

"Yes, Captain, I will."

I walked the customs inspector around my main deck and let him peer into the ship's holds, their hatch covers having been removed as a routine precaution for such an occurrence. Seeing how upfront I was to allow him free access to the ship, his reason for continuing with his inspection could only be to verify I wasn't carrying contraband through his port.

Finally, Senhor Albreggo was satisfied. "Good luck, Captain. I do not envy your trip to Cotonou."

"Oh, and why is that?"

"It is just sea legend, senhor—mariners' tales handed down over the years. But you know how rumors and traditions are. It probably stems from the Voodoo the Catholic priests encountered when they first went there to convert the natives. There's an old sea chantey that goes: 'Beware and take care of the Bight of Benin; there's one comes out for forty goes in'."

"That's quite a foreboding rhyme, senhor."

This was the second time within a week I had been warned, in a manner, about Benin and its environs.

"I've never been there, mind you. Make of the verse what you will." Then, with a nod of relief at being able to change the subject, he added, "Well, all seems to be in order, Captain." Facing me directly, he added, "By the way, I also work as the purser for the dock and am authorized to surrender payment to you for the Irish goods. I was told the price agreed to is £2,128."

"Very good, senhor. I admire your efficiency. Here is an account number you can transfer the funds to." I handed him my Dublin bank number. I was only too pleased to note that I had made a nice £1,310 profit. This trip was looking up.

"Thank you, Captain. When you have finished fueling, shall I bill this same account?"

"No, senhor, if you please, I'll pay you cash. My consignment owner has given me the funds to cover fuel as well as the cook's bill for the provisions. I assume these also fall under your jurisdiction. Will that be satis-factory?"

"It is, Captain. Have a safe voyage. Perhaps I will see you on your return to Dublin. Oh, I almost forgot." He reached into his coat pocket and withdrew a telex envelope, which he handed to me. "This came for you last night."

I thanked him and watched him depart across the brow. Standing alone now with a rare free moment, I followed to the pier to enjoy a cigar. Tengazy, Wahral, and Tasmoon-Shamlyn were on the pier finishing up the last steps of the fueling operation. Putting a good hundred yards between me and the stern of the ship to avoid the diesel fumes, I lit up. Then I opened the telex Senhor Albreggo had given me.

Johnny,

Good decision to maximize profit from Marigold. *I wish you'd told me before beggin' to that arsehole O'Connor, though. As I told you, O'Connor and I didn't part ways on good terms, but we had no time to resolve differences then because he was one step ahead of British authorities for his IRA doings. I was just lucky enough to part ways when the coppers closed in on him. We never got the chance to settle the issue.*

Don't trust him, laddie. He's no good.

GF

I tucked the letter away, puffed my cigar, and mulled over the warning he'd repeated. Still unresolved, however, was what to do about it.

My eyes focused on *Marigold's* transom. The raised letters forming the ship's name plate were bleached from years of exposure to salt, sun, and sea. The dot over the top part of the *i* had faded, as had most of the *l*. I made a mental note to have the crew repaint the letters at our next port call, then realized, why bother? I took another satisfying puff on my cigar. I could kick myself. I should care about this detail. I always had, but now it no longer seemed to matter.

"You seem very lost in thought, Capitáno."

I turned, caught off guard by such a friendly greeting in a place I'd only visited a few times years ago. "Ms. Occhipinti, I'm sorry, I didn't see you. I must have been daydreaming."

"You seem a little troubled. Is there something wrong?"

"No, I was mulling over some information I've heard recently about our next port of call in Cotonou, that's all."

"And that is upsetting, Capitáno?"

"At breakfast the other day, Andjou made a point of describing a certain mysticism that surrounds Benin. He mentioned rituals, Voodoo, and black arts in graphic detail. I must admit, he painted a very dark picture."

"And this is what is bothering you?"

"No, but it made me stop and think a bit. Perhaps I wouldn't have given it another thought, but Senhor Albreggo, our customs inspector, went on about Benin in a similar vein. In fact, he took me aside to give me, well, almost a warning about what happens to mariners sailing near Benin. He said, at the very least, they encounter trouble. And at the very worst, seamen might not survive—that is, according to legend."

Miranda didn't respond, and as my words trailed away, her silence became uncomfortable. I was about to say something, anything to break the clumsy moment, when she said, "Capitáno, you know that sailing men often mix legend with truth. Not everything they say has a basis in fact. For centuries, the dark mystique of Africa was built by such men. You cannot take everything they pass on in sea stories to heart. Otherwise, you will always be worrying about your shadow."

"I appreciate what you say, Ms. Occhi—"

She squeezed my forearm tightly. I didn't know if her interruption was because she wanted me to use her first name, or something else. I took her gesture, not as warning, but perhaps advice. But her grip persisted.

"Capitáno, if it will help settle your mind, there is a small sailor's chapel down the quay. I was just there while I waited for the ship's chandler to deliver my order. I find solace when I pray to my saints."

For the first time, I noticed the thin gold necklace and cross pendant she wore. However, I didn't reply. She loosened her grip. "I have offended you, Capitáno?"

"No, Ms. Occhipinti." Her hand still rested on my arm. "I do attend church most of the time when I'm home in Dublin. And I definitely don't take sailor's warnings as a threat to my soul. I just thought it odd for two different people in two different places to voice similar concerns."

Before she could respond, Tengazy approached, wiping fuel oil grime from his hands. "Excuse me, Captain. We have finished fueling and should have the engines ready in a few minutes."

"Very good. It's Tengazy, right?

"Yes, Captain O'Scanlon."

"I couldn't help noticing that the entire time you were working the refueling rig, you never stopped singing. Is that something native to you and your countrymen?"

"Oh no, Captain, certainly not. It's quite personal for me. I sing songs to myself to occupy my mind. If I didn't, I would worry too much about all the bad things happening in the world today."

"Indeed, not a bad philosophy. Very well then," I said, turning to Miranda, "If you have your pantry restocked, Ms. Occhipinti, I guess I'd better get the ship underway. Benin isn't getting any closer sitting next to the pier."

I flicked my cigar butt to its hissing demise in the bay and nodded to the two crewmen. I decided then and there that the two of them were people worth trusting. Call it a sailor's intuition. Their good-natured outlook on life had brightened my mood and pushed the warnings of First Mate Andjou and Customs Inspector Albreggo to that part of my mind that was best left unconsulted. I wasn't about to have unsubstantiated cautions spoil my first trip to Africa.

By 3:20 p.m. the deck was secure and Patel had the *Marigold* underway for the 2,480 mile trip to Cotonou.

Chapter 5

MIRANDA OUTDID HERSELF in preparing the evening meal. Besides taking on fresh vegetables in Funchal, she had managed to purchase a few delicacies normally not a part of shipboard cuisine. She served a delicious roasted rack of lamb with Mediterranean spices, Greek potatoes, salad, and a medley of sliced fresh fruit. In addition, she placed two bottles of Madeira wine on the table. For Waajid Prankiop and Rajip Tasmoon-Shamlyn, Miranda prepared a special dish of olive oil poached fresh snapper with rosemary and a soy curry paste made from scratch to accommodate their religious preference for not eating meat.

Perhaps because of her good nature, or because we were coalescing as a crew, a festive air prevailed as we dined. I looked around the table, pleased they were getting to know each other after a week at sea. Then again, it could have been the wine.

I couldn't fathom this festivity so early on a cruise, but those gathered didn't seem to care. With the exception of First Mate Andjou on the bridge and Pravesh Wahral, the crewman from India, in the engineering spaces, everyone else was at the mess table, even the ones who could have been in bed resting before their next watch.

I clinked my glass for their attention.

"Gentlemen, Miranda. I'm pleased that all of you are enjoying yourselves and wanted to thank you for the hard work you've put in this past week. Miranda, I especially thank you for this fine dinner. I hope I can afford it."

A chuckle went through half of them, followed a few seconds later by more laughter from the two who had to wait for their shipmate's translation. Laughter spread, with the exception of Radeep Rajman, who maintained the stoic aloofness he had displayed when I first encountered him at Chamberlain's in Dublin.

I thought this odd, since by now I figured he would have overcome his reluctance to associate with the others. Perhaps my joke was lost in translation. In any case, I dismissed my observation. Though coincidence had thrown us together, I was realistic enough to know that upon journey's end, I would never associate with any of them again. The meal put me in a good mood, and I wanted them to enjoy it while we had the opportunity, so I continued with the toast.

"This journey is bittersweet. It will be the last one for the *Marigold* and for TC Miriam shipping. I know I haven't worked with any of you before, but *Marigold* and I have been plying the Atlantic and adjacent environs for over twenty years. She is like family to me. So, it's not without emotion that I announce that when we deliver our next cargo to the Congo, that will be her last voyage. After that, I will take her around the Cape to the breaking yards in Chittagong, Bangladesh."

There was a slight intake of breath from Patel and Miranda. It seemed at least two of the crew were as sentimental about ships as I was.

"That means you are sharing this special experience with me. Please raise your glasses and join me in a toast."

They clinked their glasses. A chorus of *"Marigold"* followed. The emotion that welled within surprised me. Looking at the happy faces one by one, I smiled, until I stopped at Rajman's. True to his lack of enthusiasm so far, he conspicuously didn't drink the toast. This, however, I discounted as religious preference.

With dinner over, I stayed behind on the mess deck to await those who would be coming off watch to share with them the same good will the others had enjoyed. As I sat drinking coffee, I noticed Rajman loitering at the after part of the mess deck.

It wasn't long before First Mate Andjou and engineer Wahral arrived. The three talked briefly, out of earshot, and then Rajman departed. Were they simply carrying on the friendship I'd witnessed on the docks when they boarded at Chamberlain's in Dublin? Most likely, but I took note of it nonetheless.

The off-going watch standers came to the table ready to eat. It had been a long day for everyone. They were not only hungry, but ready to retire for the night for some much needed rest. But, as elaborate a table setting and meal as Miranda had laid out, neither Andjou nor Wahral showed much appreciation for the great lengths to which she had gone. When I offered a toast of thanks for their hard work and shared with them my misgivings at having to leave my life's work on the sea, they listened without reaction. Their behavior was so obviously detached that when they left the table, I felt obliged to comment to Miranda.

"I can't figure out the first mate, Miranda. I apologize for his lack of appreciation for your effort in preparing this first-rate meal."

"Capitáno, it doesn't bother me. I'm only happy you now call me Miranda and no longer refer to me as Ms. Occhipinti."

Surprised, I looked at her. "That doesn't offend you, I hope."

"Oh, no, Capitáno, quite the opposite. It's just that this will be a long voyage, as well as your last one on board your own vessel. I simply think it's more comfortable on a daily basis to be less formal."

"I can assure you, Miranda, that I—"

She held up her hand and smiled. "Capitáno, I don't criticize. After all, it's not like we're long-standing partners. I happen to think we'll be working close together over the next few weeks and it would be good to be less straight-laced. I am Miranda and you are Capitáno. That is all there is to it. As far as those two go," she nodded in the direction where Andjou and Wahral had departed and said something in Italian.

"I'm sorry, I didn't understand that."

"I was just saying, Capitáno, that the world is made of many people who are also different, no?"

Her candor and insight left me speechless. So I simply sipped coffee and watched Miranda clear the dishes.

THE BUZZER FROM my sea cabin phone awakened me at three in the morning two nights later.

"Captain, it is I, Daniru Malik on the bridge. I have slowed to eight knots because Waajid Prankiop in the engine room reports there is something wrong with our number one engine. He has secured it and I am making the best speed I can on number two engine by itself."

"What is Mr. Prankiop doing about the bad engine?"

"He has called for the other engineers, Tasmoon-Shamlyn and Rajman, to come back and check it out."

"Very well."

I cradled the phone and stared at the overhead in my cabin through the darkness. For the first time, I was aware of an exaggerated pitching motion. The seas were building. I turned on my over-the-bunk light and looked at the aneroid barometer. It had fallen several millibars since last evening. *Marigold* was in for a blow.

I rolled over, trying to get more sleep, but the engine problem wouldn't let go of my subconscious. Finally, I gave in to my best nautical judgement and got up from the growing discomfort of my bunk. I put on trousers and shirt and headed aft to the engine room to check on what progress the engineers were making in repairs.

The pitching was such that I needed one hand on the safety rail as I made my way aft on the weather deck. Though the engine breakdown was unfortunate, as well as being ill-timed, it reinforced my decision to scrap *Marigold*, rather than go through the expense of an overhaul, which in the end might never reap sufficient financial payback.

Rajman noticed me first. "Good evening, Captain."

I nodded. "What do you have, Mr. Rajman?"

"At first I thought it might be a clogged fuel injector, because compression was missing in cylinder number three. But now I think that injector has failed completely."

"Can you fix it?"

"Most certainly, sir. I just need to check in stores to see if we have a replacement."

"How long do you figure?"

My grave concern was keeping to schedule. I had almost a day and a half to play with to reach Cotonou by the twenty-first and take delivery. On my original track and speed, I was scheduled to arrive with time to spare on the afternoon of the nineteenth. But at only eight knots, I was eating into my leeway.

"I will know within the hour if we have a spare. If we do, I figure it will take us two or three hours to replace it and test the engine."

"Keep me informed, Mr. Rajman."

"Aye, aye, sir."

Rather than look over his shoulder, which would do no one any good, I went back to the mess deck for a cigarette. I had just taken my first drag when Miranda appeared in the galley doorway.

"I see you couldn't sleep in the freshening weather."

She was right. We were taking substantial rolls and pitching significantly. Freshening was an understatement I assumed she used to express her familiarity with and ability to withstand rough weather.

That, or she was putting up a good front to avoid getting seasick. Either way, I gave her credit for manning the galley, regardless of circumstance, to keep the crew fed.

"Honestly, I hadn't noticed. I was aft checking on the repair status of the diesel engine."

"That explains why we slowed."

Experienced sailors become attuned to the ship's vibrations and readily sense when the ship alters speed and direction by the changes in vibrations coming through the deck plates under their feet. Her observation told me that Miranda was an experienced sailor.

"Would you like some coffee, something to eat, Capitáno?"

"Coffee would be good, Miranda, but no sense in raiding the freezer just for one person."

"You are the Capitáno. It is no trouble at all."

"In that case, thank you. Black would be fine."

"Then coffee it is." She disappeared into the galley.

By the time I finished my cigarette, Miranda returned with two mugs of coffee and joined me at the table.

"Tell me, Capitáno, what really made you take such a long last trip? Why not simply sell your ship closer to home, in Great Britain or Europe?"

Miranda's question was an honest one. Her interactions with the other crew members and her diligence in performing her job were trademarks of her professional experience. Most of all, she was genuine in her wanting to know more about her captain. I liked that.

"Part of it I'm sure is denial, not wanting to face the reality that this part of my life is coming to an end. It also has to do with being sentimental about the old gal."

I waved my hand at my surroundings. "I don't think I want her last resting place to be anywhere near home, the place where I sailed to and from for all these years." I went on to tell her about my grandfather, how his declining health and the downturn in the shipping business climate had forced the decision. She listened with interest and respect.

When I paused, she said, "Is there more to going so far away from Ireland than just fighting nostalgia?"

It was a fair question. While I mulled how to respond, Miranda returned to the galley only to reemerge carrying the whole pot to refill our cups. She said nothing as she sat. I swirled my cup with a spoon to cool the coffee.

Finally, I replied to her question. "I think I'll feel better that I won't be burying her in the same place I'll have to eventually bury my grandfather."

There was a lurch as *Marigold* corkscrewed, shuddered, and pitched at a much steeper angle than before.

"I think the seas have picked up, Miranda."

She smiled with a confident glow about her. "Are you worried?"

"My only concern is that we reach Cotonou with sufficient time to make this business transaction. Honestly, I'm counting on the profits from this trip to offset my grandfather's nursing home bills and to feather my nest egg while I change careers."

"You're too young to retire, Capitáno. Is that what you really want to do?" She leaned over the table, holding her coffee cup in both hands. She pouted her lips and blew gently on the coffee. The upheaval of the decks wasn't the only thing affecting my emotions. It was hard for me to ignore her pursed lips and not wonder if she knew precisely what I was thinking. Surprisingly, I had a good feeling about all of it.

I said, "You had better go check your galley and insure everything is battened down. I'm going to the bridge."

She smiled a knowing smile. "Of course, Capitáno."

When I stepped onto the bridge, Malik was hunched over the radar repeater. His back was bent and bathed in the red glow of the bridge night lights and his face reflected the eerie green of the radar screen. The view through the bridge windows afforded a 270-degree view of the tempest raging outside. But between the wind-blown spray from the wave tops and the near-horizontal rain, visibility was only a few yards ahead at best.

"Any radar contacts, Mr. Malik?" I asked.

Without looking up from the radar repeater he replied, "The backscatter is intense, but we do have one, sir, about four miles southwest of us and opening. I have tracked her for over an hour. It looks like she is headed west, probably for the Caribbean."

"Maybe it's a good thing we slowed. With the weather and all, we'd probably be down a few knots anyway. I'm glad we got that deck cargo off at Funchal; otherwise, we'd be out there now checking the lashings and exposed to the elements."

"Yes, sir, she's riding just fine. These freighters were built well for heavy weather. Built to last."

There was a hidden irony in his statement, since I was sailing *Marigold* to her last resting place.

Miranda appeared at the back of the bridge, one hand holding onto a stanchion, the other holding a paper bag and a carafe of coffee. "I brought you some sandwiches and coffee, Daniru. It might help you weather the storm."

Malik raised his head from the radar. It was obvious to me there was something about her tone and honest, caring demeanor that endeared her to other crewmen.

"Thank you, Miranda, you are too kind," he said.

"No need to thank me," she said, putting the bag down in a secured tray near the plotting table. "It's my job."

As she turned to go, her hair flipped and her long skirt twirled. This woman knew she had the attention of both of us. Then she was gone down the ladder.

THE STORM CONTINUED unabated for another seven hours. It was draining on everyone. The ship's constant, irregular motion, and the unsettled feeling of having to hang on to stay upright, took a tiring toll on anyone who was up and about. For those in their bunks, sleep wasn't possible. The constant weighting down and floating, as bodies followed the sudden rise and fall of the ship while supine, made sleep, even rest, beyond reason. If that weren't enough, would-be sleepers had to deal with crashing into their bunk's side rails as the ship suddenly lurched sideways, just because the storm decided up and down motion wasn't sufficient punishment.

The methodical westward track of the storm and our slow southward travel finally brought us respite as *Marigold* emerged from the southern edge of the storm into calmer seas. The engineers reported they had finished their repairs and finally had the balky number one diesel back online. I increased *Marigold*'s speed to almost thirteen knots and began to make up for lost time.

THE CLOUDS CLEARED nicely. I checked our position with a running fix using successive sun lines. When I completed the calculations, I figured we had only fallen behind by thirty-two miles, a little under four hours. I was reassured I could still make my rendezvous with the broker in Cotonou before the twenty-first.

Satisfied I knew where I was and confident I was still on schedule, I decided to walk about the weather deck to check for damage. As I came around the after loading hatch cowling, I noticed markings above the base of the ventilation intake funnel. To the best I could remember, these hadn't been there the last time I came by.

As I got close to the funnel, the dark marks resolved into three parallel smears. I also noted on the deck leading to the funnel a three-droplet trail near the weather railing, which itself was marked by more dark blotches. My shoe accidentally smeared something on the deck.

It was blood.

I stepped into the after deckhouse and rang the bridge. Patel answered immediately, "Bridge."

"Mr. Patel, this is the captain. Have someone find the First Mate and tell him to meet me on the main deck aft. It looks like someone had an accident up here during the storm."

Within five minutes Andjou arrived and we examined the evidence together.

"Mr. Andjou, what do you think? Was someone foolish enough to come out here on deck during the storm, slip, and hit his head?"

"Captain, someone may have cut themselves, but it was not during the storm. No one has reported an injury."

His reply was confident, if dismissive of my concerns. I hadn't taken a liking to his demeanor from the beginning, but his professionalism was not lacking in this instance.

"How do you figure that?"

"Captain, the rain was very intense and we were taking rollers across the bulwarks during much of that blow. I'm sure any blood that could have been here would have been washed away by the storm. This has to be fresh blood. See, it has not fully coagulated." He pressed his finger into the smear and held up a red, wet fingertip.

He was correct. "If anyone had reported for first aid treatment, by the extent of these blood markings, I'm sure they would need bandages, if not stitches."

"Captain, I recommend we muster the entire crew in the mess to verify their well-being. Patel and Wahral are on watch right now. Malik and Tasmoon-Shamlyn are off watch; Prankiop and Rajman were up most of the night fixing the diesel. We should know the condition of everyone very soon."

Within fifteen minutes, the remaining off-watch crew members reported to the mess deck with Andjou and me. To my surprise and immediate relief, they all seemed fit enough, though a bit storm-weary. There were no signs of injury or medical treatment.

It was Miranda who made a crucial observation.

"Where is Rajip Tasmoon-Shamlyn? He shouldn't be on watch now."

Alarmed at this realization, but thankful at least these five were okay, I directed everyone to search the ship stem to stern to locate Tasmoon-Shamlyn. If we were lucky, he had simply slipped and bumped his head. Perhaps he lay dazed somewhere.

After half an hour, no one reported finding Tasmoon-Shamlyn. I asked Andjou, "When was the last time anyone saw him?"

He scanned the faces of the assembled crew, then asked, "Radeep, you were up last night. How about you; did you see him?"

"Osaze, you know we were working on the engine. Radeep was the one who retrieved the spare injector we installed."

First names—Andjou had used the engineer's first name and he replied similarly. And their exchange came very quickly, when just a short while earlier, not one of them was forthcoming with information to help establish time or place.

Andjou, Wahral, and Rajman were the three who had stood together on the dock at Chamberlain's in Dublin. It was becoming clearer now that they most likely had known each other before coming aboard *Marigold*. So why weren't they being completely forthright now?

"Tasmoon-Shamlyn has to be somewhere. Recheck the entire ship, including the storeroom and his bunk area."

An hour later, with no success in finding the missing engineer, there could be only one conclusion. At some point the engineer had come topside for fresh air, had somehow cut or injured himself, and had fallen overboard. The tragedy could have occurred anywhere from three to twelve hours ago.

I quickly set aside any notion of turning around to search for him. Finding his body, for certainly he was dead from the amount of blood loss, would be a long shot of almost infinite impossibility. The probability that we could backtrack across sixty-some miles of open ocean and find a body bobbing nearly flush with the surface was exceedingly small, a probability that was worsened since he wore no international orange flotation jacket. And to radio other ships who might be within a few hundred miles to be on the lookout for him was equally fruitless, since we had no precise coordinate to provide, only a sixty-mile track that had by now been thoroughly washed by wind, waves, and sea currents.

In my years of seafaring, I had experienced man overboard incidents. Even when we saw the disaster occur, only once were we able to turn around, sight the man, and recover him safely from the icy Baltic. On that occasion the weather had been clear and we knew exactly when he had gone in. Though we lowered a boat to recover him, he died from exposure in spite of our efforts. The waters here were warmer, but it was a big ocean.

I wrestled a few minutes, weighing the pressures of adhering to my now compressed schedule against coming about to search in light of the extreme improbability of finding his body. If I did turn around to search, I had only nine hours of daylight remaining, and to continue searching after nightfall would be futile.

"Captain."

It was Andjou. With that simple prompt, he reminded me that he and the crew were awaiting my decision. The looks on their faces showed they all knew what the odds against success were, and that they understood the hazards inherent with making a living on the sea.

"Maintain course and speed, Mr. Andjou. I will hold a service on the main deck for him at dusk. Right now, I will compose a message to transmit to our maritime insurers in Dublin to report the incident. If you will check with me in a bit, I would like you to read it over before I send to make sure I have not left anything out."

"Yes, sir."

"Miranda, would you go below, gather up his belongings, and secure them so we can send them to his next of kin when we reach Cotonou?"

"Yes sir, Capitáno, that won't be a problem." As she brushed past, she placed a comforting hand on my forearm. I thought this odd, but welcome—certainly not what a captain expected from one of his crew.

It took me the better part of an hour to compose the message to the insurer and for my first mate to review it. Satisfied, I took it to the bridge. "Mr. Patel, here is a dispatch I would like you to send off right away."

"Yes sir." His composure was solemn as he read and understood what he was to transmit.

Now that we were making good speed in much calmer seas, fatigue descended on me, brought on by the extraordinary events of the day. I told my first mate I was going to lie down in my cabin for a few minutes and to call me if need be.

My sea cabin, just off the aft end of the bridge, was convenient for resting from the demands of being on call twenty-four hours a day while at sea. As I lay in my bunk, I noticed something out of place on the shelf where I kept a few odds and ends: the book I was reading, a battery-operated shortwave radio for monitoring maritime weather, and a small statue of a Swiss Guard I'd picked up on a visit to Rome almost a decade ago during my one port call to Fiumicino, Rome's seaport on the Tiber River.

Something was hanging from around the neck of the statue. It was a medical alert bracelet for Rajip Tasmoon-Shamlyn, my missing engineer.

I hadn't put it there. I'd have remembered something like that. As I examined it, I realized Rajip's disappearance was no accident. If he had slipped and fallen overboard, the bracelet would have gone with him. Or, if it had somehow come off in his desperation against the elements, we might have found it during the search. Someone had deliberately placed it here, violating the sanctity of the captain's cabin in the process.

I got up, wanting to talk to someone, but that wasn't a good idea. Who was I going to tell? No crewman should dare enter my cabin without my knowledge or permission. Sneaking into the captain's cabin and leaving a calling card such as this meant someone was sending me a message, but who? And what was the message? Until I learned who the culprit was, I had to keep this to myself.

The next morning, I received a message from the EU trade representative in Dakar acknowledging my incident report. It went on to read that Chamberlain's ship chandler in Dublin had arranged for an Admiral Pendali Gangho of the Benin Navy to conduct an inquiry into the affair upon my arrival in Cotonou.

The EU trade rep offered me the alternative of pulling into Senegal for the inquiry, an idea I immediately dismissed, since my timeline to reach Benin was tight as it was. I couldn't afford the time to divert to Senegal and the option of having an admiral conduct the inquiry in Benin was the more practical of the two options. I replied immediately that I was continuing on to Cotonou and expected to arrive at first light on the twenty-first.

The message's mention of Chamberlain's gave me pause. How could Chamberlain's have known of Tasmoon-Shamlyn's death? I certainly hadn't informed them. And how did a ship's outfitter get involved in the official decision-making process of maritime law? This wasn't a matter for anyone except properly authorized functionaries of the maritime courts.

I was annoyed and frustrated. The bad weather had already delayed me and now the pending inquiry nagged at me. Other than the oddity of finding the missing man's bracelet where it couldn't have gotten without someone's overt action, I had nothing to point to other than the fact that an unfortunate accident had occurred. It wasn't uncommon to lose sailors overboard in storms without a trace.

Proceeding to Cotonou and presenting everything I knew to Admiral Gangho of the Benin Navy as quickly as I could were the only ways I could clear up this mess and complete my contract.

Chapter 6

WITH A WEEK to go before reaching Cotonou, I finally brought *Marigold*'s course east and rounded the Bulge of Africa. I'd never been this far south. Ever curious about worlds I hadn't seen, I closed the coast to within ten miles to see if I could make out any of the continent's details.

It was moments like this, times when I could become lost in my own thoughts, that I enjoyed the most about being at sea. Here, the passage of time was measured in the light of the day and by its absence at night, constrained only by latitude and the season. In the north Atlantic in mid-spring to mid-autumn, days were long and there was time to spare. A sailors' duties matched the expanded opportunities offered by the abundant daylight. But from winter's cusp to the ides of spring, sailors worked with an intensity to finish chores while they could still see and before dark brought the cold of night.

Normally, I would have maintained at least a hundred-mile standoff from the coast, to steer well clear of local shipping traffic. It was as I daydreamed as to what I might see that I recalled the picture book I'd perused in Chamberlain's Dublin office. I wanted to see the origins of those colonial-era photographs of this fabled coastline.

The West African coastal regions were called the Ivory and Gold Coasts, which both the Europeans and Arabs exploited. From the Bight of Benin to the Gulf of Guinea, opportunists had pulled much sought-after treasures from Africa's interior. Setting up strongholds on rivers called Brass, Calabars, and Niger, traders crammed ship after ship with pepper—at one point worth its weight in gold—palm oil, cotton, elephant tusks, and gold. Fortunes were made and lost in a heartbeat amidst the swelter and disease of this tropical clime.

Thoughts of the book's pictures brought back a memory of something my grandfather had told me at the Temple Swan a month earlier. He let drop a comment, which at the time I gave little regard, but which now had new meaning.

"Sailing along Africa's west coast, the Bight of Africa," as he called it, "it matters not what you call the coast, Boyo. It's a place where they've not heard of, nor do they give a damn about Christ or Mohammad. Their only religion is greed. They'll entice you with gold and steal your soul. It was up to us ship captains to look out for each other. Not everyone who sailed here came out a winner, including me."

His prophetic words, the photo journal's account of Africa's history, Andjou's warnings about Benin, and Senhor Albreggo's cryptic comments about my destination gave me pause to wonder if I were doing the right thing. I suddenly realized I really didn't know what I was getting into. My idea to seek Dillon O'Connor's help was beginning to expose downsides I hadn't considered, the most significant being that I could lose it all to him. Grandfather's most recent communication hadn't been a whole-hearted recommendation. It was more of a mention in passing. As he had said, "Some of my contemporaries in the business at that time didn't fare too well at Dillon's expense."

I flicked my cigar butt over the side and watched it fall into *Marigold*'s wake, sparks trailing on the wind. Despite the admonitions I'd heard and read, I was excited at getting my first glimpse at this mysterious land.

For the better part of the remaining daylight hours, I stared at the coastline, enjoyed a cigar or two, snapped occasional pictures, and took my noontime and evening meals on the wing bridge. Other than the occasional harbor where a river discharged its burden of inland mud and debris into the ocean, the coastal landscape was unremarkable. Several freighters crossed my path on their ways to or from their places of business, looking for the world as normal as any other merchant vessels I might have encountered in the Baltic or the English Channel.

Twilight overtook *Marigold* quickly here in the tropical latitudes, so I gave Patel the order to open the coast as the sailing directions recommended and follow a rumbline course towards Cotonou.

My disquieting glimpse of the hump of land called Africa offered me no evidence of the nefarious trade dealings outlined in that coffee table book at Chamberlain's. Likewise, I had encountered none of the treacheries my grandfather and the others had warned me of. However, what did come to mind was Miranda's question about my insistence on making this final voyage: Will this make it sit better with you?

The answer to that I still didn't know.

Chapter 7

JUST AFTER DAWN on the morning of the twenty-first, I brought *Marigold* around to the north-northeast and made the final run to the coast. The blinking lights of civilization grew steadily brighter as I steadied on course for the harbor entrance.

I was startled to see the menacing grey form of a naval gun boat idling outside the sea buoys, a vessel of the Benin Navy judging by the ensign flying from her jack staff. Though smaller in length than *Marigold*, she brandished a 76-mm gun on the foredeck and two gun tubs on the superstructure, each of which contained manned, fifty caliber machine guns. The patrol boat made no attempt to hail me nor hinder my progress inbound to the port, though her advantage in speed would have made such an effort easy. The ominous warship simply marked time, as if to say in a polite but daring manner, "Please enter the channel."

I aligned my course with the lagoon channel marker and made the final turn west into the wharfing basin. The patrol boat fell into line astern and followed me in. There was another freighter tied up at the opposite wharf, but there was no activity at the piers, save for the line handlers sent from the port control officer to assist in tying us up. As the line handlers made busy making *Marigold* fast, the patrol gun boat moored fifteen yards directly astern of me, effectively blocking my exit. I wasn't sure if the Benin Navy was protecting me from foul play or perpetrating it.

Though midmorning, the sun had climbed rapidly and was well overhead. Looking to seaward past the entrance channel, the sky was bright and the water a brilliant blue green. In contrast, as I looked across the wharf towards the Benin harbor's support buildings, the mangroves formed a dark backdrop that milked the brightness from the sky above.

Beyond the long warehouses fronting the wharf, the buildings in the surrounding section of town failed to rise above the spreading tops of the tropical trees extending towards the interior. The water in the basin was the outflow from coastal mangrove swamps where a rotting vegetative smell mingled with the refuse odors of civilization, which sluggish water had carried south from the interior lagoon. This would be my lasting impression of Benin proper.

I didn't have to wait long before a battered and rusting Land Rover made its way down the dock and pulled up opposite *Marigold*'s gangway. Beside the driver sat a heavyset man in a khaki tropical uniform. He spoke quickly to the driver, turned to the back seat to recover a portmanteau, and alighted to the pier proper.

I greeted him at the gangway and welcomed him aboard. He was slightly taller than me and outweighed me by a good hundred pounds. In a deep, authoritative voice he said, "I am Dembo Johnson, the Cotonou Excise Tax Officer and Head of Longshoremen."

Definite French colonial intonations inflected his English and his girth was only exceeded by the length of his official title.

"Pleased to meet you, sir. I am Captain Johnny O'Scanlon."

I presented *Marigold*'s registry, but he didn't seem interested enough to examine it. He simply nodded to acknowledge that I had at least made the effort to present my bona fides. I motioned toward the ladder leading below. "Why don't we get some coffee or tea, sir?"

"Indeed, sir. I should like to inform you of my few port requirements."

I raised an eyebrow at hearing his comment. He'd gotten right to the point by saying "my requirements," not "our requirements." And by that I assumed that his point was: this could be a problem.

Miranda had a mess deck table set up with coffee and pastries. I thanked her for her trouble and whispered, "Tea," and she stepped back into the galley. The big official in his sweat-stained khakis sat heavily on a chair, all but eclipsing a good portion of his side of the table with his bulk. He set his satchel on the table and rummaged in it before finally removing a document.

"Capitaine O'Scanlon, here is a listing of the port facilities available for your use, their costs, and the mandatory labor required if you subscribe to them."

Once again his comments were preemptive. He'd said, "if you subscribe to them." But did I have a choice? I looked askance at him. He'd made no attempt at even the slightest acknowledgement of pleasantries before he delved directly into the business of running the port.

I examined the document. The prices for provisioning food and water seemed in order, but the labor costs for porters to deliver them pier-side were very dear.

"Is there something wrong, sir?" the tax officer asked.

Not wanting to get off on the wrong foot, I decided to say nothing derogatory. "No, Mr. Johnson. It just seems your labor costs are higher than they were in my last port of call."

"Perhaps at your last port of call they didn't have the same difficulties to overcome as we do here in Benin, sir." This man was all business—his business.

"I can abide by them, I assure you. I won't be here long. As soon as I can arrange for my cargo to be delivered and loaded aboard, I shall be gone."

"Whom are you dealing with? Perhaps I may be of assistance," he offered.

I hesitated, my instinct being he'd charge me for that service, too. But I decided on expediency.

"Thank you, I'm looking for a Mr. M'Nasi. He has a United Nations consignment of hardwood logs, storage bladders, and bundled shake shingles from Niamey, Niger."

I pulled the note I'd carried in my packet with M'Nasi's address and phone number, which Dillon O'Connor had told me to memorize, but which I'd committed to paper right after the meeting. "I have his contact information right here—"

He cut me off, waving away the slip of paper. "Where might these be bound for, if I might ask?"

He inquired not about my relationship with Mr. M'Nasi; he simply wanted to know where I was taking the cargo, as if this were a test of some sort. Already sorry that I'd given him more information than I wanted to, I had no choice but to answer.

"I'm to deliver them to a United Nations mission project in Brazzaville, Congo. Do you know Mr. M'Nasi?"

The port official rubbed his double chin with a ham hock of a hand and made as if he were pondering whether or not to answer my inquiry. "I know Mr. M'Nasi," and then offered nothing further.

I recognized now the conversation was going to be tit-for-tat. If I asked, he would answer—maybe.

"Do you know how I can make contact with him?"

Again, he measured his response. "Yes, I believe I do."

Miranda returned with a teapot, cup, and saucer and stood behind the big man. As she leaned around him to pour, she caught my eye. I saw her rub thumb and two fingers together in the universal sign for money. He was looking for a bribe.

Not having negotiated consignments in this part of the world, I didn't know how much "extra" I would have to offer, much less know how much of the money Dillon had fronted me I had to play with. I screwed up my courage and made a stab at appealing to his vanity.

"Since I am on a tight schedule, the sooner I can make contact and get my cargo loaded, the better off I'll be. If you can provide me with a few longshoremen, it will be worth €500 to you."

Evidently, Miranda had put me on the right track. The official's eyes brightened.

"Mr. O'Scanlon, my men are highly skilled. I don't think you can get their quality labor for anything less than, let's say, €1,500."

I noted his choice of "Mr." rather than the more formal Capitaine he had used previously. He was posturing for control of the negotiation.

I pretended to consider his price. "I understand completely, sir. If you can get your best longshoremen to do this for, say, a thousand euros, I think I might be able to come up with €200 as an agent's fee for you—off the books so to speak." I put the deal squarely back into his lap.

He smiled broadly. "I think that is most acceptable, sir. I shall get in touch with Mr. M'Nasi post haste and get our transaction going."

It didn't surprise me that the port control official referred to my dealings with Mr. M'Nasi as our transaction, that is, *his* transaction. I didn't have time to care. All I knew was I was moving ahead again in fulfilling my contract with Dillon O'Connor.

Dembo Johnson lost no time in packing up his portmanteau and departing *Marigold*. We escorted him to the brow, and as he drove off, Miranda said, "You know he is a charlatan, don't you?"

"I figured as much, but what could I do? If he gets me what I need and I get out of here by tomorrow at this time, it will have been worth it."

"Don't count your blessings quite yet, Capitáno. You have another visitor." Miranda nodded towards the pier.

Approaching pier side from the ship's stern was a tall black man in a naval uniform with a retinue of three naval personnel trailing closely behind. From the gold encrusting his sleeves and shoulder boards, not to mention the aiguillettes on the uniforms of three officers in lock step behind him, I guessed this man must be important, at least in Cotonou.

My new guest strode across the gangway before I could gesture for him to board. Only one of his aide de camps followed him aboard.

"Are you captain of this vessel, sir?" He spoke in thickly accented English, with the authority and assurance of his position in the local government.

My first inclination was to raise an objection to his barging unbidden on board, but my experience with Mr. Johnson cautioned me not to.

"Yes, I am, sir. I am Captain Johnny O'Scanlon out of Dublin, Ireland, and how may I be of service?"

"I am here to conduct an inquiry into the loss of your crew member last week at sea. I have been commissioned by my government to make a report to the EU through the Pan-African Maritime Commission. So, if you please, let's go somewhere and talk."

Still not sure I wanted this man, regardless of rank or charter, on my vessel, I asked, "You have me at a disadvantage, sir. I don't know your name."

Without apology for his breach of protocol, he said, "I am Admiral Pendali Gangho, Benin Navy, a vessel of which I have stationed just off your stern."

The name rang a bell, as I remembered the EU trade rep's reply informing me there would be an inquiry headed by this man. But the message he delivered now was very clear. You are not my guest; you are at my pleasure until I have completed my business—my very important business.

As I escorted the admiral and his lieutenant towards the mess deck, Andjou and Wahral stood not fifteen feet from the gangway, each expressing a contemptuous look, not towards the naval officers, but towards me. Catching my interest in them, my first mate's stoic face morphed into a malevolent grin, which Wahral mimicked. As we reached the ladder, Wahral gave a familiar wave, not to me, but to the admiral's lieutenant, as if they knew each other. Something was going on and I needed to get to the bottom of it as soon as I satisfied the admiral's inquiry.

"Is it this way, Captain?" The admiral's question brought me back to the matter at hand.

"That is correct, sir," I said, pointing the way.

Miranda had reset the table. This time, however, her demeanor was different. Gone was her usual stance. Now she stood with one hand on a hip tilted forward. Had we been in a village bistro, I would have regarded her pose as provocative. But here, at the door to her galley, she sported a welcoming pose as only a comely woman could. It was the perfect ploy to deflate the air of importance this pompous naval official projected. She was becoming a very valuable ally.

Admiral Gangho sat and positioned his cap with its impressively adorned brim of gilded 'scrambled eggs' on the table facing me—further intimidation. Miranda was there almost as quickly with a coffee carafe, cups, and a plate of pastries, which she placed on the table after removing the admiral's hat to an empty chair next to him. She played this game well, I observed.

Caught off guard, the admiral made no objection. Rather, he smiled. "Very good. Do you have any sugar?"

The contentiousness in the air had cleared from his officious entrance, so I began. "Tell me Admiral, what information can I offer you that I haven't already provided in my report?"

He took a sip after cooling it with a soft blow through pursed lips. "Very good, thank you, Miss…"

Miranda met his gaze but did not answer his question. She simply said, "You are welcome, Admiréle."

"Admiral," I repeated, wanting to finish his business as quickly as possible. "What other information can I give you that wasn't in the report I radioed from sea?"

Not knowing for sure how much authority he or the Pan-African Maritime Commission had, I assumed the admiral's inquiry was merely a formality, something to put a bow on an unfortunate, though all too common maritime incident.

Realizing his charms were ineffectual on Miranda, the admiral turned to face me. "Uh, yes, the report. It was thorough, I assure you, Captain. But by the time I received it, it had gone through translation and I would benefit by hearing your story directly, if you don't mind."

His tone and attitude were a bit more conciliatory, so I was only too glad to relate the story again for his benefit. I told him how we'd ridden out the storm and realized after it had passed that engineer Rajip Tasmoon-Shamlyn was missing. I described how we had incidentally found blood on a bulkhead and stanchion topside. A thorough search of the ship had been made and no sign of the missing crewman was found. Nor could we find a single clue as to how the tragedy had occurred.

I didn't share the mystery of finding his medical alert bracelet in my sea cabin. This haughty admiral didn't strike me as the one to confide a secret in.

"Had he been distraught of late?" the Admiral asked, taking another sip of his coffee.

"Not that I could discern. When we left Madeira, in fact, we had an impromptu party the first evening out, and everyone, including Rajip, seemed to enjoy himself."

The admiral looked at his fingernails, which he had splayed in front of him. He was quiet for almost a minute.

"And what now are your intentions, Captain?"

There was a tinge of challenge in his words. "As soon as I can, I'm meeting with my shipping agent to arrange

93

for the purchase and loading of my consignment. Then I'll be off."

"And who would that agent be?"

The admiral had lost interest in his investigation and was now determined to discover why I was in Cotonou. I gathered from this question three things: one, very few outsiders came here except on business; two, very little commerce was conducted in Cotonou, so my being here was both an anomaly and a novelty; and three, whatever my business was, it was his business, too. Armed with these realizations, I answered.

"As I told the port tax man, Mr. Johnson, I'm to pick up a consignment from a Mr. M'Nasi and deliver it to Brazzaville, Congo. It's in support of a UN project to improve infrastructure in that country."

I tried with some difficulty to wean impatience from my demeanor, but I was already tired of the intrusiveness of these officials. I could see no reason for their insistent, probing questions. The sooner I could satisfy this tin pot potentate, the better off I'd be.

"Hmmm. I would warn you, Captain, that Mr. M'Nasi is not the most forthright man to deal with. It would be better if you dealt with him through an agent."

I shifted in my chair, detecting a not-so-subtle warning in his suggestion. I was certain with half a second of thought, the good admiral would be only too glad to serve in that capacity—presumably so I would suffer no harm—and more to the point, earn him and his cronies another fee. But I was not going to fall into his trap.

"Admiral, my shipping agent in Dublin has already made all the arrangements with Mr. M'Nasi. I am simply here to carry out his wishes."

With this statement, I stood, indicating that as far as I was concerned, our meeting was over. I think the gesture of being dismissed caught the admiral off guard.

Moreover, the medal-bedecked, pretentious naval officer didn't follow my lead. Rather, he took another sip of coffee and looked to the galley doorway for Miranda's attention. She approached with a smile, which he eagerly returned.

"Admirále, I am so glad that you enjoyed my refreshments."

Then she summarily picked up his half-filled cup and the plate of pastries and returned to the galley. If he hadn't gotten the hint of my impatience, he certainly understood so from her actions.

"Come, N'Diaje," he said to his toady lieutenant, reaching for his cap on the chair beside him. "We must leave the captain to his very tight schedule." Then turning to me as he stood, "Captain, I think the investigation is done. Thank you for your input. However, the business of the port is my business. Please understand that there will be a fee for the escort I provided you into the harbor."

"Fee! I don't recall..." I caught myself and lowered my tone. "And what would that fee be, sir?"

He had me over a barrel. Moored directly astern of me was a vessel that had enough firepower to render me and my crew useless, if not dead. I had no idea if this was the standard way of doing business in this unfrequented port, but it was certainly in vogue today.

"The standard fee for escort into the harbor and out is €53K."

I was flummoxed. His demands were even more blatant than Dembo Johnson's.

"And what does that fee cover, sir?" It was all I could do not to spit the word "sir" in his face.

"It covers the escort into the harbor, the expense of my investigation, and the escort out of the harbor when you leave."

"Expense of your..." Again, I caught myself. "And why would I need an escort to leave?"

The sternness in his eyes morphed slowly into a smile.

"Why, pirates, Captain. I cannot control the miscreants who roam the swamps and jungles along our coastline. I'm sure they have agents watching every ship that picks up cargo here. In fact, I have no doubt they're watching you as we speak. I would think that a UN sanctioned cargo of building supplies would be something an enterprising pirate crew could make a handsome profit from."

"I will not pay that, sir. What you demand is nothing more than extortion."

Miranda, who had come to stand next to me, surreptitiously tapped my foot with hers, out of the admiral's view. I got her message.

"I am sorry to hear that, Captain. I think you should understand that I must insist. If you read the Cotonou Port Authority Instructions, you will find that a competent authority has the right to levy all necessary fees for services rendered to visiting vessels."

"And that competent authority would be you?" I glared at him.

Nonplussed by my ire, he said, "It would appear so, Captain."

His smile couldn't have been more annoying. I was so angry, it was all I could do to control myself. I almost blurted out what I thought he could do with his fees, but years of Grandfather's training constrained me and I didn't.

"In that case, Admiral, I am only too happy to pay for the escort and for your investigation. But I don't think I'll require your navy's assistance leaving the harbor. I saw no sign of pirates as we approached your coastline. I'm sure I'll be perfectly safe."

My diplomatic parry at his thrust made me feel better. I only hoped it wasn't a Pyrrhic victory.

His face softened from his roguish grin. "As you wish, Captain. In that case, the charge will only be €42K. You see, I am a reasonable man. And may I suggest that this evening you enjoy the festivities in Cotonou, more specifically in Ganvié, just a few miles north of city center, along the lagoon to the lake. That town has often been referred to as the Venice of Africa. My understanding is that there's a festival there tonight. You and your crew should go and enjoy it."

I couldn't think of a thing to say to his change to a cavalier tactic, so I went to my cabin to get his payment, only too eager to be rid of him. My only consolation was that I had managed to stem the financial damage by refusing his offer of escort from the harbor. Between his payment and the one pending for Dembo Johnson, I would have to be on my toes when I negotiated the delivery price in the Congo.

As I surrendered the negotiated fee at the head of the gangway, I noticed Andjou, Wahral, and Rajman standing by the handrail near the gangway. Their demeanor was almost giddy as they watched the departure. As the admiral's lieutenant passed them, he said something to the three, the only snippet of which I could hear clearly was when he referred to each of the three by their first names.

The admiral strode arrogantly to his open-topped Range Rover. Glad to see him off my ship, I turned to my three over-inquisitive crewmen smugly watching the proceedings and walked directly up to them.

"Andjou, explain why you seem to have an obvious relationship with members of the Admiral Gangho's staff."

Andjou's smile changed to a glare. "Captain, I was only glad to see him go." But as he spoke, both Wahral and Rajman snickered, drawing an equally penetrating glare from the first mate. Returning to face me, Andjou said, "I hope that he was satisfied with his inquiry about the loss of Tasmoon-Shamlyn."

My anger threatened now to get the best of me. "And how would you know the subject of the business the admiral and I discussed?"

He didn't respond and his face took on the expression of a guilty man caught in a lie. I turned to the other two. "How about you two? What do you know of this, since you obviously know the lieutenant?"

They didn't say a word. Very quickly I was putting answers to questions I'd been trying to resolve for days. Questions about coincidences: the mysterious disappearance of a sailor overboard after a storm had passed, not during it; the routing of my message reporting the incident to the ship's chandler who outfitted my ship and who was somehow privy to the assignment of the subsequent investigation; the appearance of the missing man's medical bracelet in my cabin; and the strange assignment of an admiral conveniently stationed in Benin to investigate the sailor's disappearance—an admiral who had somehow learned of the tragedy while I was at sea.

Someone, somehow was tipping off people along my sailing route of happenings on board *Marigold*. Were these three men spies, put aboard to observe that I picked up the cargo, safeguard it, and ensure its delivery to the Congo? Had Tasmoon-Shamlyn somehow learned of the reason for their keen interest in this cargo and was he eliminated by these three, using the storm as cover?

I came to the only logical conclusion I could—yes. I might not know how they got their information, but I couldn't have them remain aboard *Marigold* any longer.

"All three of you, you have five minutes to gather your things and leave."

They offered no explanation or rebuttal for their behavior. And within a few minutes they were sitting in the back of the admiral's open-topped Range Rover. They didn't appear to be in distress. Appearances confirmed the coincidences that had been vexing me. But what I didn't know was, why?

From the Range Rover, Andjou looked up at me standing on the weather deck and gave me that same cautionary look he had when he pronounced his veiled admonitions regarding Cotonou. His eyes, in contrast to his dark features, shone like beacons, even from the distance of the pier. And then he smiled, his white teeth forming a counterpoint to his eyes. His warning of Benin went from ironic to prophetic.

It was all too obvious, this man and his two cohorts were henchmen in league with a devil. Since it was O'Connor who had provided the crew, my assumption now was this treacherous trio had been embedded aboard *Marigold* to either keep an eye on me or to learn the possible location of gold Grandfather had hidden years ago. Equally clear to me was that Johnson and Gangho were either his henchmen or were extortionists of opportunity.

Before having his driver start the Range Rover, the admiral said, "Good day, Captain. Oh, it would appear that you may be in need of some additional crew. It seems that in spite of your hospitality, three of your men would rather stay here in the relative luxury of Cotonou. I am sure my colleague Dembo Johnson will be able to find extra crewmen willing to sign on for your trip to Congo."

He gave a casual two finger salute to the bill of his cap and ordered the driver to proceed. As he pulled away, he turned in his seat towards me, further unnerving my demeanor. He gave a full white-toothed smile, or more accurately—grin. In what I could only regard as a mocking voice, he said, "The festival at Ganvié—I recommend it highly, Captain." With his newly augmented entourage, he sped down the pier to his gun boat.

I seethed but didn't want to succumb and make a public outburst. At least three of my crew had betrayed me. How many of those left on board could I trust? I had been fooled by those three. Were there others? Was I completely blind? And exactly who could I turn to in this remote region of the world to voice my call for justice?

I reached the mess deck in a nasty mood and threw my cap on the tufted divan along the bulkhead. I bellowed, "Miranda, do we have any coffee?" Then I lit a cigarette.

Miranda appeared with a carafe, a cup, and an ashtray.

"Here you are, Capitáno. Is there anything else you need?"

She didn't seem affronted by my outburst. Her matter-of-fact, professional demeanor had a calming effect. It made me realize that being bellicose wouldn't resolve my problems, problems which were essentially behind me now in any case. Or at least I hoped they were.

Miranda reached around the corner of the galley door to grab her own coffee cup and sat opposite me. Without saying a word, she poured herself a cup and gestured by wiggling two fingers that she would like a cigarette. I pulled the pack from my shirt pocket and bumped one up, which she daintily removed. When she put it to her lips, I reached across with my Zippo and lit it. She took a long drag and blew out the smoke from the corner of her mouth, away from me.

"I don't think I've ever seen you smoke."

"I usually only have two or three a day. But you look like you need someone to talk with, Capitáno. So, go ahead. I am a good listener. Talk."

With a few well-chosen words and a simple gesture, she had disarmed my anger. I was still upset, but I was no longer consumed by the rage of betrayal I'd felt just moments before.

I didn't want to come off as being naïve in front of a crewmember. So I kept the subject matter on business while she listened without interruption. But once more, Miranda surprised me.

When I mentioned I'd fired Andjou, Rajman, and Wahral for their apparent shift in allegiance to Admiral Gangho, she said, "I thought those three were shady characters when I first saw them at Chamberlain's in Dublin. I wouldn't describe what they did as a shift in allegiance, Capitáno. It didn't take me long to realize they were in league. I never considered them as shipmates of mine."

I wasn't prepared for her revelation. "Weren't all nine of you together?"

My question was more for confirmation of her allegiance than a request for information. Until this moment, I couldn't rule anyone out of my suspicions. I was determined not to drop my guard too soon.

"I never sailed in a crew with any of them before, Capitáno. Those three came together into the jobber's office that morning in Dublin, their duffle bags in hand, just a half hour before you arrived. I'm telling you, somehow, they knew that Griswold needed a crew for the *Marigold*.

"The rest of us had been waiting for several days for a crew assignment, in my case for a week. A delay like that isn't uncommon in our line of work. The five of us had arrived separately looking for a contract sailing. At the last minute, those three showed up.

"The life of a merchant seamen is transient. We ship out on contracts, sometimes with individual ships, sometimes with shipping lines, sometimes on a spot basis at a port looking for work. As long as our papers are in order, the shipper doesn't care anything else about us. He is simply looking for qualified bodies."

My comfort level with Miranda was growing, so I asked, "Where did you come by your sea experience?"

"Up until two years ago, I was a stage performer on the Big Red Boat, Capitáno."

"Big Red Boat?" I wasn't familiar with the name.

"Disney, Capitáno. I worked on the Disney Cruise Lines in the Caribbean. But it didn't pay as much as being a cook on the bigger cruise vessels. For the past two years, I've been working mostly European and Mediterranean cruises. I'd never been to Ireland, so I took two weeks off to visit the Emerald Isle and was looking to get back to work when I inquired with Griswold." Taking a long drag on her cigarette, she blew out the smoke, her lower lip directing it above my head.

Her body language was inviting, as well as distracting, in a pleasant way. I had to pause before refocusing on the information she was sharing.

I began thinking out loud. "So, if those three were plants on *Marigold*—plants by someone interested in the United Nations development supplies...." My voice trailed off, but she didn't comment or prompt me to continue. She let me think.

Could I count on my remaining four crewmen? I already regarded Miranda as a trusted agent.

Miranda stubbed out her cigarette. "Capitáno, you should not worry. I have great confidence in you. Things will work themselves out. You'll see. Now, if you will excuse me, I must return to the galley and make preparations for our next meal. Is there something special you might want?"

"No, whatever you were planning is fine with me, Miranda." I stood and left the mess deck for my sea cabin.

I sat at my desk and pondered the day's events, trying to grasp their full import. I was faced with acquiring three replacement crewmen for the men I had fired, as well as preparing for my dealings with Mr. M'Nasi. Obtaining new crewmen no doubt meant having to deal with

Dembo Johnson, a likelihood I didn't look forward to. My concern with making a deal with M'Nasi had me worried he was of the same ilk as Johnson and Gangho. I could only hope that transaction would go as O'Connor had described it a month ago in Wexford.

My composure was almost back to normal when my eyes focused on the ship's logbook sitting on my desk. My breath came up short. Laid across the current open page was a brightly colored, braided amulet.

I'd seen it before, but with all my anxiety I couldn't immediately recall where. I picked it up. The cords were made of tightly woven hemp, its strands dyed red, black, green, yellow, and blue. This was no souvenir trinket. A skilled artisan had woven the intricate patterns that intertwined around the bracelet.

I dropped it as if it were on fire. For the second time in a week, someone had the audacity to invade my cabin and leave a gift, though I didn't consider it as such. In addition, that someone had the nerve to open my deck log, an official legal document in which I recorded every occurrence of importance on the vessel.

I quickly examined the pages and was reassured that at least the perpetrator hadn't defaced, or worse yet, removed any of them. This was of no solace, however; it did nothing to dispel my quandary as to who would do something like this.

I was mad and had to control myself not to give into that crimson impulse. Instead, I knew it best to rationalize who had betrayed me, and why.

While I mulled over possible options to take, I took out my crew sailing roster and looked at the names, focusing on four of them.

Osaze Andjou	first mate
Radeep Rajman	engineer
Pravesh Wahral	engineer
Rajip Tasmoon-Shamlyn	engineer

I crossed out Rajip's name, since he was dead. If there were a conspiracy, he most likely was not a part of it. More than likely, he'd been killed to keep the conspirators' secrets from being discovered.

I caught myself. Why had I just concluded it was not an accident, as our onboard investigation had concluded? No, the mysterious appearance of the two bracelets all but proved this had been murder. As I tossed around possibilities for responsibility, a few facts emerged.

One, Rajip was from Pakistan and the other conspirators were from Africa and India, nationalities not prone to fostering close alliances or becoming coconspirators.

Two, since that first day I initially spied my crew on Chamberlain's pier, Rajip had associated with his countrymen, Prankiop and Tengazy, and the Sri Lankans, Malik and Patel. On the other hand, Andjou, Rajman, and Wahral had stood together, and once onboard, always kept company with each other. Miranda's observations had confirmed this conclusion.

Clearly, the three keeping separate from the others indicated the possibility of conspiracy. There was that word again. And Dillon O'Connor had told me in The Morrow he would provide my crew for the voyage to Benin and Congo.

The proof of the link was in the medical alert bracelet I'd found in my cabin. And now the sudden appearance of a mysterious amulet. Each had to have been deliberately placed there. I tried to come up with some common thread to tie up these loose ends. The only one who had access to my cabin was Miranda, but I ruled her out.

It became all too clear: my First Mate Andjou was on the bridge when I had gone to my cabin and found the medical bracelet. And while I was dealing with Johnson and Dembo, he had plenty of time to plant the amulet today.

My thinking was focused now. The first time I'd remembered seeing the colored amulet was when I'd first had breakfast with Andjou. So as not to stare at the tribal scarring on his neck, I had diverted my attention elsewhere—his wrists. That's when I'd noticed the amulet next to a strange bangle he wore. I'd attached no importance to it at the time, but I had seen it.

And today, Andjou had revealed his true colors by displaying his allegiance to Admiral Gangho. The only way a contract merchant marine could be in league with a corrupt official, both of whom I first met separately some five thousand miles apart, was if the person who hired the crew and positioned them at Chamberlain's and had access to international merchant marine personnel incident reports were one and the same—Dillon O'Connor.

It looked like O'Connor had more riding on the success of *Marigold*'s voyage than making a few million euros on building supplies. So his three plants were there to ensure I picked up the cargo and successfully delivered it.

Maybe Andjou was to report back to him periodically as to my progress, a feat easy enough for a first mate who would be inconspicuous going to and from the radio room.

But O'Connor had a plethora of maritime shipping connections throughout the ports of Europe and Africa. He could have easily called on these to keep him abreast of *Marigold*'s whereabouts without insinuating agents on board. No, he had people loyal only to him aboard *Marigold* because either he didn't trust me with getting his cargo to its destination, or he was looking for something.

Could that something possibly be the gold Grandfather had skimmed from O'Connor years ago? Grandfather had only said he'd hidden it where O'Connor couldn't find it. He'd never told me where, though.

As I sat putting pieces together while still smarting from the assault on my authority, Malik rapped lightly on the cabin door jamb. "Captain, there is someone from the port authority who would like to see you."

I looked away from the logbook and acknowledged his report. "I will be right there, Mr. Malik, thank you."

Arriving on the main deck, I saw a very fit Black man at the brow. "And whom might you be, sir?"

"Yes, yes, I am Mr. M'Nasi, sir. I was only too happy to see you come in today. Otherwise I was going to have to seek other means to handle my business transaction."

My face brightened. "Come aboard, sir. Let's do business."

Based on my dealings with Dembo Johnson and the scurrilous Admiral Gangho, I wasn't confident in how to consider this man: friend, foe, or opportunistic business-man. I decided that at the least, he was the latter—and at the very worst, the second.

But at least I could complete the first part of the transaction I had been contracted for. One thing was for certain, however; I was not going to share any information about my dealings that morning with Mr. Johnson or Admiral Gangho with this man. Either M'Nasi was in league with them, or he wasn't. Either way, my dealings with him were at the behest of Dillon O'Connor and not of concern to anyone associated with the Cotonou Port Authority.

I did, however, take one precaution and asked Miranda to stay close by the mess deck during my meeting with Mr. M'Nasi. She responded by setting out refreshments and stationing herself ready to assist. I was rapidly recognizing how valuable a crewmember she was.

Mr. M'Nasi wore a smart European suit, not Gives and Hawkes of Savile Row, but not off the rack at Marks & Spencer, either. He stood a bit shorter than me and was slight in build."Mr. O'Scanlon, I'm prepared to consign my cargo with you for €4.5M."

I all but swallowed my tongue and tried hard not to show my disappointment. Dillon had given me €4.1M for the job, a sum which provided me no profit. I also knew the going rate for building supplies, as the manifest claimed they were, was valued on the European market at far less than what Dillon's price warranted. But then again, this was not Europe and I was dealing with the United Nations bureaucracy.

But with Mr. M'Nasi's opening gambit, I figured there had to be something else involved—something of which I was yet not fully aware. Most likely I would never know what about this cargo made it so valuable, but I understood all too well that I was assuming all the risk to secure my future.

I knew one thing for sure, based on the strict schedule dictated by Dillon O'Connor: time meant everything to

Mr. M'Nasi, a fact I suspected he would never admit. I probably had leverage, but as to how much, I needed to determine.

"I tell you what, Mr. M'Nasi. It's a seven-day trip to the mouth of the Congo, and another three days to get up the river to Brazzaville. I can do that, but I can only pay €3.5M."

I knew full well I could make it to the river mouth in three and a half days, with another two to get upriver. That would give me four and a half days to negotiate with, something he most likely didn't know. I was banking that his need for speed was greater than his greed.

It took a few back-and-forths, but we finally settled on €3.875M if I could deliver the cargo within seven days from the time I left Cotonou. This left me €225,000 to the good, less the €1,200 I had committed to that crook Johnson and the €42,000 extortion fee for Pendali Gangho.

We shook hands. His grip was strong and confident. There was something about him, not reassuring, but definitely not alarming—or at least not as alarming as were my two previous visitors today.

SEVERAL TRACTOR TRAILERS loaded with M'Nasi's cargo consignment rolled down the wharf an hour later. Dembo Johnson lived up to his side of the bargain by providing a crew to handle the transfer to *Marigold*. It took them a little over seven hours to load the tarpaulin-draped cargo and secure it into *Marigold*'s three holds.

By then, darkness was setting quickly, as it did near the equator. Right on cue, with the last holddown turnbuckle in place, the portly Excise Tax Officer and Cargo Handling factotum of Cotonou, Mr. Dembo Johnson, arrived for his payment.

Putting up a false front to make what had just occurred to appear to be friendly commerce, he asked me, "How many logs have you loaded, sir?"

"The entire consignment is for a United Nations building project in Congo. I have three holds. Five tarpaulin bundles are in the center hold. I assume those are the logs of which you speak. The other two holds have containerized cargo. The forward hold carries con-boxes full of rubberized storage bladders, I assumed for fuel and fresh water storage. The after hold contains con-boxes with roofing shingles. I gather from this manifest that the UN is trying to break the natives from the practice of thatching their huts with banana leaves."

I don't know why I said that. Maybe it was my excuse for humor in a situation that warranted nothing of the sort. Dembo Johnson only grunted. I handed him the manifest document, which matched what I had told him. He examined it carefully to ensure that I hadn't short-changed him.

As I waited for him to read through it, I noticed that Tengazy, my refueling supervising engineer, had sidled over to the deck near where the two of us were standing. He faced the pier but was within earshot of both Johnson and me. I felt no alarm that he might be noting our discussion. I figured he'd repositioned himself to better check on his work. In the back of my mind, however, I couldn't help but entertain the fleeting thought he might be another silent conspirator still embedded in my crew.

During the time the crew and I had spent developing goodwill amongst each other on the trip from Funchal, I remembered having only one brief discussion with Tengazy. He told me he was a Tamil and had grown up in the Calcutta suburbs, his neighborhood being surrounded by a city of Bengalis. He was worried, correctly as it turned out, that domestic prejudices would significantly dampen his work opportunities, since he was not a native Hindu. To avoid persecution and possible discrimination in trying to make a living at home, he had signed on with a maritime jobber.

None of that history, however, shed any light for me of his current politics or loyalties. For the time being, I considered Tengazy as someone on whom I could bestow my guarded trust. The longer Dembo Johnson took to examine my manifest documents, the more stationary Tengazy became, and the less frequently he watched the pier fueling activities. When I turned to catch Tengazy's eye, he noticed my attention and eased himself away.

I called after him. "Mr. Tengazy, when you finish taking on fuel, let me know what the bill is."

"Yes sir, Captain."

He had an odd look about him, as if he were unsettled at being that close to Dembo Johnson and me. Or was I just being paranoid? I shrugged it off.

"I see that my men have your cargo safely stowed, Capitaine," Dembo Johnson said, finally satisfied with his inspection of my manifest.

"Yes, they have." I handed him two money envelopes, one for him and one for disbursement to his men. Strongly apprehensive about his association with Gangho, I was most anxious to finish our business and be gone from this devil's den. But that was not to be the case, at least not as quickly as I wanted.

111

"Capitaine, I understand you are in need of some additional crew."

I didn't need to ask how he had become aware of my dilemma. I simply said, "Yes, I could use two engineers with experience running marine diesels. It would only be for the run to Brazzaville. Once there, they can pick up another maritime job."

"I am sure I can accommodate your needs, sir."

I had no doubt about that. "And what would you think that would cost me, sir?"

"The going rate for engineers is €300 a week, with a two week minimum. Plus, there is the matter of air fare home, just in case there are no ready jobs waiting there in Brazzaville. You know what I mean?"

I knew exactly what he meant. "So what would that come to, sir?"

He mumbled softly to himself, "Three hundred times two times two, plus five hundred times two." Then in a regular tone of voice, "That would be €2,200, sir."

I held my breath, waiting to see if there was going to be an agent's add-on fee. My retirement fund was being bled by a thousand cuts.

Before he could sense the reason for my pause, I said, "I think a fairer price would be €1,700. That should make everyone happy."

A broad smile broke across Dembo's face. He seemed to enjoy my discomfort and realized that I was learning how the game was played.

"I see, Capitaine, that you have good negotiating skills. How about we settle on €2,000? That way I am happy." He emphasized the first person.

"All right, when can you have two men for me?"

Without hesitation, Johnson looked first to a pier crane operator and then to a stevedore by the crane's loading hook. "Kande, Ngobe, you are going with this ship."

The men immediately stepped away from their positions and came to the gangway.

"As you can see, Captain, they are only too eager to help."

I didn't ask the obvious question as to where their belongings were. I simply motioned for the two men to lay below. I was relieved only in that I had enough crew to man all of my watch stations safely for the week it would take me to deliver my cargo.

I was none too happy at having two of Johnson's, and most likely Gangho's, agents on board. But once I cleared the harbor, what could they possibly do to mess things up?

I paid Johnson and his next action was to go to the wharf and pay off his men. As a parting gesture, he had a stevedore drop off two seabags, presumably belongings for Kande and Ngobe. This coincidental convenience was getting to me. That complete, he drove a hundred yards further down the pier to the naval patrol boat berthed astern of me. My conspiratorial suspicions were confirmed when I saw him board the gunboat. He and Gangho would probably be toasting their good fortune at my expense very soon.

Knowing there was nothing I could do anymore about that situation, I went to my cabin and wired Dillon O'Connor. I reported I had the cargo securely in *Marigold*'s hold and listed the total cost. I included the extortion fees in the price, just so he knew what my expenses were.

My surprise was not that bribes were part of doing business. I had encountered plenty of that in my dealings on the Baltic and in the Mediterranean. What had astonished me, and the point I was trying to convey to O'Connor, was the blatant manner in which they were demanded and the amounts they sought.

I hoped he would take this added expense from his fee rather than from my profit, but he made no reply to my offer. I further informed him the investigation into the loss of crewman Tasmoon-Shamlyn was complete, as cursory as it had been. Finally, I told him of Johnson's and Gangho's willingness to offer replacements, for a fee, for the two engineers and first mate whom I had fired.

I decided not to mention anything about Gangho's veiled threat of pirates. At this point, I wasn't sure about anything concerning Benin, except that it was a rip off from beginning to end.

I also didn't mention my suspicion of his master-minding the untoward events I had suffered to date. Bringing this up in anything but a face to face encounter would not be beneficial for me.

As I sat in the comfort of my cabin, my sole refuge aboard *Marigold* where I could collect my thoughts without interruption, I revisited my earlier contem-plations of betrayal. Though I had suspicions as to the who and the why for my current state of affairs, proof still eluded me.

O'Connor had to be the central figure connecting the incident with Tasmoon-Shamlyn, the coziness of the three crewmen who first appeared together at Chamberlain's, and the coincidence of those same three to "seek asylum" in Cotonou.

My eyes went to the message copy I had just transmitted to Dillon O'Connor. He certainly could have arranged for those three to be in my crew. But why kill an innocent man at sea? Had he been a coconspirator, too, who somehow changed his mind, giving the others reason to eliminate him to keep him from alerting me? Or had an innocent Rajip overheard the other three talking, discovered their reason for being on board, and then been killed to prevent his reporting it?

I couldn't answer those questions, but it put my regard for Dillon O'Connor in a darker light. Perhaps he wasn't the answer to my financial trouble. But I had no explanation for why he would foment the tragic events that had befallen us on *Marigold* to date. After all, he had several million euros at risk in this cargo of building supplies.

And about those building supplies in my hold: who spends that much for building supplies from the Central African Republic when much better quality, and certainly less expensive goods, could be sourced from Europe?

Something about this cargo was worth a hell of a lot more to Dillon than simply roofing shingles and commercial water bladders. Interestingly enough, neither Gangho nor Johnson insisted on examining the cargo. They simply took the manifests at face value.

The only reason could be that they weren't as good at this extortion game as they would appear.

Now I was pretty sure the sole reason for the three interlopers in my crew and for the strongarm tactics of the Cotonou Port Authority was to ensure the cargo was loaded for the journey south, thus protecting O'Connor's investment.

That implied Mr. M'Nasi's role was that of the banker, a conduit for the transfer of money. The reason for the intrigue that had permeated this journey so far had to lie in the true nature of what I carried in *Marigold*'s holds.

But I couldn't just go breaking security seals on the con-boxes to look inside. If I found exactly what was manifested, I'd have broken the trust all clients have with their shippers, that is, to transport their goods securely.

And if I found contraband, who would I tell? After all, Gangho was tied up just aft of me, in his country, on a heavily armed gunboat. I was certain I would not survive any attempt now to resolve this issue.

Any attempt to get underway in the dark and sneak by the gunboat would be pure folly. As soon the sun rose tomorrow, I had to clear Benin, get to the high seas, and deliver whatever was in *Marigold*'s holds to those waiting for it in Congo. To do anything else would jeopardize getting to the breaking yards, selling *Marigold*, and starting a new life.

My feelings were not unlike having to take cod liver oil when I was a boy—I simply had to pinch my nose to tolerate it. It didn't make it taste any better, but at least it would be over soon.

The one bright part was the realization that the only one I could trust in the crew was Miranda. She'd proven her loyalty to me on more than one occasion, the only thing on the plus side of the balance sheet at the moment.

Chapter 8

IT HAD BEEN a tiring day and I needed to shake today's problems. Since darkness was gathering and I wouldn't be leaving port for at least another twelve hours, I decided it was time to relax. What I liked most about having my own ship was not the work of hauling cargo, but the chance to visit new places and experience new cultures. I most certainly would never be in Benin again, so I might as well see what I could of the place while I had a few hours.

I didn't want to venture out alone. If Dembo Johnson and Admiral Gangho represented the hospitality in Cotonou, I needed moral, if not physical reinforcements. Miranda, Patel, and Malik were eager to see a few sights and joined me in the short walk up the quay to the Hotel de la Plage, apparently the best hotel in town.

Built in French Colonial style, the exterior was well maintained, a significant departure from other storefronts we passed along the way. Sunset didn't appreciably change the heat of the day and sweat stains quickly appeared on our shirts, that is, except for Miranda. She had sensibly worn a sleeveless blouse to save her that embarrassment.

Not feeling adventurous when it came to choosing food from a menu in a foreign land, I'd suggested the hotel restaurant rather than one of the other eating establishments along the main street. Fortunately, English was spoken by much of the staff and their menu offered food which was familiar to us.

After dinner, I asked the hotel manager what there was to see in Cotonou.

"Yes, yes, mon Capitaine, you are in luck for tonight there is a Voodoo festival in Ganvié. It is something you should not want to miss. It is a very short ride from here, just past Abomey-Calvi. It is a village built on stilts above the water. You can get there easily by taxi. Or, if you are more... eh... eh, how you say... venturesome, you can take the *zemidjans*, what you call a motor scooter. That is cheaper than a taxi."

I recalled Gangho's parting recommendation about seeing the Voodoo festival. That in itself had not spurred my interest. But the hotel manager seemed to be a straightforward and honest man. I asked my crew and they gave me an it's-your-choice shrug. I said "Why not?"

I opted for a taxi, feeling it best not to split up on separate bikes. The hotel manager assured me the taxi would take no more than thirty minutes to cover the eleven miles to reach the festival. Thus fortified with knowledge of at least how the public transportation worked, we set out along the Lagune de Cotonou road.

For me, the term lagoon always had a romantic connotation. Unfortunately, it didn't apply to Cotonou's tidal basin, which consisted of shallow, nearly stagnant slough containing submerged, decomposing vegetation subjected to incessant tropical heat. I likened it to an odiferous tidal cesspool. The taxi couldn't get away from the foul smell quickly enough. Reaching the main coastal highway, we turned west and then north to where the town on stilts was located.

Being situated on the water was the only thing Ganvié had in common with Venice. The buildings were wooden structures, simple thatched roof huts atop rickety pilings driven into the lake bottom's festering muck.

What passed for a town's square was where the driver dropped us off after collecting 2,000 CFA francs, the equivalent of €4. His knowledge of English and our collective mastery of French precluded us from knowing how to contact him, or any other cab driver for that matter, for our return to the wharf where *Marigold* was.

At least the good admiral hadn't steered us wrong about one thing: there was a festival that evening. We only had to follow the sounds of percussive music and the glow of festival lights to find it.

As we approached the center of activity, the crowd grew. The stench of unwashed bodies accosted my olfactory senses differently than had the lagoon, though neither was pleasant.

Soon we reached a broad park where the people were packed almost shoulder to shoulder. We were so crammed together we couldn't walk four abreast, and soon enough, the dense mass of people separated us. We were like same-colored pawns on chess board squares; we could move slowly, but were always one person away from one another. To ensure we didn't lose sight of each other, we kept talking loudly to be heard above the ever increasing din.

The jostling made me nervous, fearful of pickpockets. But Miranda, who carried no purse, seemed to be perfectly at home. Patel and Malik, both used to dense populations in their home countries, weren't bothered in the least. I finally gave in to enjoying the festive mood, the music, and the adventure of finding something different in my life.

On a raised platform, there were several men in colorful costumes of yellow, green, and brown with batik and paisley patterns. They were beating long drums strung from straps across a shoulder. Random blares from horns, seemingly coming from multiple directions, added to the festivities. There was no melody or syncopation to either the shrill sounds or the beat; it was just a cacophony of hundreds of people in exotic celebration. Their collective uncoordinated movements, in time with an elusive rhythm known only to each individual, contributed even more to the revelers' gaiety, and added further to the pervasive body odor.

Within fifteen minutes, Miranda struck up a conversation with a couple in the crowd. She introduced her newfound friends. "Capitáno, these are Helen and William Sandler. They are from New Iberia, Louisiana."

"Happy to meet you." I shook the man's hand. "How did you happen to come across these festivities?"

The professor offered, "I teach African Cultures at Bayou State University. We came to West Africa on a sabbatical for research. And please, call me Bill."

With a skeptical eyebrow raised, I asked, "Bill, is tonight part of your research?"

"It's a little bit of that and part vacation," his wife said. "Several of the priests will be overseeing the rituals we came all this way to see. Back home in New Orleans there's a significant Voodoo culture. Those are mostly for the tourists, though we certainly have our share of dedicated followers. It's very much a part of the Creole culture throughout the bayou country. We thought we'd come over here to check out where it originated. I think we're all in for a treat."

"So what exactly happens in these rituals?"

Her professor husband spoke up. "Since I teach old world cultures at BSU, I might as well give you some background. There's Voodoo culture in New Orleans and Haiti. But that's because the slaves who were brought there originated from Benin. They carried their beliefs with them to the new world.

"Voodoo's a movement that harvests unsettled souls. These ritual festivals excite the followers who are spurred on by music, chants, and body movements. The priests then usher the suggestable ones, who are in a state of rapture, to become true believers and subsequently, disciples.

"Pretty soon you'll notice that the drum beats will synchronize and many of the people will begin a pronounced swaying to the music."

I was fascinated by Bill's enthusiasm and obvious expertise, but I couldn't quite give in to what he was describing. Thinking back to my teen years for a comparison, I asked, "Do you mean like we have at western rock concerts?

"No, it's more of a semi-religious experience here. Some of the people in this crowd are mediums trying to contact the spirit world. They use the music to help channel their thoughts. Before long, the diviners and the healers will join to reveal secrets of the spirit world. They will move amongst the crowd dispensing magic in a variety of ways."

"Magic? You mean like sawing women in half?"

Bill laughed. "That's circus magic. No, Voodoo employs witches as the go-betweens for humans and the undead."

121

Now my mind was reeling. "Witches? You can't be serious."

The professor continued. "Oh, but yes, witches are the ones who deal in spells and curses. They are extremely important in Voodoo, in spite of their being loathed by non-believers."

I nodded. "I will have to agree with you on that point."

"In the Voodoo rites, witches are both feared and respected. Mostly they reside in women beyond their childbearing days."

Malik piped up. "See, Miranda, you are safe for several more years."

Miranda frowned and simply said, "Go ahead, Professor Sandler. I find this fascinating."

Bill chuckled and continued. "Witchcraft is a social cleanser, since witches are eventually driven from society; thus, their magic must be spread by other than hexes or spells, that is, by a newly recruited crop of witches."

My skepticism obliged me to interject. "This sounds a lot like Christianity's exorcism rites, or at least confession."

"You're not totally wrong, Captain. The term Voodoo means mystery power in Benin's native tongue. Voodoo uses zombies and Ergungun to dispense justice while in a trance. These ghosts, night watchmen, and the living dead pass on magic while in a trance brought on by rhythmic drum beats. They speak in tongues while their eyes roll back."

"Sounds like historical accounts of the Spanish Inquisition, Professor."

Sandler gave me an odd look, but didn't smile. He simply continued his explanation. After a few more of his

DAN MOORE

revelations, I was compelled to ask, "Tell me you're not just describing a pagan analogy to the New Testament."

When he didn't respond, I added, "I guess the only thing I can say is I hope I don't run into any of these magic dispensers, or however you refer to them."

Bill remained unflustered by my cynicism. "You're already surrounded by them—followers and mediums alike. Don't worry, Captain, the Ergungun and witches are forbidden to touch you. To paraphrase your vernacular, this isn't a tent revival with the laying on of the hands. Theirs is a mind game only.

"So, no Captain, it is not that kind of magic," Bill went on. "They believe they can bridge the gap between the human world and the bizarre world of ghosts and the gods. It's their way of communicating with their nether worlds.

"You'll notice supplicants waving their arms and swaying to the drum rhythms. If you look closely, their eyes will be open, but they don't see. They'll be in a trance. We refer to that condition as a high religious state of being."

"I see." But of course, like the entranced revelers, I did not.

He continued, "Passing in and amongst the crowd, there will be sorcerers casting spells and witches interacting with anyone who wants to make the journey to the spirit world."

"Remind me again about the no touching rules..."

Before I could finish, the beating of the drums became more noticeably rhythmic. On a raised platform, not quite a stage, twelve men straddled tapered, cylindrical drums. They struck their drum heads with muffled, mallet-like drumsticks, festooned with feathers. The thong stringers that tightened the drumheads to the drum bodies were interwoven with red, yellow, green, black, and blue beading.

I searched my mind to remember where I had seen intertwined colors like that, but my attention was overpowered by the pageantry. The drums themselves were painted with strange symbols: spirals, parallel wavy lines, or stylized standalone human figures, all in brilliant, primary colors.

Whump... thrump... brunk... drump...

I could make out individual drum sounds, each making a counterpoint to another drum. The drummers had their eyes closed and moved to their own cadences, which were not yet syncopated.

The performers wore traditional African tribal garb, pantaloons and draped shirts with boldly printed patterns. Some had completely shaved their heads, but most had short cropped hair, the most common fashion I'd seen. The women wore printed, shapeless caftans with their hair wrapped in brightly printed scarves.

I glanced at the Sandlers, both of whom swayed with the rhythm and clapped their hands, more as if in an aforementioned tent revival than a Voodoo ritual. Their eyes were smiling, focused on absorbing the sights and sounds. I figured they would soon succumb to the rituals of the trance, as the swirling crowd enveloped and moved us along from where we stood.

What next caught my eye was a man holding a four foot long drum. He had raised pattern scars visible on both of his cheeks. His arms extended from the shapeless sleeves of his over garment and were bare from the wrists to his fingertips. Wrapped tightly around one wrist were several brightly colored amulets. I had seen those same adornments on the wrist of my now departed first mate, Andjou.

The drummer's amulets were identical to the ones he'd worn and the one I'd found stuffed between the pages of the ship's log in my sea cabin.

The professor saw my attention to the drummer's adornments and yelled above the tumult, "He's a Voodoo priest and right now is only focused on communicating with the other drummers. He'll slowly work them into a common rhythm. Once they start sounding as one, then the crowd will sway together, step in place with the common beat, and wave their arms back and forth in the air. A few will fall to the ground in a full trance. As they writhe there, no amount of attention by anyone attempting to aid them will bring them back to reality."

A man in African garb about my height danced slowly towards me, twisting his way through the crowd. He had on a loose outer cloak similar to the drummer's, except his had colorful fringe tassels edging its length. Fully covering his head and face was a knitted hood. There were no openings for his eyes, nose, or mouth, just zigzag vertical rows of gray and black knitted yarn.

I backed up and raised my camera to take his picture when Elizabeth Sandler cautioned, "Don't do that, Captain. He is an Ergungun."

"But I'm not going to touch him?"

"He is a Voodoo priest in direct contact with the dead and the spirit world," Bill said.

"You mean like zombies?" Miranda asked, raising her voice above the tympanic beating of the drums.

125

"Exactly," the professor replied. "We of the living world cannot communicate, touch, or interact with him in any manner. He's looking for the ones who will be chosen to speak with the gods to cleanse their souls for forgiveness."

I lowered my camera but continued snapping pictures from hip level, trying to be as inconspicuous as I could and hoping some would come out. That's when I noticed the welts on the masked man's neck descending to his shoulders and disappearing under his cloak's collar. On his wrists were colored amulets, some of which contained miniature charm-like attachments. Also encircling his wrist was a multihued, braided hemp bracelet—exactly like the one Andjou had worn.

I looked down at the feet below the hem line of his robe. He wore work boots—boots just like the ones Andjou had worn. Christ! In that instant, though I couldn't see his eyes through the knit pattern of his mask, I knew this man recognized me. Had I harbored a Voodoo priest the whole time on *Marigold* and not known it?

While my sudden thought made no sense, neither as to why I had made it nor as to why it mattered, I had conjured that image just the same. The reminder of my first mate's duplicitousness made me shudder.

There were too many coincidences: scars, Voodoo distractions, colored amulets. If I were to examine every dancer's face in the crowd, I would probably find Rajman and Wahral as well. All three of them plants, put aboard *Marigold* by O'Connor and perhaps in cahoots with Gangho.

The circumstantial evidence I pieced together in my mind—crewmembers not of my choosing, aloofness from

126

the rest of the crew, colored amulets, and the ready acquiescence of all three when I discharged them from my service that morning—fit together. It wasn't enough for me to prove something in a court of law, but sufficient enough for me at least to be glad I had fired them.

It took all of my will power not to snatch the hood from his head. But something told me that this wasn't the venue in which to bring this rascal to account for his betrayal. The crowd would turn on me with an outcome not as I intended.

Going for help was equally out of the question. If Andjou were teamed up with Gangho and Johnson, then he was most likely well connected with whatever passed for a local police force. I had no choice but to allow the Ergungun past. He continued weaving through the crowd, looking for someone's lost soul, if Bill could be believed. I just hoped it wasn't mine.

The drum beats grew louder and became more in sync. The writhing throng in the square moved in unison and waved their arms above their heads, moaning and mumbling incoherently.

Bill raised his voice above the din. "They are speaking in tongues. It's all part of the ritual. Soon a few of them will start—"

Two nearby participants fell to the ground, their eyes rolled back in their sockets. They babbled and flailed. The throng parted as people danced around them, ignoring them completely, as if they sought their own methods to achieve the same state of disorder as the poor souls thrashing about, not four feet away.

Off to one side of the drummers' platform, the sea of gesticulating people suddenly widened to form an opening for a drably dressed woman who approached holding a rope and leading a yearling bull.

"She is a high priestess," Elizabeth said. "She will tie the bull to that ceremonial post at the edge of the stage. In a few minutes, one of the Ergungun will sacrifice the bull."

"He'll what?" Miranda asked.

But Elizabeth didn't respond. I couldn't tell if she simply couldn't hear Miranda's question or didn't understand with all the noise going on. But it was clear the professor's wife was wrapped up in the happenings around her.

Bill's voice broke through the noise. "They'll sacrifice the bull to call the spirit world to them."

Miranda shook her head and leaned to whisper in my ear. "At least in Pamplona, they give the bulls a running start."

By now, a dozen or so worshippers, if I should call them that, were on the ground, and the drums were at their loudest. *Whump... whump... whump... whump.* The rhythm was getting to my psyche, almost forcing me to sway with the beat, not unlike the heavy metal concerts I had enjoyed in my youth. It was a strange feeling indeed—part reminiscent, part unbelieving.

The man with the biggest drum increased the tempo and the other drummers followed suit.

Whump ... whump ... whump ... whump. Soon the drummers' hands were a blur as they beat faster and faster. Suddenly, the lead drummer hit his drum loudly, *WHUMP!* The other drums abruptly stopped.

A squatty man approached—I assumed it was a man, but I couldn't verify that by his appearance. He was covered head to toe in black and brown robes. Not even his feet peeked from beneath his cloak's hem.

He strode slowly towards the ceremonial pole where the bull was tied. Hanging loosely around his waist was a scabbard on a rope belt. Two long, multi-colored knotted tassels hung from the hilt of a short sword protruding from the scabbard. He stopped in front of the bull. Not a sound could be heard in the square, except the heavy breathing from an exhausted crowd. Not even the night crickets, toads, and other normally vocal creatures of the nearby mangroves stirred.

Sweat rolled down my face, torso, and arms from the incessant equatorial heat. The priest slowly raised his arms above his head. Every eye in the square was on this strange figure—except for the bull's. He simply looked straight ahead at the pole. I clicked away with my camera, which was tight on its strap at my side. Fortunately, I had disabled the flash. I could only hope that the low light feature captured something.

Suddenly, the portly high priest, or whatever he was called, drew his sword and held it aloft. He began a singsong oration. It made no sense to me, but evidently its meaning was clear to those who had been squirming on the ground, because they ceased their commotion.

After an incoherent phrase or two, the wielder of doom reached around the bull's neck and drew the sword's blade across its gullet, slicing from one side to the other. The bull was nonplussed. He turned his head slightly, perhaps in disbelief. Blood spewed onto the ground.

For several seconds, the bull didn't move. Then his front legs buckled him to his knees. He wavered in that nose-down pose for several more seconds before his back legs folded. He began to low, as if he knew his end was near. With the bull's belly on the ground now, the priest withdrew the sword, wiped it quickly on the bull's flank, and reinserted it in his scabbard.

Whatever had happened, it broke the magical hold that bound everyone to silence. People who'd been dancing and waving their arms moments before murmured, mesmerized by the spectacle. Those on the ground pushed their torsos up with their arms, like a boxer who was being counted out and had regained consciousness.

I sensed that to remain in the square was not a good thing and motioned to Miranda, Malik, and Patel.

"I've had enough. I think we should find a taxi or one of those Jimmy Johns and head back to the ship."

"I agree with you, Capitáno."

"Leaving, Captain?" Bill asked. "I assure you, there's much more to come."

"I'm not sure I can take more of this excitement," I replied.

Just then an Ergungun, the nastiest smelling of the ghosts so far, stopped not five feet from me. I couldn't see his eyes through his knit mask, but I was certain he stared right at me. He raised one arm above his head.

His wrist was circled by amulets, some with engraved metal links and one with a multi-colored braid. I tried not to tremble and reflexively raised my arm as if preparing to ward off a blow.

"Don't touch him!"

It was Bill. "It is forbidden. He is of the spirit world. He won't harm you, and he definitely will not touch you."

I tentatively lowered my arm, staring the whole time at that terrible knit mask. Even though I couldn't make out any features behind the mask's knitted patterns, I was certain that he was smirking at me—mocking me. That's when I saw, peeking from beneath the bottom of the mask along his neckline, the all too familiar raised pattern welts, just like Andjou had displayed.

I was frozen by this sight, both in thought and in time. Just as suddenly, my mental paralysis was gone. I'm not a religious man—I attended mass on an irregular basis and made confession even less frequently growing up—but I'd just experienced a brief glimpse into what true believers of any of the great religions strive for. Call it God's grace, rapture, nirvana—it was otherworldly.

I snapped out of it when Malik pulled my sleeve and broke my engagement with the Ergungun. I followed my crewmen through the crowd.

It took us ten minutes to force our way back to where the taxi had dropped us and another five minutes to find *zemidjans* drivers who would agree to transport the four of us back to Cotonou. I hoped the open air ride on the motor scooter would clear my shaken senses; I was shaken, whether or not I wanted to admit it.

The vegetative stench of overripe mangroves and sewage forced the sights and sounds of the Voodoo ritual from my bewildered mind, like a dose of smelling salts. The scooter drivers followed a lake road, bordered on one side by tropical forest gloom and on the other by the fetid lake, until they reached the outflow to the lagoon proper where they turned south and followed the tidal runoff stream back to the wharf.

The smell of decay grew stronger until the bikes stopped at *Marigold*'s gangway and I got a welcome whiff of sea salt air. Before heading for my cabin, I stopped into the mess deck for some water. Miranda, Patel, and Malik joined me.

"Capitáno, do you also need something to settle your nerves?" Miranda asked.

"I was getting some water before going to bed," I replied.

"Patel and Malik were about to join me in a Campari. Would you like one, too?"

That sounded like a much better idea than water. I took a chair opposite them, relieved to be able to relax with people I knew well and could trust. "That was an experience I'm not sure I want to have again."

"Yes, Captain. I don't believe in the spiritual world, but clearly, many people in this part of the planet do," Malik said.

"I agree with Daniru. That is not a part of any of my upbringing," said Patel.

I hesitated to ask the question that was on my mind. But Miranda could see I was thinking of something, so she asked. "Capitáno, I take it you saw more than just a ritual spectacle tonight. Did you see what I saw on those ghost priests, as Mr. Sandler called them?"

Ah, she had recognized it, too?

I couldn't have replied more quickly. "I could've sworn I saw welts on the neck of the Ergungun."

"Just like the lead drummer had!" Malik said.

"And just like that *cabrón*, Andjou, had!" Miranda all but spat her words.

Malik's tone was not as vehement as Miranda's, but held derision nonetheless.

"He was not a good shipmate, Captain. And neither were Wahral and Rajman."

132

"Andjou was bad people, Captain," Patel added. "I think I suspected it when I first laid eyes on him at the pier in Dublin."

"I take it none of you liked him." I gestured with my glass inviting any of them to reply.

It was Patel who said, "No, Captain. I'd never met them before setting foot on the quay at Chamberlain's. And I hope I never do again. The three of them sat together at the dinner table when off watch, but I didn't think anything of it. But one time, while I was on the bridge after leaving Funchal, I saw Andjou coming from the radio room with an intimidating look on his face, as if to convey, 'You didn't see me if you know what's good for you'. That's when I knew for certain not to trust him."

"I wish I had known of this sooner, Mr. Patel."

Miranda cut in. "But Capitáno, what could you have done? He was first mate. Is it not common for him to go to the radio room?"

"That's true, Miranda. Perhaps that in of itself would not have set off any of my alarm bells. In retrospect, I'm not sure there was any way I could have known that I was harboring a disloyal crewman on board."

Malik sipped his Campari. "Captain, do you think those three had something to do with Rajip Tasmoon-Shamlyn's disappearance?"

"I would bet on it, Mr. Malik. But I'm afraid there's no way to prove it. And even if I could, who would I report it to? It looks to me like those three were under the thumb of someone else the entire time they were on board. But …"

Though I didn't voice my concerns, the evidence against Andjou was clear to me. The similarities of amulets, colored bracelets, and scars on the priests tonight with what Andjou wore brought these into focus. Tonight's festival revelations, at the very least, reminded me that Andjou held others, Wahral and Rajman, in his sway.

He alone had unquestioned access to the bridge and would know when I was present or absent from my sea cabin. For whatever reason, he was instrumental in Tasmoon-Shamlyn's death. He had placed his medical bracelet multi-colored amulets in my cabin to upset me. He hadn't hidden them. Rather, he had put them in plain sight where I was sure to see them. He wanted me to know someone on board could go anywhere, anytime he wanted to, and I couldn't stop him.

But he had overplayed his hand as Admiral Gangho's lieutenant was departing the ship. But firing them and ridding them from *Marigold* didn't put me out of the reach of Dillon O'Connor. Of that I was certain.

I couldn't allow myself the distraction of worrying about what O'Connor might have in store. Regardless of Andjou's actions during the transit to Benin, he was gone now and I no longer needed to worry about him.

To speculate what further obstacle might lay ahead of me did me no good. I couldn't protect myself or *Marigold* from something of which I had no specific knowledge. I had to focus on the prize, that is, to reach the Bangladesh breaking yards and secure my financial future. And the delivery of the cargo in my holds was key to that success.

Chapter 9

IT WAS A FOUL tide that pushed me clear of the Cotonou turning basin the next morning. With the gunboat not blocking my way, I backed to the channel, turned outbound, and headed to sea.

I cleared the harbor entrance sea buoy to the sight of the breaking dawn. The constant *thrump* of my diesel engines was a welcome beat. I felt its throbbing through my soles, not unlike the drum vibrations from the night before, but much more comforting.

The stench of the lagoon immediately gave way to the welcome freshness of saltwater air as a stiff sea breeze lifted my spirits. Not seeing Admiral Gangho's gunboat at the pier had been a much needed welcome sign. The bribe I'd paid him, though damaging to my pride, seemed to have worked. Between him and Dembo Johnson, I was down €46K, money my grandfather and I would sorely need once I disposed of *Marigold* and sought a new livelihood.

"Mr. Malik, steer course one eight zero at full speed for the next six hours. We have almost six hundred miles before we reach the outfall of the Congo River. I saved a great deal of money by saying we could make this run in under seven days, so don't let anything slow us down."

"Yes, sir, Captain, one eight zero degrees, full speed, I have it." His smile was genuine.

I stepped out of the bridge house onto the small flying bridge for some privacy. The events in Cotonou had me wondering again about the cargo I was carrying for Dillon

O'Connor. If he had insinuated crewmen loyal to him on board to ensure that this cargo was in fact loaded on *Marigold*, then what other measures had he taken to satisfy himself that it would be safely delivered?

The lengths O'Connor was apparently going to—the heavy handed crewmen, the loss of a man at sea—told me my difficulties had to be more than just about the content of the cargo. There had to be more to this than the few tidbits Pop had chosen to tell me—more than two Irishmen who were business acquaintances years ago.

Something had kept their mutual grudge alive all these years—something that neither one would tell me. If my grandmother Miriam were here, I might learn the answer. Whatever happened back then, I knew she blamed Grandfather for it. If I could ever hold Dillon O'Connor to account, I would demand the truth from him, for I was sure he was at the heart of the matter.

I was pleasantly taken from my troubling thoughts when the bridge house door opened and Miranda stepped out. "A penny for your thoughts, Capitáno. May I join you?"

She was lovely in the new morning's dawn. The ship was making thirteen knots and the breeze of our forward progress pressed her gypsy blouse against her. The sound of her accented greeting and her welcoming smile were more than I needed to lift my spirits.

"Certainly, Miranda. I was just getting some fresh air."

"You were deep in thought, no? I would think that after the hassle those two officials put us through in Cotonou, you would be happy to be rid of that place."

"I am. Don't get me wrong. I was just contemplating the coincidences surrounding the events. The mysterious loss of Tasmoon-Shamlyn at sea, Mr. Malik seeing Andjou exiting the radio room, and having to fire Andjou and his two cohorts, Rajman and Wahral, in Cotonou. And there were those strange marks on the necks of the dancers last night, just like Andjou had. Somehow, I can't believe they aren't all connected.

"If they are and I can figure them out, it would go a long way towards explaining how the word of Tasmoon-Shamlyn's loss conveniently preceded us to Cotonou, which alerted Pendali Gangho and Dembo Johnson. Someone relayed my radio report about Tasmoon-Shamlyn's death to Chamberlain's as well as to the intended EU trade representative. Then there's the Cotonou Port Control Officer's shakedown and the collusion between him and his navy friend, Pendali Gangho. If he is an admiral, then I'm a saint."

Miranda did something that took me totally by surprise. She touched me, not in a longing way, but she touched me nonetheless. She placed her hand softly on my forearm and said, "You are correct, Capitáno. Your instincts are true."

This unexpected and sudden personal contact didn't seem as out of place as it should have. If she'd been a man, it would have seemed a brotherly pat, a mild attempt to reassure. In any case, I didn't recoil. Neither did I draw any overt attention to it. I half turned to her.

"I'm worried, Miranda."

Miranda had demonstrated her loyalty to me and I needed someone to bounce ideas off, and this seemed to be the opportunity. Her reaching out to me enabled me to express my thoughts. In an unhurried, measured way, I related to her what was troubling me: Tengazy's curious interest in my discussion with Dembo Johnson on the pier while refueling, Johnson's coincidental availability of the two new crewmen I needed and who just happened to be working on the pier, and the eerie eye contact the Ergungun with the knit mask, scarred neck, and multi-colored bracelet had made with me at the Voodoo festival.

I didn't reveal finding the bracelet and amulet in my sea cabin, because I still couldn't confide in anyone how personally I took that action as an assault on me and my authority as captain. Additionally, the fact that it was Tasmoon-Shamlyn's bracelet I had found suggested that his loss was murder, rather than simply falling overboard, a suspicion for which I had no proof.

She listened, never interrupting, always looking straight into my eyes, taking in my every nuance. I had just begun to tell her of my new suspicions as to the nature of the cargo when her eyes shifted slightly to focus behind me, ahead of the ship.

"Capitáno, I think we have a friend."

In the hazy distance, about six miles ahead, I made out the unmistakable outline of a naval vessel. Its grey silhouette wasn't unlike that of the gunboat that had blocked the pier in Cotonou the night before.

It was, in and of itself, not that alarming. What did raise my hackles was the sight of a ribbed Zodiac kicking up a rooster tail racing towards *Marigold*, a few hundred yards away.

"Now what do we do?" she asked, more calmly than I would have imagined her reaction should be. "Are they pirates?"

"Pirates my ass! I'd have to assume this is no coincidence, Miranda. I'm sure that our friend Admiral

Gangho is out to make a double score. Yesterday's pier shakedown and now my cargo."

I bolted back into the bridge house and yelled, "As fast as we can go, Mr. Malik!"

At full speed, *Marigold* could make a little better than thirteen knots. At flank speed, the two diesels at best could answer only another knot and a half. I knew this would be insufficient to outrun the ribbed raider with its powerful dual outboard motors, but it bought me a little time and let me open the coast further in international waters. Then I heard the first pings of automatic rifle fire ricocheting off the sides of the bridge house.

"Helm to port! Steer a zigzag course, Mr. Malik! Thirty degrees one way, then twenty degrees the other, then back ten and then shift twenty. Don't set up a pattern; turn the rudder every thirty seconds. We have to make it as difficult as possible for them to close us. And above all, we can't let them board us."

The *Marigold*'s wake formed an elongated *S* in the sea as the ship plowed its sinuous course. This made us a more difficult target but still let us open the African coast, over twenty-one miles distant.

I went to the radio room off the bridge, picked up the transceiver's microphone, and tuned to the international distress frequency. "Any vessel, any vessel, this is Motor Vessel *Marigold* out of Dublin. I am under attack by pirates, repeat, under attack by pirates!" I informed whoever might be listening of my latitude and longitude, and then repeated my distress call.

I released the send button and heard the speaker crackle with static. After a few seconds, I started to key the mic again when I heard, "*Marigold*, this is Benin naval vessel *Gomo.* Are you certain that you are under attack? Could your hailing vessel simply be a welcoming party?"

Even through the garbled nature of the radio air waves, I recognized something familiar about that voice. By now, the Zodiac had passed a hundred yards down my port side and was circling behind to come up on my stern, all the while firing repeated bursts that occasionally dinged my hull. Evidently it was harder to hit a moving target from a bobbing small boat in the ocean than one would think, even with an automatic weapon.

"*Gomo,* this is *Marigold.* Are you able to render assistance?" I demanded into the microphone.

Click ... static ... click. "*Marigold,* this is *Gomo.* Captain O'Scanlon, if I were you, I would let my good friend Jaspar Kongali come aboard your vessel. I assure you, he is no pirate."

Pendali Gangho, that bastard! Now I recognized the voice of that two timing snake who had all but robbed me at gunpoint on the wharf in Cotonou. He was back for more, or more likely, for it all.

I went to the bridge wing. The Zodiac was only fifteen yards off my stern. Standing on my fantail, Kande and Ngobe, the new men Dembo Johnson had hired out to me, were waving to the Zodiac. Those bastards weren't trying to wave the raiders off. They were urging them to close the distance! One of them even had a throwing line ready to help them board us when they were close enough.

"Shit! Right full rudder!" I yelled to Malik. The bow immediately swung to the right, momentarily throwing off the Zodiac's approach.

"Steady as you go!" I yelled, straightening out our wake.

The Zodiac veered and circled around for another pass. My sudden change in course had knocked one of the two crewmen on the fantail off balance. With nothing to grab and arms flailing, he tumbled into the water. He foundered, thrashing his arms, as his head bobbed to the surface.

Neither his compatriot on the transom rail nor his countrymen in the Zodiac made any attempt to rescue him. His arms and head quickly receded in the *Marigold*'s wake. I could only imagine what his fate would be in these shark infested waters.

But I had no compassion for him. My anger was at the boiling point. Thugs were assaulting my ship, trying to steal my consignment, and attempting to kill me. The cargo was the least of my worries, but I would do everything I could to defend *Marigold* and my crew.

Just then, Patel and Tengazy reached the bridge carrying rifles and a pistol from the armory. I gave the pistol to Miranda and took up one of the rifles and several clips.

"If they try to board, shoot them," I yelled over the wind buffeting the bridge. "And Mr. Malik, keep up the evasive maneuvering!" I turned to Patel and Tengazy. "Follow my lead!"

Patel, who had probably never fired a firearm in his life, put the rifle butt to his shoulder and began shooting at the Zodiac. And any thought I might have had about Tengazy's loyalty disappeared when I saw the determination in his eyes.

I yelled, "Take the other bridge wing, Patel. We'll stay here and fire from this angle. One of us at least should always have a shot for them to worry about."

Both men began returning fire with gusto. Between Patel's and Tengazy's amateur marksmanship and the constant motion of both vessels, not a single round from the Zodiac found a vulnerable mark. Unfortunately, neither did any of ours.

I needed a different plan to fend off this attack if we were going to survive. That's when I noticed the lone turncoat crewman on the fantail was moving in sync with the ship's motion. I steadied my rifle on a stanchion, took a bead on him, and fired three times. One of the bullets hit home and he dropped to the deck clutching his thigh. Good, one more foe was out of the fight.

"Miranda, you stay here on the bridge with Mr. Malik. And Mr. Malik, come back to base course 180 and maintain your speed. Keep opening the coast. I'm going down to the fantail to see if I can dissuade these Zodiac pirates. Mr. Patel, keep firing. Mr. Tengazy, follow me!"

Before I could leave the bridge, the radio crackled.

"*Marigold*, this is *Gomo*. Captain, I see that you have a few tricks up your sleeve. Even if you repel my friend Jaspar Kongali in the Zodiac, you cannot outrun my warship *Gomo*. I can do over twenty knots and have a 76-mm gun at my disposal. I recommend you heave to, right now."

I hesitated. My first reaction was to pick up the microphone and engage in some heated diatribe with this villain. Instead, I bolted for the afterbridge door that led to the ladder down to the main deck, Tengazy right behind me. Stooping to keep a low profile as we made our way to the fantail, we found the remaining new crewman on the deck writhing in pain. It was Tengazy, my feisty marksman sidekick, who kicked the defenseless deck hand in the ribs. So much for my concern about his loyalties.

Seeing the assault on their compatriot, the Zodiac concentrated their fire on us rather than the ship's superstructure. The pitching seas sent their shots awry, thank goodness. Feeling nothing but rage, I couldn't help taking this assault on *Marigold* as anything but a personal affront, both to me and to everything I had worked for my entire life. How dare these bastards try to take it from me! Consigned cargo be damned; this was my ship!

I grabbed the gunshot sailor by the shoulders and dragged him to the transom rail. He screamed in pain, but I didn't care. A spark from a ricochet hit deck plating a few feet away. The intended boarding party's accuracy was no better than Tengazy's. With a firm grip, I lifted the wounded sailor's back to the rail and, with a heave, levered him over the side.

He kicked and screamed the short way to the wave tops and made a big splash. His flailing in the wake was short lived as he soon sank from sight beneath the waves, his leg wound streaming a red trail of blood—chum for the sharks.

I should have felt at least some solace in ridding myself of the second of those two treacherous snakes foisted on me by Dembo Johnson, but I was facing a more immediate and desperate reality. Several large plumes blossomed in the water just astern of Marigold. It was 76-mm gunfire from the *Gomo*. Shit! Once his salvos bracketed me to find their range, I was done for.

"Shoot at the Zodiac!" I yelled at Tengazy, who was fumbling to insert a fresh clip into his rifle. We both knelt behind the transom bulwark for cover and opened fire on the approaching raiders. I thought I saw one of the five in the raft fall backwards, hopefully hit by our rifle fire.

As for Tengazy, I realized I'd made an incorrect assumption that his aim was ineffective. Two of his shots hit the inflatable and its two bow floatation cells crumpled. Whatever my shipmate had aimed at, he was having better results than I could have hoped for.

The Zodiac's speed dropped as her seaworthiness became their crew's main concern. Realizing Tengazy's good fortune, I too aimed at the body of the Zodiac. Between the two of us, we managed to put a hole in two more of the Zodiac's flotation cells, which reduced the speedboat to a motorized life preserver rather than a steerable assault vessel.

The remaining Zodiac crewmen became more interested in their own survival than in continuing to fire at the *Marigold*. Seeing them fall behind our wake, I grabbed Tengazy by the scruff of his shirt to get his attention. He reluctantly stopped firing. I wasn't sure if he was flushed with some newfound discovery as a sharpshooter, or was simply high on the adrenalin rush of the moment. I motioned for him to follow me to the bridge.

There I found Malik diligently steering his cardinal compass heading of 180 degrees, plowing the seas as fast as he could make the *Marigold* go. Patel was busy reloading his rifle and I could see spent shell casings all around him. A salvo of splashes hit the water twenty yards off *Marigold*'s port beam.

Miranda came from the radio room. "Capitáno, your friend Admiral Gangho has repeated his order for us to stop and to let his friend Jaspar Kongali board."

"Did you answer him?" I asked.

"No, I figure he had binoculars and he could see what was going on well enough."

Something caught my eye from the distant horizon to the northeast, roughly from where Gangho's gunboat had first appeared. I saw a great puff of black smoke billow from *Gomo*'s stack. She had cranked on speed. I grabbed my binoculars from their bridge holder and fixed them on *Gomo*. The gunboat's bow was turning quickly towards us, but then continued swinging to intercept the sinking Zodiac, now well astern of *Marigold* by a good five hundred yards.

This was no time to breathe relief, though. With his speed advantage, I knew it would be simple for him to rescue his fellow conspirators and then continue his pursuit of *Marigold*, all within the next hour and a half.

This running gun battle had started roughly twenty miles from the coast of Benin. By now I was at least twenty-three miles off the coast. I contemplated my options. Were Gangho to pursue, he would overtake us, but not before we had both opened to forty miles from the coast, well beyond any nation's territorial claim. The whole time, of course, I would be on the radio maritime distress frequency telling the entire world exactly what was happening—of little consolation if he continued firing with that 76-mm cannon of his.

Before I could run through another option, the Pride of the Benin Navy stopped his pursuit entirely and turned back towards his home waters, still belching black smoke, abandoning his friend Jaspar Kongali to his fate in his less than stable rubber raft. I swung the binoculars back to the northeast, and the reason for my good fortune and Admiral Pendali Gangho's terminating his assault became apparent. The looming grey silhouette of a much larger warship appeared on the horizon.

My godsend was a Nigerian Navy frigate which hailed both me and the *Gomo*. Exercising a judgment developed while patrolling these waters over recent years, the Nigerian commander sent me a message wishing me well and headed directly for the *Gomo*. Gangho, outgunned and outmanned, was no match for the Nigerian ship of the line. At my last sighting of him, he was steaming due north as quickly as he could back towards Benin.

My competent officer of the deck, Malik, who had never wavered in adherening to my orders, slowed to a more fuel efficient speed and came to the south-southeast, on course to close the mouth of the Congo River over five hundred miles away.

My heart returned to a normal rhythm for the first time in almost an hour. Flushed more by relief than any sense of victory, I lit a cigar and went about inspecting *Marigold* for damage.

Peering over the gunwales and checking the super-structure, I noticed multiple dings where bullets had chipped paint and dented metal. The searchlight in the mast rigging had a shattered lens. On the fantail, I grabbed a hose and washed the pirates' blood over the stern transom. I wanted any contagion gone from the ship.

When I leaned over the taff rail to ensure it was clean, I noticed bullet stitch marks had tracked a path through *Marigold*'s nameplate. The entire *i* was obliterated, as were most of the *l* and the *d*. My one remaining nautical possession had been rechristened *Mar go*. But the word Dublin remained unscathed.

As the magnitude of what had just transpired sank in, I wanted to shout at the top of my lungs at the marvel of *Marigold*'s, and hence my, survival.

After settling myself, I returned through the mess deck on the way back to my cabin. Miranda called me. "Capitáno, you have not eaten today. I made lunch. You should have some. It will make you feel better and help you regain your strength. I just returned from the bridge to tell Daniru to get the word out to the rest of the crew."

Her tone was arresting and insistent. She spoke as someone who sincerely cared about my well-being. Her invitation was the prescription I needed to soothe my nerves after the morning's fiasco. I pulled up a chair and she placed a cold beer next to a hot bowl of stew.

Then she did something I was becoming pleasantly accustomed to, and which was completely against protocol. She sat down opposite me and wiped her hands on her apron. "Tell me, how are you doing, Capitáno?"

No longer surprised at her forwardness, I welcomed her offer. Strangely, the question that came to mind was, when did she have time to prepare this while shooting it out with pirates?

Being the captain had its lonely moments. By choice, I'd never gotten close to a crewman and certainly would have never thought to confide my personal concerns. I'd grown up under a rigid system espoused by every sea captain I'd served with, including my grandfather, all of whom believed that the business of the ship was the captain's and no one else's.

The crew was hired to load cargo, sail the ship, and run the engines, not to share in whatever troubles the skipper might have, professional or personal. After all, running a ship was a business, the captain was the boss, and he was paid for the troubles he endured.

Miranda's interest in my condition, however, seemed honest, and, I must admit, I liked it.

"All of my body parts are in the places where they started out this morning. That's a good thing. There for a while, I wasn't sure that was going to be the case for very long. You, Malik, Tengazy, and Patel were very brave, firing on those men who were trying to bring aboard the pirates."

She shrugged her shoulders. "We only did what we had to, Capitáno."

I took a sip of my beer. It tasted good, just what I needed.

"To tell you the truth, I was mad. I was angry at being duped by that unscrupulous harbor agent and that so-called admiral. I should have realized their treachery hadn't ended simply because I had pulled away from the pier."

I stopped talking, realizing that I was going on about things I should probably not share with a crew member, much less my cook. "I'm sorry; I'm just rambling. I don't mean to burden you with my concerns. You endured quite a bit yourself."

"That is quite all right, Capitáno. I'm glad if it helps you. What else could you have done?"

"Of course, you're correct. I had the schedule to adhere to and a cargo to deliver. I guess there was always the chance the attackers weren't really bad guys. They could have been Benin patriots trying to ward off some corrupt opportunist, doing their best to rid their nation of outside meddlers."

I searched her face. She raised an eyebrow and her face broadened into a smile.

"Be that as it may, you were still very brave." She reached across and patted my hand. "Now eat. You must restore your strength." She pushed back her chair to leave.

From an impulse I couldn't explain, I said. "You don't have to go. Stay and talk. I could use some polite conversation right about now."

Without hesitation, she settled back into her chair. "I guess it was a good thing the Nigerian Navy happened along when they did."

"Yes, it was." Realizing I hadn't eaten what she had prepared, I took my first bite. "Mmm, you're a wonderful cook."

She smiled a thank you. "I wonder what brought the Nigerians into the Gulf today? It was our good fortune, don't you think?" I noticed a brief sparkle in her eyes.

"They're patrolling as part of the International Piracy Flotilla, a duty shared by several African countries who possess a navy worth speaking of. I guess today was Nigeria's day."

How did she know to ask that question?

Then her expression changed, and I was sure she was reading my mind. "Do not look so surprised, Capitáno. After you and Tengazy left the bridge, I went to the radio room and kept repeating your plea for help on the distress frequency. The Nigerian captain intercepted my distress call. He left Lagos last night and was taking up station as part of the Pan-African anti-piracy effort to guard the trade routes along the coast from Sierra Leone to Equatorial Guinea."

My spoon hung there over my bowl. "You did that?" This was incredible. How could I have doubted her? "So, your previous questions were just to toy with me?"

"Of course, Capitáno. After all, I also am a member of the crew. I have many talents you don't necessarily know. Not all of us are experts in shooting *pistóles*." She smiled.

"Hmm, I never doubted it for a moment." I shook my head and finished the spoonful of stew.

"Would you like some more, Capitáno?"

"No thank you, Miranda. I'm going to shower and then get a little sleep, now that things have quieted down. Would you tell Mr. Patel of my intentions? He has my instructions for the next several hours. We should have clear sailing from here on out."

"Of course, Capitáno. If there is anything else you need, do not hesitate to let me know."

THE HOT SHOWER coursing across my head and down my torso felt good. I'd never been shot at before and my nerves were still on edge. I scrubbed extra hard, trying to rid myself of the gunshot residue, which my subconscious assured me still clung to my skin. I secured the water and dried off. In the equatorial heat, it was never possible to shed the sheen of sweat that persistently clung to one's body. At least I was rid of the smell of cordite and calmed of my fear.

Never was climbing into a bed more welcome than now. It was just after midday, but I was undeterred by the bright sunlight streaming through the porthole. Right now, I could sleep through anything.

Chapter 10

A GENTLE VOICE awakened me, soft and close to my ear. "Capitáno, you may want to get up now. It is almost nine in the evening."

My eyes fluttered open to pitch darkness. I didn't move. I smelled the freshly washed scent of hair and sensed a woman was in my cabin trying to wake me. The clawing fatigue of sleep, however, was thwarting her efforts.

Again came the insistent words. "Capitáno. Are you awake?"

Rolling over, I saw her move away from my bunk. It was Miranda. It took a few more seconds before I could assure myself I wasn't still asleep. Finally, I said, "What time is it? How long was I asleep?"

She stood by the cabin door, a respectful distance away. "Capitáno, it's okay, there's no problem. I just thought it might be good for you to get up and have something to eat. The bridge officers report they have everything well in hand."

I pursed my lips and ran my tongue across my teeth. My mouth was dry.

"Good ... how long was I out?'

"You slept almost nine hours, Capitáno. Would you like some coffee? I brought you a cup and placed it in the holder on your desk."

I switched on my bunk light. Miranda's face shone like hazy moonlight as she leaned back against the door. When she motioned to the steaming cup of coffee at my desk, I realized I was back in the realm of the fully conscious.

"Who's on the bridge?"

"Daniru Malik is, Capitáno. Everyone has had a chance to rest and cycle through their watches since the events of this morning. You have a very good crew working for you.

"Come on, you should get something to eat. I will heat up the lasagna I made. I still have half a bottle of table red open. I will see you in a bit in the mess, no? Now watch your eyes, I am going to switch on the overhead light."

I heard the switch click and squinted to ward off the sudden brightness. I slowly opened my eyelids to see the steam rising from the coffee cup, just out of reach.

Damn it, her conspiracy was complete. I would have to get up.

My first stop was on the bridge where Malik had *Marigold* on course and heading into gentle swells ninety-three miles off the west coast of Africa.

"Good evening, Captain. You look refreshed."

"Thank you, Mr. Malik. I feel much better, but you shouldn't have let me sleep so long."

"That's perfectly all right, Captain. We are very experienced. Chenal Patel has already taken the evening star sights of our position and logged them in. He updated the navigation fix on our charts. It tracks accurately with the RDF bearings we are taking from the African coastal radio beacons." Without skipping a beat, he added, "I highly recommend you eat some of Miranda's lasagna. It's delicious."

"It seems you don't need any assistance on the bridge. I think I'll take your suggestion about dinner."

I made my way to the mess deck and took my seat where my meal awaited. It seemed Malik and Miranda had their own signaling system as to my whereabouts. I wasted no time digging in and was grateful that Malik's menu forecast was accurate. It was excellent; or I was simply hungry. In any case, I thanked Miranda for holding a ration for me.

She was ever diplomatic with her reply. "You are the Capitáno, after all. We must take care of you."

I liked the way she called me captain: very Latin, very Italian... different.

"I hope you didn't do this because you thought you had to. I'm a member of the crew, too. If I sleep through a meal, I can survive until the next one."

"Of course you could, Capitáno. But you are not . . . not so regular a guy, as you say. You are very special." She smiled.

I realized she'd gotten the better of me in this exchange, but I didn't care. She was different in many likeable ways.

When I finished, I pushed back from the table. "Thank you, Miranda. I'm going to the bridge to check the charts. I had better earn my keep after spending all afternoon and early evening in my bunk."

"Very, good, Capitáno," she said. She took my dirty plate and glass to the galley as I left for the bridge.

Malik greeted me. I pulled a cigar from my shirt pocket and offered one to him. "No thank you, Captain. I'm just about to go off watch. I wouldn't have time to enjoy it."

"Mind if I do?"

"Captain, this is your ship. You can do as you wish."

I knew full well I could, but still felt compelled to ask.

"The seas are calm tonight," I said, lighting up.

"Yes, Captain, the sea gods are looking kindly upon us. The weather forecast from here to the Congo is quite favorable, based on our last satellite update."

"Have you ever been there before? The Congo River, I mean?"

"No, sir, I haven't. But I hear it's quite spectacular. When big rivers dump that much fresh water into the ocean, one can run into very strange sights."

"Like what?"

"Mud. All that silt from inland has made its way to the sea and has to go somewhere. It attracts all sorts of fish, which then attracts birds, and the bigger fish come to feed on the smaller ones. And then there are all the fishing boats taking the opportunity to catch the big fish. It is a very productive fishing ground."

"For not having been there, you certainly know a lot about it, Mr. Malik."

"Yes, sir. I haven't been to the Congo, but I have encountered plenty of the world's other big rivers: the Yangtze, Danube, Indus, and Amazon. But I have yet to make it to the Arctic. Maybe it is different there, I don't know."

"Hmmm," I puffed out a blue white cloud of smoke. "I've never thought about it. Although I have sailed the Baltic. But there aren't any great rivers flowing into it that I recall."

Patel appeared on the bridge. "Good evening, Captain. Did you finally get enough rest?"

"Yes, yes I did, thanks to both of you. I only hope you've gotten your rest."

"Yes, sir," Patel said. "We are used to six hour shifts."

154

"But you can't tell me you're used to having running gun battles mixed in."

They both laughed.

"No, sir," Patel said smiling. "That was a first for me."

"And me, also." Malik grinned.

"And me," said Miranda. She had given up her apron and come to the bridge for fresh air.

I realized that, except for Tengazy, who was deep within the bowels of the ship tending to the diesels and being relieved by Prankiop, I had the majority of my reliable brain trust in one spot. These were the people who'd stood by me when I needed it the most.

"I want to thank each of you for that fine performance earlier today. I'm sure we all realize we wouldn't be here now had you not been as decisive as you were. I want you to know that when we reach Brazzaville and settle up the books, there will be something extra in it for you."

"Thank you, Captain." Malik smiled. Patel nodded his thanks. Only Miranda said nothing. Instead she looked at me with her big brown eyes as if to say, 'It was my pleasure.'

Perhaps I was reading too much into her expression. I was horrible at reading women. But this was not about a man and a woman. She was every bit a part of the crew, just like the men in that regard. She had even said as much.

The professionals that they were, Malik and Patel went about the business of turning over the bridge watch. To give them some space, I stepped onto the bridge wing for some solitude and to enjoy my cigar.

At least for a few days, it would be calm: just a gentle ocean, sunrises, and sunsets. In spite of the sweltering heat, which hit me instantly, I was in a good place. As I watched the swells roll by only to become consumed in *Marigold*'s wake, beads of sweat formed on my brow. Only fifty miles north of the equator, Marigold's thirteen knots didn't generate sufficient breeze to counter the heat.

As I contemplated returning to the air conditioning in my sea cabin, Miranda stepped onto the bridge wing, I assumed to keep from interrupting Patel and Malik as they conducted their business. She made no comment as she gently clicked the door closed behind her. Normally when she entered a space where I was, she asked to join me, as tradition dictated. This time, she simply stepped onto the bridge wing.

Though I gave her no overt greeting, privately I couldn't help but notice. In fact, I found myself noticing everything about her. There was something about sharing the brink of disaster with someone that rounded off the edges of formality.

I was acutely aware she was standing only a few feet away, closer than I had ever known her to do. If it were possible, my temperature climbed and I flushed, and not because of the tropical heat.

"Oh, it is hot, Capitáno." She fanned her neck and chest with her hand.

"Yes, it is, Miranda. We're almost at the equator. I'm afraid it will be like this until after delivering the cargo at Brazzaville. We won't reach cooler latitudes until we almost reach the Cape of Good Hope."

She wiped the back of her hand across her forehead and pulled the yoke of her blouse to the edge of each shoulder to allow air to circulate more freely. The adjustment to her blouse, however practical and innocent it may have been, caught my attention. I hoped she wouldn't notice my momentary distraction.

"Miranda, I know I told you and the rest of the crew that this is the last voyage for *Marigold*. The cargo hauling competition I face with TC Miriam makes carrying on with such a small operation impossible.

"But what I didn't dwell on was how poor my grandfather's health is. Selling this last cargo should go a long way towards securing his comfort in his remaining years. Additionally, the scrap price I will get at the breaking yards will give me the financial means to get started in a new career."

Unbidden, I felt my passion for my life's work rise in my throat. To hide my emotions, I pushed closer to the bridge bulwark and feigned contemplating my cigar.

She recognized my sudden awkwardness and exhaled softly. She stepped to face me directly. "What will you do?"

I took a long drag on the cigar. The tip flared, illuminating our faces before fading. *Damn it*, I thought. *Why am I mentioning this—noticing her? Why are there suddenly too many details in my life?*

"*Marigold* is the last of my family's shipping line. At one time my grandfather and I owned five ships, each engaged in delivering small bulk freight to ports within four hundred miles of Dublin. As times changed, business dwindled. Grandfather and I gradually sold off parts of the fleet, until now only *Marigold* remains. And I can't even sustain her upkeep. To pay the taxes on the business, my home in Dublin, and the bills at Grandfather's nursing home, I have to liquidate."

"Can't your parents help?"

My mind flashed back to that day thirty-one years ago when Grandmother Miriam told me my mother and father had been killed in an incident on the border with Northern Ireland. She gave no details, saying I was too young. She never discussed it again and I never heard her talking to Grandfather about it, either. Grandfather, I'm sure out of deference to Grandmother, never mentioned it to me.

I paused as Grandfather's Temple Swan revelations of his dealings with Dillon O'Connor and the IRA flooded back to me, which suddenly triggered a new suspicion that one of O'Connor's IRA schemes was responsible for my parents' death. And if that were true, it explained Grandmother's failure to discuss the matter and probably meant she held Grandfather at least partially responsible for bringing O'Connor into their lives.

Being much too young at the time to think anything but the best about Pop, I never considered he have ever been involved in what happened to them. But thinking now, this might explain at least for some of the animosity Grandfather had voiced about O'Connor—about how O'Connor only had his own interests at heart. This in turn reinforced my conclusions that I needed to be wary of O'Connor. Either way, I wasn't going to share these personal thoughts with Miranda.

"No, Miranda, it's up to me. My parents died a long time ago and my grandparents raised me. Ever since Grandmother passed away a few years ago, I've had to care for Grandfather."

"That's very noble of you, Capitáno."

"I don't know how noble it is, but it is my duty. My immediate concern, however, is what am I carrying down in my holds? Our family has always operated well inside the law, and I don't want to break with that precedent now."

"But what is your concern, Capitáno? I thought we carried logs, shingles, and some kind of water bladders."

"I know that's what the manifest says, Miranda. But what kind of building materials come from Niamey, Niger? On top of that, those two scallywags in Benin certainly wanted their hands on whatever's in my holds. Otherwise, why go to the trouble of accosting me on the high seas as I was leaving their territorial waters? I seriously doubt they would've gone to the lengths they did simply for building supplies.

"It's all very suspicious. And no, I don't think I'm being paranoid. The loss of Tasmoon-Shamlyn and Admiral Gangho's attack seem too coincidental for my liking. Someone really wants to do us harm."

Perhaps Dillon O'Connor had contacted Gangho and put him up to investigating Tasmoon-Shamlyn's death. Gangho being an opportunist had taken this tacit permission to seize the cargo for both his benefit and to curry favor with a potential benefactor in O'Connor. If the former, there was more value to the cargo than was evident on the manifest. If the latter, then Dillon O'Connor was more deeply intent on resolving his grudge with Pop by bankrupting me.

In either case, I needed to inspect the cargo, seals or no seals, to ensure it was legitimate. I would deal with the consequences, good or bad, later.

As if reading my mind, Miranda said, "Maybe you should inspect the cargo. At least that would help settle your doubts."

I took another puff on my cigar to consider my next steps. The best way to deal with this dilemma was to think out loud.

"If I do, then I'll have to do something should I discover contraband instead of what's declared on the manifest. I don't know who I'd disclose such a discrepancy to. Interpol? The United Nations? Who do I trust? And what port do I head for to turn over such a cargo? At some point, and well short of either Bangladesh or returning to Ireland, I'll run out of money."

I was talking myself out of my resolve when Malik opened the bridge wing door. "Captain, you have a message that just came in."

Within the weather safety of the bridge, I read the message. It was from a longtime friend, Gilbert McCallister, in Dublin. Pop was in danger of being moved at the end of next month because of new management fees at his private nursing home. If I didn't send an additional €500 a month in rent plus an €800 surety deposit, they would have to move Pop to a public facility in Balbriggan, miles away. He closed by saying Pop didn't want him to tell me, but he figured I should know.

I stuffed the message in my pocket and stepped back out onto the bridge wing. "Miranda, we'll have to finish our talk later. Something has come up I must attend to."

Back in my cabin, I composed an answer to Gilbert that I was having the money sent to the private nursing home and asked him to contact me if they hadn't received it within a few days. Then I sent a message to my bank having them make the appropriate transfers. That was €1,300 I wasn't counting on. At least I had a little financial room still to deal with it.

I took a deep breath. My emotions were getting the better of me. The gun battle with Gangho, my concerns about what Dillon O'Connor was up to, and Miranda's intriguing choice of words had all unsettled me. Which-ever it was, she had forced me to the heart of the matter — what was I carrying to Brazzaville, Congo?

I booted my computer and searched for a satellite link. Maybe a thorough internet search would help me find some answers to the nature of the building supply industry in Niger. As I worked the keyboard, the entire business with Andjou, his violation of my professional trust as a crewman, and what I suspected was his surreptitious taunting of me at the Voodoo festival still made my skin crawl.

And now I was wrestling with the validity of the cargo Dillon O'Connor had contracted me to carry. I wanted a bit more information of what possibly could be in my holds before I simply broke the seals to inspect. There had to be some answers and I was going to find them.

I scrolled the browser looking for links to Niger, a locale which could explain some of my misgivings. Several images popped on the screen. I paged through travel agency ads and bogus business web sites. After several false tries at clicking on what I thought might be promising, I stopped on a seemingly legitimate news photo.

It showed the president of Niger in full military garb seated on a reviewing stand for a military parade in Niamey. And who stood one step behind him in the presidential box, dressed in full military regalia and bent whispering in the president's ear? It was Mr. M'Nasi — the same Mr. M'Nasi Dillon O'Connor required me to deal with and who had consigned the building supplies to me in Cotonou, which I now carried to Congo.

Why had M'Nasi represented himself as a construction material agent? More importantly, was he hiding something illegal on board *Marigold*?

I thought about my string of transactions with the quasi-officials of Niger and Benin and wondered which one, if not all of them, was in league with the other. I hadn't seen a single United Nations logo or letterhead remarque on the manifest documentation accompanying the shipment I carried. There were no powder blue UN brands on the cargo pallets I'd loaded.

What the hell was the pedigree of the cargo in my hold right now? One thing was undeniable: Mr. M'Nasi wasn't at all the person he represented himself to be. Far from settling my suspicions, I had more questions now and no answers.

I closed the laptop, stormed from the cabin, and strode across the bridge to the weather deck ladder. I had to find out what those perfidious bastards had tricked me into delivering for them. When the tropical heat of the main deck hit me full force, I slowed, giving me time to overcome my impulses and consider things more rationally. I gripped the safety railing, stared into the bioluminescence of *Marigold*'s wake, and listened to my conscience.

Where are you heading, Johnny? Don't look at where you've been. Get a plan before you jump off the cliff...and get some allies while you're at it. There's too much at stake to go it alone.

WHEN I MADE my way down to the mess deck the next morning, I found Miranda had prepared a quiche, sausages, and fresh biscuits for breakfast. As I ate, I contemplated what I must do to safely deliver my cargo, regardless of its nature. I'd never been on the Congo River and every nautical chart I had described a piloting and navigation nightmare for novices navigating the river.

Though the Congo was one of the largest rivers in the world, almost cutting the African continent in two, it was navigable by ocean going vessels only for a few hundred miles, and only along its lower reaches. The river was plagued by cataracts and falls for most of its three-thousand-mile length. To worsen matters, the river current was almost seven knots at the mouth, significantly greater than any river I'd ever encountered.

With these concerns in mind, I reluctantly decided to call the only person I knew who could give me advice and had a vested interest in my success for delivery—Dillon O'Connor. I wanted to confront him about who had been harassing me, but when the connection finally went through, the concern I voiced was about my navigation issue.

"Dillon, how am I supposed to get this cargo to Brazzaville? According to my charts, the good water only extends 110 miles upriver, as far as Matadi."

"Aye, laddie, good to hear from you. Regardin' the river, now you know why I promised you such a premium. Remember, I warned you—donae venture on the Democratic Republic of Congo side of the river."

"Stay to the west bank. I got it." I could only wonder if that was the real reason for the premium.

"Matadi is in the DRC," O'Connor went on. "Whatever you do, don't stop there. They'll steal your cargo, maybe your ship, and you could end up in jail, or all three."

"Why would they do something like that?"

"Because they can."

A chill ran down my spine.

"They donae have to have a good reason. They consider every vessel fair game and the owners are free booters, swindlers, or maybe even both. They donae have to put up with gun runners."

What the hell was he talking about? "Why would they ... what's that got to do with..." I stopped speaking as the words *gun runners* sank in.

Was it a slip of the tongue or had he just admitted what I was carrying in my hold was a disguised arms cache? If so, how devious of him. He knew he couldn't legitimately transport contraband across the African continent from its source to the ultimate buyer. That bastard was smuggling it at sea under the auspices of the United Nations. And I was his unwitting accomplice—more like a nitwitted accomplice.

"You still there, Johnny?"

"Yeah, I'm here, you SOB. How could you set me up like this? I damn near got killed in a gunboat skirmish with that third-rate Benin Navy."

"Stop complaining, you pantywaist shite! You're several hundred thousand euros ahead right now, and in line to make a good deal more very soon. You're the one who came crawling to me to bail you and your grandfather out. So shut your bloody yap and listen.

"When you reach the Congo, head up river, past Matadi. Favor the west bank of the river. Stay on the Congo side, not the DRC side. I'm going to give you a number to call as soon as you near Matadi. The name is Godfrey Rochelle Gund. I call him GR. He works for

MONUC, the UN peacekeeping mission stationed there. I have a contract in place with him to lighter your cargo the rest of the way upriver to Brazzaville, past the shallow water."

I remembered our conversation about payments back in Wexford. "Who am I supposed to negotiate the payment with, Ótubé, this GR person, or someone in Brazzaville?"

"Leonard Ótubé. He will be there when you meet GR. When you transfer your load to Gund's vessel, Ótubé will hand you a package—the payment. Accept the package without opening it in his presence. Later, when you're alone, send me my cut. Then forward the amount we discussed to Arman Byassian in Greece."

"I thought I was going to be able to negotiate with Ótubé to see if I could squeeze a little more out of the deal."

"You can, but that's between you and Ótubé, not GR. He works for the UN. Ótubé's no saint, mind you. Squeeze him hard, if you have to. Your grandfather would. Call me when you get to the mouth of the river. Now I have to go."

The connection went dead. Treacherous thoughts raced through my head. Was Ótubé working with O'Connor? Did this Gund guy know about the guns? Had M'Nasi known about the guns when he sold me the lot in Cotonou? Was Ótubé in the same category? Oh, sweet Mother Mary and Joseph, what had I gotten myself in for?

I had to inspect the cargo to put my mind at ease as to whether or not I was abetting an international arms deal.

I found Chenal Patel on the bridge and told him to have Miranda come up from the mess decks. With the others working a demanding six hours on and six hours off schedule, I knew she was the only one up. When he put down the phone, he said, "Captain, this message came in for you about an hour ago, but you were busy."

He handed me the message. It was Gilbert McCallister reporting that the nursing home had received the bank drafts and that Pop was resting well. At last, some good news.

Just then Miranda reached the bridge and asked, "Capitáno, how may I help you? Chenal said it was important."

As she said it, Chenal pointed to the bow and said, "Look, we have an escort."

My heart skipped a beat thinking back to the last time I was faced with the specter of Admiral Gangho and his gunboat. But my fear was short lived. A pod of dolphins had taken up station off each bow and were surfing on *Marigold*'s bow wave. Off to the port side, dozens more were leaping their way in the water to join in the fun. Within a few minutes, over a hundred of those graceful mammals were frolicking in a broad V off each bow, leaping and plunging as they paced *Marigold* through the sea green waters.

For the time being, with proven allies alongside me on the bridge, the news that Pop was all right, and one of the great spectacles on the open ocean before me, my psyche was in a good place.

But concerns still plagued me and for the next day and a half I brooded. I was sure the mates on the bridge noticed and I was certain Miranda did. In fairness to her, she didn't intrude into my space. That was good because I couldn't, or wouldn't, burden them with any of this.

My suspicions about what I was carrying was one thing. For my shipmates' sake, I couldn't in good conscience implicate any of them in an illegal enterprise. Should the worst I feared come about, I wouldn't put them in a position to suffer blame.

But to go to authorities, and which authorities I still couldn't figure out, would put an end to my plan to sell *Marigold* and finance Pop's well-being. *Marigold* and her cargo would be impounded. I would lose the business and he would end up in a state-run nursing home, which would spell the end of him.

No, I had to protect the crew and Pop's future; I had to deliver the cargo and conclude the contract. Then, my suspicions and O'Connor's slip of the tongue notwithstanding, I had to figure out a way to right this wrong. Perhaps after the fact I could tip off the right people so O'Connor and his colleagues could be found out for the crooks they were. Who those 'right people' were I didn't know.

EARLY IN THE EVENING on the second day, we crossed the equator. Other than Tengazy, none of us had ever crossed that imaginary line on the globe. I must admit, I did go to the bridge wing, whimsically half-expecting there might be a buoy or some sort of marker there. The only thing I noticed was that in the heart of the doldrums, it seemed hotter, if that were possible.

When I asked, my crewmen didn't want a crossing-the-line ceremony. However, being the traditionalist I was, I couldn't allow the crossing of zero degrees latitude to transpire without some official acknowledgement. Once again, Miranda salved my anxiety, as mild as this bout was, by finding a few good bottles of red wine in the pantry, with which I toasted the special dinner she prepared to mark the occasion.

Though the small celebration for crossing one of King Neptune's mythical challenges helped my mood, I couldn't shake my concern over how I'd reached my troublesome state of affairs. I wasn't so naïve not to remember I had taken consignments, unknown to me at the time, to a variety of parts of the world: Norway's North Cape, St. Petersburg, and Malta.

To carry sealed cargos wasn't uncommon, especially in the world of nation-to-nation aid or NGO sponsored assistance. But never before had I become so mired in an endeavor that sucked me further down the more I struggled to understand. Likewise, never had I been burdened with the stakes I faced now: a secure future for my grandfather and a head start on a new career for me.

I was hamstrung, locked onto a path whose end I couldn't see and which I knew I had to sidetrack. But how?

Chapter 11

As STINKING AND putrid as the mangrove swamps in and around Cotonou had been, the roiling heat and smell of decay blowing off the sea along the Congo coastline was worse. It was useless to bathe; sweat poured from me as soon as I put up my towel. And the only spaces on the *Marigold* that had any semblance of air conditioning were the mess deck and the bridge enclosure, which included my sea cabin. When off watch, crewmen found their way to one of these two, if for nothing else than to cool their brows for a bit.

At 1353 local time on the fourth day out of Cotonou, I turned *Marigold* onto the Congo River entrance range and headed upstream towards the interior of Africa. The out-fall of the Congo River was easy to identify from seaward. A thick, miles-wide tongue of muddy river water flowed from the continent towards the sea. This boundary, de-marcated by ocean blue next to river brown, wouldn't dissipate for more than a hundred miles out to sea. The muddy current was strong. Even at a full bell, *Marigold* only made five and a half knots good against it.

Now that I was on the approach to Matadi, I again attempted a call to Dillon O'Connor on the sat phone as he'd directed, but there was no answer. After too many rings to count, I disconnected the call. For a man who had several million euros riding on the balance of our trans-action, I thought it odd I couldn't contact him.

I had little time to consider what mind game O'Connor might be playing; I was more concerned with the buffeting *Marigold* was taking at the mercy of the swiftness of the passing river current. What little information I had gathered about navigating up river was correct; this effort would take every bit of my seaman's skills, and then some. Realizing I'd be spending the better part of the next few days on the bridge, I mentally prepared for an extended effort.

To satisfy my sense of adventure, I had my camera at the ready to capture the passing scenery. As the coastline of the greater Congo landmass passed astride *Marigold's* beam ends, I forged upriver. On either side of the river mouth and well up into the river proper, sandbars were prevalent, which seemed incongruous with the sounding beneath the keel—an astounding five hundred feet deep. At first I thought the fathometer had malfunctioned, but subsequent soundings were consistent with very deep water. At well over three miles wide, this river was gigantic: deep, fast moving, and cluttered with half submerged debris.

The business part of the river channel teemed with small boat traffic. Fishermen used nothing more than motorized dugout canoes in their cross-river mad dashes as they eked out a daily living. Once or twice I saw ferry boats plying their way from one bank to the other. With no bridges, these vessels were the only commercial connections between the towns that occupied opposing banks of the river.

After a few hours, I realized I had a handle on what to watch for and thought about why Dillon O'Connor was not answering my calls. He was making this trip more difficult for me at every turn. As I ticked off the reasons for suspecting his treachery, I realized I had only a few hours left to make good my intent to inspect the cargo. As much as I needed to do this, I also knew I could not jeopardize any of my crewmembers. I looked at the chart and the next few miles of the river appeared to be relatively manageable for my bridge team.

I slid from my bridge chair perch and was about to head for the cargo holds when Daniru Malik said, "Captain, we have company."

A small patrol boat approached *Marigold* from the DRC side of the river. He pulled alongside, struggling to keep pace while contending with the combined effects of my bow wake and the natural upheaval of the swift river current. Armed, camouflage-clad soldiers stood on the patrol boat's bow and port side gunwales. A man holding a bullhorn and wearing a holstered pistol stood at the bow of the patrol boat. I figured he must represent the DRC Riverine Force de Frappe.

I couldn't understand his first hail, which he rattled off in French. I motioned with a shrug that I didn't understand. His second attempt was in heavily accented English, which I understood with difficulty. The essence of his message was that I should follow him to shore.

Not slowing *Marigold* one iota, I asked him why, the whole time checking to make sure I was on the Congo side of the river channel, as O'Connor had so vigorously warned me. He replied that my wake had capsized some fishermen a few miles downstream and I must pay reparations.

In fact, I had seen dozens of fishermen going about their business having no problems with my wake, or any other vessels' wakes that were plying this busy waterway. This maritime militiaman was simply attempting a scam.

I accepted it for what it was—a shakedown. My ill-spent time in Cotonou was paying off after all.

I slowed by a knot, to make sure he could hear me properly over the wind blowing across our respective vessels, and told him *Marigold* was on international business for the United Nations and could not miss her appointed docking time in Brazzaville. I went on to remind him that Brazzaville was a city on the Congo side of the river, and thus out of his jurisdiction.

This didn't deter him from insisting again that I follow him. He reinforced his demand by having his soldiers fire warning shots into the air.

There was no way I was going to pay this maritime thug, much less allow him the opportunity to inspect my cargo. I aimed my camera in his direction and snapped some shots. Then I did the only thing I could do. I gave him another shrug, a wave, and pushed *Marigold* ahead once again at top speed.

By the time I had traversed another mile, he gave up the chase, finding it impossible to keep pace with *Marigold* in the stiff current that was battering his small boat. I slowly pulled away, opening the distance from him towards the safety of the western river bank.

Wary I might encounter other opportunists along the way, I roused Tengazy from a sound sleep and had him bring two rifles to the bridge. He had already proven his mettle, if not his accuracy with a rifle. I felt much more comfortable with him close by. Any thought I might have had to inspect the cargo would have to wait.

Fortunately, we received no more threats. When the sun disappeared below the jungle canopy a few hours later, I told Tengazy to lay below and get some rest, but by then it was time for him to go on watch. His rest would have to wait until his watch ended at midnight.

I spent the night on the bridge just in case, as Patel and Malik spelled each other every six hours on the bridge. I caught cat naps in my chair, not wanting to waste any time in having them roust me out of my sea cabin to render assistance if either of them needed me.

For amusement during the night, I used my searchlight periodically to illuminate the passing riverbank, at times only a few dozen yards away. Not uncommonly, I found myself staring into the reflections from eyes in the water, most likely crocodiles or hippos, both of which occupied the mudflats and sandbars on the river's shoreline.

At two in the morning, I was surprised when Miranda came to the bridge.

"Good evening, Capitáno, Patel. I thought you might like some fresh coffee." She held up a carafe and two coffee mugs.

"Ah, Miranda," Patel said. "You are a sight for sore eyes. I always seem to hit the wall about this time on the mid-watch, no matter how much sleep I've had."

She poured him a cup and then turned to me. "How about you, Capitáno, do you hit the wall?"

At first I thought she was using a double entendre, but for the life of me, I couldn't fathom what the implied reference would be. Why was it that everything about her seemed to play with my head?

"No, Miranda, fatigue hasn't gotten to me yet. If nothing, I have gotten too much rest over the last few days. But things should pick up today. I will have plenty to keep me busy when the UN purchasing agent shows up to relieve me of this cargo."

The question of what exactly that cargo was ran through my mind again, but I was resolved to press ahead with the transaction that would ensure my grandfather's well-being and secure my future. I had no desire to share this secret with either of my now much-trusted shipmates.

"But I thought we were going to Brazzaville," Miranda said.

"The river's too shallow. About thirty miles beyond where we'll drop this cargo with the UN rep, we'd reach the first cataracts. Except for a few ten- to forty-mile deep channel stretches, the river is plagued by shallows, rapids, and cataracts all the way to the big waterfalls at Kisangani. That's over seven hundred miles of river, which can't accommodate ocean going cargo ships, even with a draft as shallow as ours."

"Let's hope, Capitáno, that this United Nations man is easier to deal with than the other agents we have dealt with so far." Then she added, "Have you decided to ins-pect the cargo before we arrive at the transfer point?"

At this late date, I knew that inspecting would do little to alter the delivery regardless of my concerns. O'Connor knew I was only hours away, I had hostile territory to the east in the form of the DRC, and I had no means to travel back down river to… where? I had no safe harbor to turn to.

Miranda knew I was in a quandary and didn't press the issue. She leaned against the bridge window, her arms folded below her breasts. The red glow of the bridge lighting illuminated her face and neck, not to mention the rest of her. "Then, Capitáno, there is nothing I can do to ease your worries?"

Though her pose captivated me, I had to remain steadfast in my duties to navigate the ship safely.

"Miranda, I appreciate your concern, but the time to inspect has come and gone. We'll be at the UN transfer point in a few hours. I'll just have to live with that."

She turned to go. "You are a wise and practical man, Capitáno. Have a good evening. Just let me know if you need anything."

I touched two fingers to my brow in salute as she left the bridge.

WHEN MORNING LIGHT first arrived, I was pointing out some shallow areas from the bridge wings to Patel when Miranda joined us for some fresh air after spending her last few hours in the galley preparing breakfast. By now, the shallows extended well away from the river bank, crowding *Marigold* mid-channel towards the demarcation separating the two Congos.

My navigation charts had been accurate so far, but I was still leery of anything charted near Matadi. The further up the river I travelled, the more I worried about river debris and shallow ledges. I slowed to three knots as a precaution. The Congo was proving to be like no other river I'd ever run.

"Miranda," Patel asked, "do you have any sweets left over from last night's meal?"

"For you, Chenal, anything. Capitáno, would you like some sweets also?"

Again, the inflection in her voice seemed to imply more than her words actually said.

"No thank you, Miranda. You've fattened me up enough this trip. I need to watch what I'm eating."

This brought a broad grin to her face and a sparkle to her beautiful brown eyes. I was learning that nothing pleased her more than a full-fledged compliment. "I will be right back, gentlemen."

As she disappeared down the ladder, Patel said, "Captain, I think that woman bears watching."

"And how is that, Mr. Patel?"

"I think it is you she has designs on."

I shrugged him off. "I don't think so, Mr. Patel. She is just a pleasant woman who knows how to provide for her fellow shipmates. She cares about her work. That is to our benefit."

"I'm just saying, with the way she looks at you, it is more than work and a paycheck that has her interest."

I was beginning to think he was right.

JUST BEFORE NOON, the outskirts of the port city of Matadi hove into view. I had Patel keep *Marigold* as close to the western bank of the river as I could. On my sat phone, I dialed up the number Dillon O'Connor had provided for Godfrey Rochelle Gund. The UN rep answered as the first ring faded.

"Hello, hello, this is Godfrey."

There was the lilt of a slight British accent in his voice. "Mr. Gund, I am Captain Johnny O'Scanlon of the Motor Vessel *Marigold*. I have a cargo I am to deliver..."

"Yes, yes, I've been expecting you. Dillon said you'd be here. But to be honest, I didn't expect to see you for a few more days. Where are you now?"

"I am approaching Matadi from the south, on the Congo side of the river, sir."

"Ah, yes, yes, I see you."

"Uh, where are you, Mr. Gund?"

"I'm about 3,000 yards ahead of you in the middle of the river. Do you see that mid-channel barge with the large blue stack?"

There was indeed a barge with a motorized pusher vessel lashed to its stern in the middle of the river, not a mile and a half ahead. Smoke idly curled from a pale blue smokestack above its after deck.

"Yes, I see you now," I said. "Do you want me to tie up to your port side?"

"No, I think I shall come to you, sir. It is always best not to chance drifting into the DRC side of the river. When I come alongside, you can tie up and I will drop fore and after kedge anchors. I will use your kingpost crane to swing the cargo from your hold to my barge."

This was going to be one of the more unusual arrangements I'd undertaken to transfer cargo. Tied up to his anchored barge, I'd have to use my engines to counteract the forces of the rushing river on his two anchors to keep both vessels from dragging. I retrieved my camera to record the pending lashup for posterity.

As Tengazy and Malik doubled up *Marigold*'s lines to the barge, I ordered Prankiop in the engine room to leave one diesel on idle. No sooner had the incessant rumble of the other engine subsided than a uniformed man wearing a pale blue military helmet, with the white letters UN printed prominently on both sides, jumped across to my deck, followed by a less conspicuously dressed man. They made their way to the wheelhouse where I awaited them on the bridge wing.

"You must be Captain O'Scanlon," the man in the light blue helmet said, extending a hand. "I am Godfrey Gund and this is Mr. Leonard Ótubé, agent for Portland Exports, Liverpool and Manchester in Brazzaville."

Leonard Ótubé was slightly built and had very dark skin. He wore a pale green short sleeve shirt and off white cotton trousers, both loose fitting, perfect for the steamy tropics. I hoped they were both on the up-and-up and we might finish our transaction before the real heat of the day set in.

Leonard Ótubé shook my hand and got right to the point. "I understand you have my shipment, Captain."

His English was accented, but not British or French. Its origin eluded me.

"Yes, sir. Would you like to go down to the mess deck for some tea or coffee? Mr. Patel will have my deck hands open the cargo hatches. Mr. Ótubé, if you have a few stevedores, I could use the help. I had more problems leaving Cotonou than I anticipated."

Ótubé turned to the barge and barked orders in Belgique. Ah, that was the accent. He was Congolese, which would account for that inflection. His effort got the attention of the men standing on the deck, and several workers rose from their lounging spots in the shade and began handling lines and cargo netting. Satisfied that the transfer of goods was underway, we lay below.

When I reached the mess deck, I found Miranda had laid out cups and pots for coffee and hot water. Additionally, she had arranged savory snacks on a tray. I wasn't surprised by this, but thankful just the same. She poured coffee for me and hot tea for Mr. Ótubé and Mr. Gund. Whatever I was paying her, it wasn't enough.

Godfrey politely refused her offer saying, "This is really Leonard's dealing, Captain. I must return topside to supervise the cargo transfer. I'll leave my bill, if that is alright with you."

He pulled an envelope from his shirt pocket and handed it to me. I took it and asked, "Mr. Gund, it seems strange to me to find a UN outpost in the middle of the river doing lighter work. I would have expected a Congolese enterprise."

"My barge enterprise, as you call it," Gund said, "is part of the United Nations MONUC peace-keeping force. The acronym stands for the United Nations Organization Stabilization Mission in the Democratic Republic of the Congo, which monitors the two countries situated opposite each other on the Congo River. The UN peacekeeping force is here to preclude a flareup of the conflict which occurred in the 90s. My part of the operation is simply to facilitate peaceful river commerce.

"As you now realize, the Congo River, for all its length and volume, isn't particularly useful for deep draft traffic for most of its geography. Though on its lower stretches, it's the deepest river in the world. To facilitate river traffic along its length above the rapids, the UN Security Council sanctioned us as peacekeepers to actualize this arrangement.

"My pusher boat has a powerful enough engine to maneuver a fully loaded barge anywhere except within the cataracts themselves. We draw less than two feet of water, so we feel very much at home among the sandbars and mudflats. Our biggest hazard is avoiding the occasional crocodile snapping at a crewman's arm or leg left carelessly trailing in the water."

"Yes, I guess it pays to be mindful of one's surroundings in this part of the world."

I opened Gund's envelope apprehensively. After my experience in Cotonou, I wasn't sure what to expect. Surprisingly, the bill was only for €21K.

"I assume this is for unloading *Marigold* and the cargo's transport to Brazzaville?" Having endured that leech Dembo Johnson, I wanted to ensure that labor and transport were covered.

"Certainly, sir. I am not a for-profit business. I only seek payment for our UN services."

"Of course. I will bring you a draft check when I have concluded with Mr. Ótubé."

Then, addressing both men I asked, "Do either of you want to inspect the cargo against the manifest?"

Gund spoke without hesitation. "Not necessary on my part, Captain, since I don't take possession. Leonard?"

Ótubé hesitated, surprised by the question. "That won't be necessary, Captain. I have been overseeing transactions like this for some time. Everything appears to be as it should be."

There was an awkward moment of silence until Godfrey spoke. "Very good, gents. In that case, I'll get out of your hair."

With his departure, I turned to Ótubé. "If we could get down to business?"

Recovering from the surprise of his not taking up my offer to inspect the cargo, I sat opposite him and Miranda poured me a cup of coffee.

Ótubé said, "Please, call me Leonard. It will make our dealings go much better." He flashed a smile, but his gesture did nothing to put me at ease.

"All right...Leonard. Here is the manifest for the building materials you ordered from Niamey, Niger."

I handed him the bill of lading without the barest hint in my voice or expression that I knew, or had suspicions about, what was actually resting in my holds. "I have been told that Portland Exports will pay me €31M."

I purposely asked for a number much higher than the €27M O'Connor had set for his cut so I would have negotiating room. What surprised me, however, was how calmly I was able to quote such a large sum.

Leonard didn't even blink. "The payment I'm authorized isn't quite that much, Captain. A significantly lower number is more in line with what I am prepared to offer."

There was no accusation or threat in his voice, but it was clear he meant business. Now what? I sensed immediately I might be out of my league with this man. Based on my experience negotiating with Admiral Gangho, I would have to keep my wits about me to ensure I ended up with a favorable outcome for me and my grandfather.

What was intimidating, however, was that I was dealing with millions of euros, something for which I had no experience. And by Ótubé's calm demeanor, I suspected he was all too familiar with the game. I couldn't afford to come out on the wrong end of this deal.

Miranda approached from the sideboard to offer more coffee and tea. This gave me a moment to think. Or at least I should have used the time for that. Instead, I was distracted; she had changed her appearance since first offering tea. The change was subtle and I'm sure I was the only one who noticed. She had added a belt cinch at the bottom of her blouse where it clutched her waist. With this alteration, the front of her blouse now stretched not-so-subtly across her breasts and tugged the scooped neckline lower.

A broad smile on Leonard's face greeted her ministrations. Though I could see the effect of her changed appearance on Ótubé's face, I was put off that it was Miranda he was ogling.

I took a deep breath and said, "Are you sure, sir? My jobber gave me explicit instructions. But his words came to me over the satellite phone and I may have misunderstood. Perhaps he said €30M." We had both seized the bait and were into it now.

Leonard removed a ballpoint pen from his pocket. Without extending the tip, he wrote phantom strokes on a notepad and then looked up to admire Miranda, who stood by patiently.

"I know all too well, Captain. I don't always hear the numbers clearly with these electronic contraptions. As I try to reconstruct that conversation in my mind, I'm sure that the salesman in Niamey said €28.5M."

He was addressing me, but his eyes never strayed from Miranda.

Miranda moved behind me and bent slightly at the waist to let gravity enhance the view for Leonard, all the while smiling at him. His eyes now darted every few seconds to a spot over my shoulder to where Miranda stood with one hand high on my back, which she tapped to encourage me to counter his offer.

Warming to the game, I feigned like I was trying to recall some mythical phone call. "Sir, could we perhaps agree on a payment of €29.5M?"

"Hmm, that's an intriguing figure, I must admit, Captain."

I wasn't sure which figure he referred to.

"Let me consider it for a minute. Uh, if your hostess might bring some more, uh, refreshments, that would be appreciated."

Miranda broke her pose and moved the plate of savories closer to him. As she did, she happened to bend a bit further and lingered, not moving away directly. Leonard's eyes never wavered from her.

"Is there anything else I can do for you, Mr. Ótubé?" Miranda murmured.

Leonard stirred in his chair. And when he moved his hand to touch hers on the serving tray, Miranda took up a new position beside me, not behind as before, affording Leonard a fuller view.

"Miranda," he said, "that is a wonderful name. I should think that you might be better at these negotiations than your captain."

I couldn't believe what I'd heard. What was he doing? I was trying to work a business deal, obviously a sensitive one, but a business deal nonetheless, and he was propositioning a member of my crew right in front of me.

"Leonard," I raised my voice to show my disapproval.

He turned and stared at me, annoyed at my interruption, his face now displaying extreme confidence, if not arrogance. Shifting in his seat, he leaned slightly forward and spoke with a malevolence that betrayed his laidback attitude of only seconds before.

"Mr. O'Scanlon, you, sir, have a very difficult problem. One which you must decide to resolve at this very moment."

I bristled and sat upright in my chair. I had an instant to take action, either let this man continue with his affront to my authority as captain aboard my own vessel, or let him dictate whatever terms he chose and lose what hope I had of coming out of this deal with O'Connor having gained anything.

"What will it be ... Captain?"

Before I could say something I would regret, Miranda tapped the back of my shoulder blade.

"Perhaps, Capitáno, you could see if Mr. Gund needs some refreshments for the men in his crew."

When I didn't respond, she tapped her foot against mine, out of view beneath the table. With her left hand on my back, hidden from Leonard's view, she whisked her fingers as if brushing off some lint.

I wasn't sure what she was up to in light of Ótubé's demand, but I decided to follow her surreptitious instruction and stood.

"Excuse me, I'll be just a minute. I must check with Mr. Gund."

He turned from me, grinned at Miranda, and said dismissively over his shoulder, "Of course."

This man was a chameleon. From intimidation to ambivalence, the change was as abrupt as my departure.

As I walked to the ladder leading up to the main deck, I had a full view of Leonard, Miranda, and the table in the sideboard mirror. Miranda stood close to the still seated Mr. Ótubé. She leaned in to say something privately in his ear.

Everything I knew about propriety told me not to leave her alone with this man. It was my transaction and my company's future. But I trusted her. She hadn't discussed this with me; and I wasn't sure what Ótubé might do. I could see she had something in mind and seemed very insistent. Part of me said I probably didn't want to know what it was, while the other part was screaming at me to return that very instant. I continued from the mess deck hoping Miranda was not going to do something she'd regret on my behalf.

Topside, I found Gund smoking a cigarette, talking with Tengazy and one of the barge crewmen across the gunwale from Marigold.

He saw me approach. "Ah, Captain, I hope the negotiations are going well."

"I think they are, Mr. Gund. I only wanted to see how things were going with the transfer of cargo while Mr. Ótubé considers my latest offer."

The UN rep said, "As you can see, sir, we have the con-boxes from two of the holds off-loaded, as well as one of the log bundles. It won't be too much longer. How much more do you have to negotiate with Mr. Ótubé?"

I wondered that, too. "We have just a few details he's taking under consideration now. Do you have another cigarette? I'm out after the long voyage. That's another thing I'll have to restock when I refuel later."

I no more wanted a cigarette than a punch in the gut, which is what I felt after seeing Miranda next to Leonard Ótubé. However, it was all I could think of at the moment to kill more time.

The UN workers and my crewmen worked unceasingly in the heat under the high sky that was common for midday in the Congo. As sweat covered their torsos, swarms of insects relentlessly attacked their bare skin. Some they swatted away, but most found their marks for a satisfying feast, all while the incessant current of the river coursed below. Circular red welts formed on backs, necks, and arms where the little buggers dined. A few persistent intimidators even made their way past my cigarette smoke screen and scored hits on me. To resist was futile.

I finished the cigarette and lit another, more out of self-defense than a desire for nicotine. I thought of going to my cabin for a cigar, which would have been more enjoyable and more effective as mosquito repellant, but I didn't want to pass at an inopportune time through the mess deck. Just thinking about what was happening there right now with Miranda and Ótubé was too upsetting.

It flashed through my mind that I should invite Gund to step over to his barge where the cargo was being loaded and inspect one or two of the parcels. This was not so much to assuage my doubts, but more to prove to myself that I was capable of doing what was honorable, something I regretted not having done earlier. Instead, I took another Benson & Hedges from Gund and listened to his innocuous stories about life in the UN peacekeeping business.

When it seemed like he was done with his tale, I said, "If you don't mind, Godfrey, I'd like to get a few pictures of this arrangement for posterity."

"Of course. I'd suggest standing on your fantail. That way you'll get the other UN barges in the background. When you show your photos off, I'll receive that much more publicity."

"Be careful, sir. The way you market your services, I might end up in a new line of work as your advertising agent."

I obliged him by taking a few extra pictures, zooming in on the other barges in the background.

"Well, that should fortify me enough for this final round of negotiations," I said, flicking the cigarette butt into the swift current. "Now, it's back to the bartering session."

"I wish you good luck, Captain. I don't know Leonard Ótubé all that well, but he has a certain . . . reputation, if you will. Don't let him get the best of you."

I eyed him. It wasn't me I was worried about his getting the best of. On the other hand, Gund struck me as an independent person, one who played his role strictly as a UN functionary doing the best he could as a peace-keeper. He didn't strike me as being corrupt, as Dembo Johnson, the Cotonou Excise Tax Officer, and his pal Admiral Pendali Gangho had been.

I hoped I was right.

As I went below, I wasn't sure what to expect when I returned to the mess deck. I hoped beyond hope that Miranda knew what she was doing and recognized the type of man she was dealing with. I certainly hadn't re-hearsed this latest tactic with her.

At that moment, I realized that I didn't know her all that well. However, of one thing I was fairly certain, she was no traitor to my cause, as had been the three henchmen of Dillon's I had to rid my crew of in Cotonou. Any possibility of her being in cahoots with Leonard Ótubé seemed to me to be a coincidence beyond thinkable. Yet, why had the thought crossed my mind?

Leonard quietly sipped a steaming cup of coffee, sitting where I'd left him. Miranda was nowhere to be seen.

"Good day again, Captain. I do hope the transfer of cargo is going well. Are you satisfied that the building supplies are as stated on the manifest?"

From his expression, I sensed he knew that I suspected something was not as it should be about the contents of the cargo. I feared that if he thought I had more than a suspicion, his next actions would be more than a negotiation. I decided to play it out as I had started. "Mr. Gund has just about finished offloading the building materials. Where is Ms. Occhipinti?"

"I wouldn't concern yourself with your cook, sir."

While I bridled at his dismissive reference to Miranda, I could see that something had changed his demeanor from pompous to more conciliatory. Somehow, our playing field had been leveled.

"She is an excellent, and I may add, very persuasive negotiator. I should be so fortunate to have someone as skilled as she is in my employ." Before I could react, he changed subjects. "Should we conclude our negotiation?"

Within five minutes, we agreed on a figure—€29.334M. Miranda, whatever her role, had performed admirably in moving Leonard to the amenable side of my ledger. It also didn't hurt that he probably thought I believed something wasn't completely up to snuff with his cargo and was now buying my complicity.

Quick mental calculations told me that after paying Dillon his €5M, and the mysterious Mr. Byassian his €22M, the balance for TC Miriam was €2.334M, a healthy retirement sum in anyone's book. I'd have plenty, even after paying Mr. Gund his €21K for cargo handling services, to complete my journey to Bangladesh and insure my future.

When we returned topside, there were five stacks of mahogany logs chained to the middle of the transfer barge's deck, with blue-helmeted workers clambering over them to tighten turnbuckles. To one end were the con-boxes containing storage bladders. The con-box which held roofing shingles was secured at the other end. As I took a last look, I could detect nothing about them to hint that they weren't exactly what they appeared to be—building supplies. And best of all, *Marigold* rode a foot higher in the water, now rid of her last burden.

Ótubé and I shook hands and he wrote out a bank draft for the agreed amount. As he stepped to the UN barge to his newly acquired cargo, he turned. "I hope we can do business again in the future, Captain O'Scanlon. This venture has been profitable for both of us."

I nodded and turned to Gund. "Here is a bank draft for your services, Godfrey. I think you'll find this satisfactory."

The UN representative looked at the check and folded it into his sweat stained shirt pocket. "Ah, I can operate for at least another few weeks, Captain. Thank you."

I didn't envy this man. Not only did he have to work hard for his supper, but he had to do it in the repressive equatorial heat.

"And where are you off to now, sir?"

"I am headed for Chittagong, Bangladesh."

"Do you have cargo to forward?"

"Not unless you have something to consign to me." I didn't want to get into my life story and describe the dire financial straits that TC Miriam shipping was in—or at least, had been in.

"I'm afraid not, Captain. I'm strictly a transfer agent here."

"Well, in that case, I'll head back down river to refuel before heading for the Cape."

He smiled. "And restock your cigarettes. I wish you well, sir."

We shook hands and he stepped to his barge, barking orders to his deck hands.

I took a few more pictures as his barge departed and then went to the bridge to get underway down river.

As I stepped onto the starboard bridge wing, I was surprised to see Miranda standing there, the wind blowing her sweat-dampened hair awry. Her body language told me she wasn't in the mood to talk. When she looked at me, a tear trailed down the side of her nose.

"Are you okay, Miranda?"

"It is fine, Capitáno. I'm not used to the heat and the bugs, that's all. They bother my eyes. I think I will go below."

I reached for her shoulder. "Did something happen between you and Ótubé while I was topside?"

She shrugged off my hand. "No, Capitáno, I had things well in hand."

She turned abruptly and took the ladder to the main deck, avoiding having to pass through the bridge house. Watching her hasty departure, I felt down rather than elated at having just secured my financial success.

Whatever she had done had been instrumental in turning the outcome of the negotiations my way. I feared, however, what compromise she may have made in her effort to serve the cause. And the more I thought about what had just transpired, the more I worried. In spite of all my reasoning to the contrary, maybe there was something I should have done to verify to myself and to the appropriate authorities that the last business transaction TC Miriam would undertake was legitimate.

Chapter 12

I UNMOORED FROM the anchored barge and headed *Marigold* downstream for the hundred mile journey to sea. Going with the current made the trip much quicker than the journey had been coming up.

Having previously encountered all the river's navigation hazards gave me little solace, since I once again had to maneuver around them, but now at almost twice the speed. At dusk, I sighted the Matadi fueling pier, but Dillon O'Connor's warning about steering clear of the DRC side of the river convinced me to continue on. It looked deserted except for one lighted shack, probably the fueling attendant's office. Discretion warned me not to tempt fate.

"Mr. Malik, I don't think it wise to put in to refuel here. As soon as we are clear of the sea buoy and in open water, set us on a course for Luanda, Angola. We should have plenty of fuel to reach there by tomorrow morning, especially with this following current."

"As you say, Captain."

I detected a twinge of relief in his voice. Apparently, I wasn't the only one leery of dealing with the DRC. Then it dawned on me. Though I had mentioned to my crew about going on after the Congo, I hadn't formally contracted them for this extension to the journey. I'd have to rectify this. The crew seemed satisfied with my manner of running of the ship to date, but I had to address with them their plans for the rest of the trip. With the events of the past two weeks, it had simply slipped my mind.

Relieved to have delivered this last consignment, I settled into my bridge chair with a cigar, relaxed, and watched the refueling pier lights at Matadi distance themselves off my port quarter. I soon found myself staring at the river.

For me, the Congo was no torrent of pure rainwater runoff from some distant mountain range. It was a river in full flight with an emptying urgency, as if the water couldn't escape fast enough from its jungle basin of decaying corruption and heat fouling oppression—a river that sucked the mire, the unwanted refuse, and the excesses of greed swiftly to the sea.

Then I realized what had me in a funk was not the swelter, not the swarms of insects, nor even the mystery of Africa that clouded my thinking. No, what had me down was having been coerced into a business deal which I suspected went against every forthright business principle I had ever held. Dillon O'Connor had misled me and I had bought into his scheme out of the need to resolve my grandfather's future. I had decided to put an end to TC Miriam, after almost four decades, to rationalize the actions O'Connor had dictated. I was mad at having to deal with petty crooks like Dembo Johnson and Pendali Gangho and being assaulted on the high seas.

Maybe the heat and self-recriminations were my penance for having been foolish enough to agree with O'Connor in the first place, rather than work harder for a different solution. In any case, I heaved a sigh of relief to have the ordeals behind me. I drew comfort from the flowing silence as *Marigold*'s bow parted the muddy water and it slid effortlessly aft, only to rejoin in a burble in the ship's wake. A following wind from upstream matched our speed, letting my cigar smoke waft upwards to disperse. For the first time since leaving Dublin, I thought of new things—what to do with my life and to settle down.

At dinner, I set about to square myself with the crew for my oversight in not contracting the matter of remaining with *Marigold* beyond Congo.

"Miranda, Mr. Tengazy, Mr. Patel. I have been derelict in consulting you about your contracts. As you know, I didn't put into Brazzaville and decided against refueling in the DRC. Instead, I unilaterally made the decision to push on. We will be in Luanda by early morning. There, I'll refuel Marigold. If you want, you may leave the ship and look for a new charter contract or fly home, whichever you choose.

"I'm most appreciative of your services and your abiding loyalties to me and TC Miriam. I'm now offering you a third alternative. That is, for you to continue in your employment with me under the same terms as before, if you so desire, while I take *Marigold* all the way to Bangladesh. Regardless of your decisions, in Luanda I will pay you €500, in addition to what I've already promised for services rendered to date."

This brought an appreciative smile from each of them.

"You do not have to tell me now, but please think about it. Whatever your decisions, you have earned this bonus. I cannot thank you enough. Additionally, I shall be checking with a jobbing agent in Luanda to take on a few more hands to help you, should you stay with me to Chittagong. So please, let me know of your intentions before tomorrow morning so I can make proper arrangements with the jobber."

Each of them agreed right then and there to stay on.

Tengazy and Patel shook my hand and excused themselves, saying they had to relieve the watch. Miranda, who had taken the opportunity to clear the table, returned from the galley. She stood, composed and relaxed, next to the sideboard a few steps away from me. I noticed there was still some redness in her eyes. But she greeted me with a broad grin and said, "Capitáno, you have a good way to make a girl happy."

"Miranda, I am doing nothing for you that you haven't already earned many times over."

"Capitáno, I'm not talking about money. I have crewed on many vessels and worked for many *capitános,* but you are *preminente, altissimo.*" Her eyes glistened. She averted her gaze so I wouldn't see her emotions.

I stood and held up both palms. "I can assure you that I appreciate—"

She took two quick strides and embraced me, both of her hands around my neck with her head buried in my chest. "You need to be quiet, Capitáno. Sometimes it is best to say nothing."

Taken unawares, my first reaction was to keep both arms extended. Then I gave in to the moment. My goodness, she was a strong woman. "Miranda, what brought this on? Is this about what happened with Mr. Ótubé?"

She relaxed her grip but didn't let go. She simply hugged without answering me.

"Look, I know you were trying to help. And whatever you did with him worked. I'm not finding…"

She cut me off, never removing her head from my chest. "Capitáno, sometimes it's necessary to do things we don't want or like to do. I have learned how to treat men like Mr. Ótubé. Please accept the results for what they are and don't ask further." She let go and stepped back. "Now I must finish my very important work."

She wiped her eyes with her apron as she stepped back into the galley.

I stood there bewildered, thankful there were no witnesses. I was fortified by her confession, but bothered at having thought that she might have compromised her integrity in an effort to help me gain the advantage with Ótubé. Had I appeared so inept in not being able to handle the negotiation that she felt the need to assist me?

The thought that I might have given that impression disturbed me. And then she had almost apologized for what she did. I was fortified to know how loyal a person she was, but my frustration grew as I wrestled with my thoughts: what had she really confessed to?

Mr. Malik came down the ladder from the bridge, rubbing his hands in anticipation of dinner.

"Chenal Patel tells me you have some good news for us, Captain. But he wouldn't divulge any information. He said I had to wait and be surprised like he was. What is this wonderful news? It would be a good time for our fortunes to turn, wouldn't you think?"

"Right you are, Mr. Malik; but before I fill you in, why don't we wait a few minutes for Mr. Prankiop to come forward from his watch? I'm sure by now he's as excited as you are, that is, if Mr. Tengazy is anything like Mr. Patel in his inability to keep a secret. Ah, here he is now." I motioned for the two men to join me at the dinner table.

"Have a seat, gents. Miranda has prepared a wonderful meal for us. She's outdone herself once again."

Miranda wasted no time in bringing out the soup and salad. I looked closely as she served, but there was no hint on her face of the emotion she had displayed before.

"So tell us, Captain," Prankiop said. "Kaamil, though my fellow countryman, wouldn't say a thing, other than I'd be liking what you have to say. Do not keep me in suspense."

"All right, seeing as how you're both here." I repeated my offer of continued employment all the way to Chittagong should they choose to stay on.

Prankiop was the first to speak. "Why of course, Captain, I will stay on. Why wouldn't I?"

"Yes, yes, of course," Tengazy followed. "I'm just delighted you want to keep us on."

I clapped my hands together. "That's wonderful, gentlemen. You don't know how much I appreciate this."

Waajid Prankiop said, "Captain, I don't know if you have ever been in Angola, but it's not a place you want to be stranded in having to look for a job. It was a long time ago when I was there, but my memories of Cabinda and Luanda aren't fond. Things may have improved now that their civil war is behind them. But as for me, I'm looking at staying right here in your employ."

"Why thank you, Waajid." I was flattered to hear his vote of confidence, not only in me, but also in *Marigold*.

"I too want to thank you for taking care of us, Captain," Daniru Malik said. "We've been through a great deal together. I would like to see this voyage through to the end. Captain, we've been with you through a battle with people who meant us grave harm. You are a good man and I agree with Waajid, you are one fine skipper. We aren't about to abandon you now."

My relief was immediate and must have shown, because both men raised a glass in salute. Whatever concern I may have harbored that some, or heaven forbid all of them, might want to leave was replaced by a touch of embarrassment at having never before thought to ask them to stay.

Until now, I had never called any of the men by their first name—men who had proven their loyalty several times over had always been Mr. Malik, Mr. Tengazy, Mr. Prankiop, and Mr. Patel. Perhaps now was a good time for me to change that practice.

Sensing my awkwardness, Miranda bustled in with the main course. I watched them dig into the meal with gusto. For the first time in a long while, I could see things coming together in a good way for *Marigold* and her crew.

I let them enjoy a few bites before saying, "In case your reliefs didn't mention it, there will be a €500 bonus for each of you in Angola and again when we reach Chittagong."

From the expressions on the faces of the two men, this news had taken them unawares. I briefly entertained the thought of telling them about the windfall I'd earned with the delivery of my Congo consignment, but thought better of it. As valuable a shipmate as each was, company business was still my business alone. Besides, with Miranda there, I didn't want to revisit the reasons for that success.

"That is most kind of you, Captain," Daniru Malik said. "But what we could really use right now is some more help in running the ship. Having six hours on watch and only six hours off will get old all the way to Bangladesh."

"I appreciate the news of the bonus," Waajid Prankiop said. "I must agree with Daniru. What we need now more than a bonus is extra crewmen. Other than that, I don't know what to say."

"Say, 'Thank you, Captain'," Miranda insisted. "Now finish your meal, you two. I don't want to stay around the mess deck any longer than I have to tonight."

I toyed with the ear of my coffee cup while Miranda cleared away the last of the dishes. Finished, she plopped opposite me, a practice of hers which was becoming routine.

"Phew, I can finish cleaning the dishes in a bit. Do you want more coffee, Capitáno?"

"No thank you, Miranda, I'm coffee'd out. I guess I have my marching orders for when we stop to refuel. I'll have to find a merchant marine office and hire more crew."

Miranda seemed preoccupied and didn't respond. I let my words die at the table.

Finally she said, "I hope you understand I had to do what I did with Leonard Ótubé. It is not something I'm used to doing, or even wanted to do. And certainly, it was nothing to be proud of. But I knew he was a bad man intending to impose a bad deal on us."

Her use of "us" surprised me. Although I had my suspicions about what had occurred between the two of them while I was topside, I didn't want to admit to my thoughts, either to her or myself. So, I put on a false front.

"I don't know what you're talking about."

"Capitáno, I was raised in Sicily. Like all Italy, it is a society of men. As a little girl, I saw what the older girls and women had to do to get along and survive. If you were lucky enough to find a good man to marry, you at least had a shield. My mother was fortunate in that way; my father was a good man.

"But my Aunt Rosária wasn't so lucky and ended up getting in with a rough crowd. She told me things she did for men just to pay the rent. She had a very difficult life. I have a niece and nephew, both of whom are outcomes of her mistreatment by the men in our village, most of whom were members of L'Azendia. I vowed never to let that happen to me. I learned that weak men like Ótubé respond to two things: physical intimidation or sensual favor. Today, I simply had to determine for myself how weak Ótubé was. So, I may be wiser in the ways of the world than you might think."

"Miranda, I don't know what to…"

But she wasn't done talking. "My father, as good as he was to me and my mother, was no saint. I heard the stories of how the men in the town caroused, and not just with the painted ladies, him included. Sometimes, if one of the housewives would be behind in her bill at the store, arrangements were made to even the books. The men lived a double standard, wanting virgins at home and whores in the streets."

I hoped to God she didn't think I upheld the same double standards as did the men of her village. I didn't want to know any more and so tried to change the subject. "I thought you grew up on Lipari, not Sicily."

"Believe me, Capitáno, Lipari is as much Sicily as the big island."

What did she want from me? Why did she think I needed her confession? I was neither her father nor her brother, and above all, I wasn't her moral arbiter.

Growing up on the Dublin docks was not the perfect setting for educating a pious man. I reached across the table and took her hand. She didn't pull back.

"Miranda, I'm pretty sure I know what you're trying to say, but you don't have to justify anything to me. I value your loyalty alone. We couldn't have come through some of the tight scrapes did if you hadn't…"

"That is the point, Capitáno." I felt the slightest pressure as her hand clasped mine.

"I didn't do what I did because I'm a member of this crew. I did it because…" She stopped mid-sentence, perhaps she'd changed her mind, and perhaps she just couldn't finish what she wanted to. A tear on her cheek threatened to run down. Then she shook her head, tossed her hair as a horse would flick its tail at a fly, and sniffled.

"I did it because I needed to. That's all."

I held her hand to let her moment pass and then asked, "Miranda, tell me. What does your last name mean in Italian?"

She smiled and said, "In Sicilian *occhipinti* means beautiful eyes. Why do you ask?"

Yes, they are, I thought. "I was just wondering."

Chapter 13

THE NEXT MORNING, I brought *Marigold* alongside the refueling pier in Luanda harbor, a port that was much busier than I expected because of the recent discovery of oil. *Marigold* was dwarfed by the tankers tied up nearby, taking on tons of gallons fresh from off-shore oil fields.

A sulfurous smell of bunker fuel permeated the air. For the locals, this was the smell of money, a product of the influx of petrol dollars from a nascent oil exploration industry which was transforming this once sleepy byway on the Vasco da Gama discovery route into a capital city worthy of the twenty-first century.

I wasn't sure what I expected to see of a skyline in Luanda, probably a civil war-torn city suffering from the ravages of the sectarian strife that dominated its history in the 70s through the turn of the century. But I was mistaken. There were skyscrapers and buildings topped by construction cranes busy at work making them taller, most of it brand new thanks to the burgeoning oil industry.

While Tengazy and Prankiop saw to the fueling operation, Miranda sought out the port chandler to resupply the galley. For my part, I went in search of a bank to transfer the proceeds from my recent cargo delivery to Dillon O'Connor and Mr. Arman Byassian at Ontotoupolos Shipping, Thessaloniki, Greece.

In the cab ride to the banking center, I pondered what O'Connor's actual stake in this enterprise had been, other than money. If my suspicions about the cargo's pedigree had been correct, he still had to be in a business just like his old days with the IRA, a business that had entangled my grandfather and quite possibly had been the cause of my parents' deaths. Whatever the case, Leonard Ótubé was his front man in the field. O'Connor had specifically told me to deal with him, just as he had handpicked Andjou, Rajman and Wahral for my crew.

While this speculation was a fine mental exercise, I wasn't sure what I could do about it other than wonder. As soon as I reached the bank, I could complete my contract and be done with the likes of O'Connor and his underlings for good. Maybe when I returned to Dublin, based on my own experiences with O'Connor, I could loosen up Pop in the Temple Swan to tell me what really sealed the fate of my parents.

The cabbie let me out in front of a quite modern structure whose glass façade rivaled any European or American building. I ascended the long flight of stairs from the street and pushed through the revolving glass entry door to a marble appointed lobby.

The bank manager, upon learning of the size of my transactions, treated me like a long lost friend. He personally escorted me to his private office and was only too anxious to assist. I put the bonus cash in separate envelopes for each crewman and put the envelopes in my pocket.

Then I processed wire transfers for Dillan and Mr. Arman Byassian. Additionally, I deposited €2M plus into my Dublin account via wire transfer. Grandfather would be set for life, however much longer that would be. When I returned home to Dublin, I would spring for drinks for everyone at the Temple Swan.

"This is a great deal of money, Mr. O'Scanlon," the bank manager offered. "You must have had some very good business dealings come your way."

Without a second thought, I said, "Yes, I did. The United Nations sponsored a housing construction project in the Congo and I was contracted to deliver a shipload of building supplies."

While the bank manager processed my deposits and transfers, he said, "The building supply business must be very good."

Not wanting to reveal more of my personal good news to a perfect stranger, I didn't respond. Making a last keyboard stroke to complete my transaction, he said, "There, that takes care of your checks, sir. I am happy for your good fortune. Please let me know in the future when I may be of service again."

I thanked the bank manager for his help and asked where the local shipping company was. He was only too happy to annotate a Chamber of Commerce map, which he gave to me.

At the shipping office, I inquired about taking on six crewmen for the trip around the Cape of Good Hope to Chittagong, Bangladesh. My skeleton crew had done well running *Marigold* shorthanded since exiting Cotonou, but as Malik and Prankiop had told me the night before, they dearly could use some help. Standing back-to-back watches had already fatigued them severely. Had an emergency occurred, as happened after leaving Funchal when the diesel engine broke down, there wouldn't have been anyone fresh to throw into the repair effort.

The jobber working out of the shipping office was accommodating. Within a few hours, he provided me with two engineers, two navigation mates, one deck hand, and a cook. I figured Miranda would welcome the help in the galley. I had to pay a €500 expediting fee to the shipping company, but the daily rates for the crewmen themselves were standard. I was relieved to find some semblance of normalcy again in my business dealings.

What I didn't count on, however, was the firestorm I ran into when I returned to the ship—a storm called Miranda.

"What do you mean, hiring a cook! What am I, last year's model? And look at him, he's Chinese! The Chinese don't know how to cook! Did I not do good enough for you? I cannot believe what my eyes are telling me!"

After rattling off something in rapid-fire Italian, which I was only too glad not to understand, she stood stock still, barring her galley door, arms folded, lower lip quivering in anger. She would not look me in the eye. She was in full sulk. No amount of, "I thought you could use the help," or "No one should have to work from 5 a.m. to 10 p.m." mattered. When I tried to approach her, she turned away, reinforcing how irate she was. As for the new cook, he was the smart one and hid in the bowels of the pantry, afraid to enter the galley proper.

FUEL TANKS TOPPED off and provisions stowed aboard by early afternoon, I made preparations for getting under-way. It was then that two Land Rovers with official government markings rolled down the pier and stopped at *Marigold*'s gangway. Two men in police uniforms stepped from the lead vehicle, while similarly clad men with automatic weapons exited from the other. All in all, eight machine gun-toting men positioned themselves at

the head of the brow and at each bollard, which held fast
Marigold's mooring lines. This wasn't a good sign; it was
Cotonou all over again.

The two officials, each with a pistol holstered on his
hip, came across the brow. The squattier of the two local
gendarmes said, "Captain O'Scanlon, can we talk?"

The man in charge may have been short, but he was
built like a rugby footballer, broad chested, with powerful
arms showing from under his short-sleeved uniform shirt.
He barked orders to the men on the pier, which were
instantly obeyed. His second in command, not as physically imposing as his boss though several inches taller and
appearing equally as fit, said nothing.

Both men wore the metal insignia of the Luanda
constabulary, if my ability to read Portuguese was any
good. I had no idea what I could have done to invite the
official attention of the government of a country I had
decided to visit briefly only the evening before. Furthermore, how did the local police know my name? Without a
twinge of guilt, I said to the more senior of the two, "Of
course, sir. Can I offer you coffee?"

It was clear to me this new development required my
utmost diplomatic effort. I left the number two man at the
head of the brow and escorted the man in charge to the
mess deck where Miranda, recovered from her earlier fit
of pique, was setting the sideboard for dinner before the
crew embarked on the rigors of leaving port. Her new
cook's assistant was nowhere to be seen.

"Miranda, we have a guest. Would you bring us
coffee?"

"Yes, Capitáno." She gave me a cautious look, but there
was nothing but civility in her voice. Most likely, she had

sensed the seriousness of the situation and had shifted into the solve-everything-at-any-cost mode she'd learned so dearly growing up in Sicily.

Before I could say anything more, the policeman spoke. To my surprise, his tone was conciliatory.

"Captain, I know you feel at a disadvantage, but it seems that the investigation into the loss of one of your crewmembers, a Rajip Tasmoon-Shamlyn, has surfaced on the international police wires. A complaint has been filed by First Mate Osaze Andjou of Benin and I am forced to investigate the allegation."

"Allegation!" I barked, but then shifted to a calmer voice. "I was told by the Port Authority at Cotonou that the investigation had been put to rest. I don't understand."

Of course, I did understand. That bandit Dembo Johnson and his unscrupulous pseudo-admiral friend, Pendali Gangho, were most likely once again haunting me, albeit from long distance, but haunting me just the same.

I took a deep breath and continued. "So what is it you need from me?"

I listened impatiently to the policeman as he laid out a bureaucratic nightmare of a story about how international procedures in matters like this had to be followed. As he went on, I inwardly fumed but said nothing.

Miranda appeared in the pantry doorway, out of the sightline of the policeman, and signaled. I listened to the government official for another minute and then held up my hand.

"Could you excuse me, sir? I have to make a quick check on something."

He started to object and perhaps warn me about trying to flee but simply acquiesced. As soon as I entered the pantry, Miranda tiptoed up and whispered in my ear.

"Trust me, Capitáno, this man is not here because he has an interest in justice. He can read the police wires like anyone else. He knows of the trouble we had at sea, and I am equally as certain he has never had anything to do with any officials from any other country except perhaps the DRC right next door. I have seen too many men like him in Sicily. He is only looking for money." She dropped down from her tiptoes and held up a hand, rubbing her thumb across her fingertips.

I put a hand on her arm to calm her. I was terrified that her voice—whisper or not—would carry into the mess deck.

"I agree, Miranda, but what can I do?"

"If you want, I can—"

"No!" I didn't let her finish the statement. I wasn't sure what she was going to say, but I was ashamed to be thinking of what it might be.

She began again, still in a low voice, "I was only going to say pay him. The only time this man ever saw €500 at one time was in a bribe. Don't let him give you a story about having to take care of his men. Offer him €150 and settle for something less than €1,000. That will send him on his way."

My God, she was a savvy woman! She was correct—this was simply a shakedown, not unlike the ones I'd endured in Cotonou.

"Okay." I released her arm and turned away. Then I looked back. "Miranda—thank you." Retaking my seat, I said, "Sorry for that, sir, but the port chandler is trying to rob me with the prices he's charging for slaughtered lamb. I instructed my cook to offer that charlatan fifty percent of what he was asking and not a euro more." I hoped this little fib would have the desired effect on the official.

"Captain, I couldn't agree with you more. As you must realize, however, I have to clear this investigation before I can release you."

Release me? Suddenly I was confronted with the possibility I was about to be detained, a thought which I hadn't considered when this started.

The official continued, "This is the only time when I will be able to send back the proper information, when I have you available to give me the answers that they seem to need."

"I am not sure who they happen to be, sir, but would €150 help you find the correct way to phrase your report and let me be on my way?"

The burly policeman started to put on an air of righteous indignation, but thought better of it. Apparently, once money was mentioned, all that remained was to settle on the price.

He dropped all pretense. "Captain, I see you like to cut to the chase. I, too, won't waste anymore of your time. But, as you may have noticed when I arrived, I have several other…"

I cut him off. "Please, don't give me that. Those people are your problem, not mine. It is you I will write the check to, not them. What you do after that is on your conscience. Give me a number."

"I think, sir that you are in big trouble." Any semblance of banter or hedging of words was gone. He looked me straight in the eye, taking the measure of me. Any possibility of amicability had disappeared entirely from his demeanor. "You don't seem to realize how precarious your situation is. I know you just left the Congo without pulling into either Brazzaville or Matadi after delivering a very profitable cargo of building supplies for the UN. Sums like you deposited could have only come from something other than lumber, nails, and tools. My guess is you were carrying contraband, as defined by the Democratic Republic of the Congo and as would be described by any reasonable international convention. Men have been brought up on charges for less at The Hague.

"Whichever the case is here, I think you made a great deal of money with your most recent transaction. You see, the manager of the bank you went to this morning is my brother-in-law. It seems after you left the bank, he thought the amounts you were presenting were inordinate for any kind of business, other than something to do with the petrochemical industry. And since he has never met you or heard of you in his years dealing with the oil companies and their clients in and around Luanda, he decided to call the UN representative in Brazzaville, who referred him to a Mr. Leonard Ótubé. He in turn gave him the name of an Irishman named Dillion O'Connor to check with to confirm the contents of your delivered manifest."

I blanched. Either the bank manager was an international watchdog on the lookout for illegal activity, or he had sensed an opportunity to cash in and take down someone, me to be specific, who had no recourse except to pay.

Seeing my expression, the policeman continued. "My brother-in-law wasn't able to contact Mr. O'Connor, so he alerted me. So you see, Mr. O'Scanlon, I don't know specifically what you delivered, but I'm guessing it was something much more valuable than building supplies. I know you deposited €2M in your home account and you wired a significantly greater sum to someone else. I'm guessing that someone was Mr. O'Connor. So, let's not belabor this further. You will come with me now and we will visit my brother-in-law's bank. He will only be too glad to honor a check drawn on your bank for €2M."

I was flabbergasted and crestfallen. My shoulders slumped. There was no way I could hide my utter despair. In one swift moment, he had gained the upper hand. The accuracy of his intelligence was undeniable. Clearly he had his ear to the ground in a very effective way. I had no wiggle room. Not only did he know how much I had cleared, but he had men with guns, and I wasn't about to test whether or not he had any compunction about using them. He had me and he knew I knew it.

When we arrived at his brother-in-law's bank, I was escorted from the lobby to a small private conference room, well away from the main banking center. Seated at the head of a highly polished mahogany table was the bank manager I had previously dealt with. He was wearing the same light-colored suit he'd worn earlier in the day. He greeted his brother-in-law with a broad grin, accentuated by very white teeth. He gave me a *tsk, tsk* look as if to scold me for trying to get away with a scam, completely disregarding what he, in fact, was doing the same to me.

I decided my only chance at salvaging some of my profits was to take the initiative and barter with the man. I made a feeble attempt to negotiate him down to some number, any number, less than what his relative the policeman had demanded.

But he wouldn't budge. The two in-laws knew they had me over a barrel, and I was squirming. They may not have known precisely what my cargo had been, just as I had not, but their experience in handling business deposits from enterprises as small as *Marigold* told them something illegal on the international scene, such as drugs, arms, or human trafficking, had to be the reason. They had made an educated guess and gotten it right.

The entire encounter happened so quickly, I didn't get either the bank manager's or his nefarious brother-in-law's name, for all the good that would have done me. Was I going to report them, and if so, to whom?

With my €2M check in his pocket, the policeman grinned and said, "Have a good day—Captain," giving undue emphasis to my title. He summarily dismissed me, not even offering me a ride back to the pier.

When I returned to *Marigold*, Malik was on the bridge and had the lines singled in preparation for leaving. "Is everything okay to leave, Captain?"

"Yes, Mr. Malik, just peachy. Get us out of here before anything else happens."

I went to my cabin.

Today's events had dealt me a blow, not quite the last straw, but my resolve had been fully tested. At the heart of the matter, I was certain the two brothers-in-law—the policeman and banker who robbed me—had to have been put up to this. Businessmen in the modern world dealt in multi-million-euro transactions in capital cities all the time without drawing the conclusions the policeman described to me. No, something was different today.

My first suspicion was to blame Dillon O'Connor. Hell, the policeman had all but confirmed that. But with Dillon O'Connor five thousand miles away in Ireland, how could he possibly have affected what happened here in Angola, considering the short time from delivering my cargo with Gund to reaching Luanda?

And if O'Connor wanted to set me up for a big score by having me carry contraband, why the persistent pursuit after I'd sold his cargo and paid him? The answer had to be the ancient bad blood between Dillon and Grandfather over late payoffs and missing gold. With his profits in hand now, that old grudge was driving O'Connor to continue to plague me and *Marigold*.

But that didn't fully explain what happened today. O'Connor had his money and had nothing else to gain from me. My only other conclusion had to be that the Luanda brothers had acted on their own when they saw a target of opportunity.

The more I thought about it the madder I got. I had too many questions to resolve on my own. I reached for my sat phone and dialed Dillon O'Connor. I wasn't sure what I'd say when he answered, but he was the source of my discomfort.

"Johnny, what a pleasant surprise. I just received your bank drafts. Good work."

Honey dripped from his voice and now I was incensed. "Don't act so innocent with me, O'Connor. I just got ripped off by the banking crooks here in Luanda after they called your man Leonard Ótubé. You and he have screwed me from one end of the Atlantic to the other, so don't try to give me that 'Hi, Johnny' shit."

"Calm yourself, laddie. You're a bit mixed up."

"Like hell I am. You stuck those three crewmen on board to eyeball your cargo to make sure it got picked up and delivered. But they tipped their hats in Cotonou, so I got rid of them. And then you had M'Nasi and Ótubé keep you informed of my progress. Now that you've got your money, you had your banker friends rip off my profits."

"Hold on, laddie, hold on. I don't know what banker friends you're referring to and I haven't tried to rip you off. I paid you good money to deliver that cargo and only took reasonable measures to ensure its safe arrival. That UN contract is only one of many I'm working to help reconstruct the infrastructure..."

"Don't give me that. What building supplies are worth that much money? You used me to deliver illicit goods, otherwise why so many millions involved for a few logs and water bladders?"

There was a momentary pause and then O'Connor said, "All right, there was something else in there besides the building supplies, but nothing illegal. I've got lots of people around the world who I have to keep happy in order to do business. In this case I owed something to my contact in the Congo."

"Was it guns?"

"No, information he could use against people he had to deal with. Information I couldn't trust to electronics or say over the phone. Documents.

"And as for the rest of it, when you fired Andjou, I was flying blind until you got to Congo. I'd already gotten a scare when Andjou said another crewman was poking around the cargo."

"Andjou told you?"

"Yes, he told me he'd killed him to keep him quiet after a storm."

"Christ Almighty, man, you've put me through hell with investigations. Not to mention my personal anguish over losing a crewman and not being able to recover his body. I'm going to the police as soon as I get somewhere that I can trust the local authorities."

"Hold on, laddie. You can't go doing that."

"And why not? I can't implicate you unless you admit to it, but I can get Interpol to go after Andjou and..."

"Johnny, if you chose to spill the beans, that's your worry. But I wouldn't advise it. How will you explain your involvement in this whole affair as being innocent? But I can solve your problems if you don't go to the police."

I didn't answer right away. Why should I even listen to this man? He'd been nothing but trouble for me. But I was intrigued enough to listen, if nothing else than to gather more grist for the mill when I turned him in. "Go ahead. I'm listening."

"It will cost you."

"Cost me! Dealing with you has done nothing but cost me so far. It's cost me everything I was trying to earn for me and my grandfather's future."

"Stop and listen, Johnny. You're in no position to bargain. Here's what I'll do. I'll take care of Andjou so he's no threat to either me or you. All you have to do is turn over fifty percent of the proceeds from the scrap yards to me."

I hesitated. I was out all of my €2M profit, everything I'd hoped to gain with this misadventure. At least this way I could get some justice for Tasmoon-Shamlyn's death and get some cash out of the sale of *Marigold*. Something was better than the nothing I had.

"That doesn't sound like such a good deal to me, O'Connor. You've got your money from the Congo and I'm out €2M because you've been double-dealing me all along."

"It's not double-dealing, Johnny, it's insurance. Now, here's what I'm going to do. I've got a consignment in Cape Town. I'll call the guy putting together the cargo to cancel his current charter with his Afrikaans shipper. When you get there, find the shipper and offer to take it."

"What's the shipment?"

"Don't worry about it, Johnny. It's just several hundred bales of raw cotton."

"What's the catch?"

"Catch? There's no catch. When you get to Chittagong, I want fifty percent of the sale to scrap *Marigold*."

I thought long and hard. "I'll do it, but only for ten percent."

"Hah, Johnny, you're finally catching on. Twenty-five percent and that's final. It's a fair deal. I'm staking you again and taking care of Andjou for you."

I hung up, dissatisfied with myself at having to deal with this man again. While he answered some of my questions, he hadn't satisfied my concerns. All I really managed to do was continue this man's association with me, *Marigold*, and by default, Grandfather. I had a chance to make some of my money back, but he was buying time—but time for what?

I was missing something. Only one person could shed light on this problem, if my suspicions were correct, and that was Grandfather. I dashed off a radio message to Pop via the offices of TC Miriam.

Though I wanted answers, what I needed more was to complete my journey, pay off the crew, and resolve my family's future. At least I had a meager plan in place to satisfy that need.

Chapter 14

NORMALLY WHEN EXITING an unfamiliar foreign port, I'd have been on the bridge to oversee the piloting past navigation hazards. But my mood was foul and I was too disconcerted from the day's events to abide by professional protocols. So I left Daniru alone on the bridge to get us underway and out to sea while I sat at the desk in my sea cabin and contemplated what to do next.

The setback at the bank was like watching a continuous film loop of my misfortunes. Just about the time my situation was hopeless, the faintest glimmer of a silver lining in my life's darkest cloud appeared, only to be blotted out again. As I recapped my difficulties, I realized if I were to maintain my sanity I had to take charge of what I could control and come up with a plan to move forward.

I made some hurried calculations and determined I had enough money remaining to refuel and take on provisions in Cape Town, even without O'Connor's help of another consignment. If everything worked out, when I arrived in Chittagong at the breaking yard, I might make enough from the scrap sale of the ship to pay off the crew and get me home to Dublin—breaking even. Small solace.

I thought about checking with shippers in Cape Town for taking on a consignment cargo on my own, without O'Connor's help. I dismissed this idea, however, as wishful thinking. Since the chances of my finding a cargo destined for Chittagong were slim, what I needed least of all now was false hope. After all, the Cape was not exactly the commerce capital of the world. Every day I lost idling in a South African port, far from my ultimate destination and hoping to find a paying freight would cost me money in operating expenses for the crew, fuel, and provisions, was money I didn't have.

No, the only sure fire way to remain solvent was to take O'Connor's offer in Cape Town and get to Bangladesh to complete the final sale of *Marigold*.

The bleakness of my prospects was overwhelming. I didn't know how much more of this I could withstand. My misfortune wasn't just about me; it was about my grandfather, too. And then there was my crew to consider. Given what they had endured, I owed them more than a paycheck for standing by me. Somehow, I had to find a way to prove myself worthy of that loyalty.

In the back of my mind, I had harbored a notion to document *Marigold*'s last voyage. I took the camera from my locker and paged through the pictures I'd taken during the voyage. The process of scrolling through dozens of snapshots proved to be good therapy. As I did, I fantasized there was a photo-journal story I could edit and sell to raise money. The exercise worked, at least as far as clearing my mind. Twenty minutes into my review, I had all but forgotten my present circumstance watching the photo-journey.

When I got to the photos of the Ganvié Voodoo festival, I found many of the shots were poor in quality. I'd shot the pictures covertly to avoid drawing attention to myself by the participants while they were absorbed in their deeply religious, animated antics. Many pictures were blurred shots of the pavement, feet, the night sky, or parts of arms and headless torsos. Enough of them, though, were sufficiently clear to contain subject matter of interest.

I was about to back up the sequence to delete the bad shots when I chanced upon a photo of the lower half of a man wearing a traditional gown which extended to the ground. A blurred hem had swirled up, showing his sandals and exposing a tattooed white ankle. It clearly showed an image of the letters FF superimposed on a black circle with strange lettering arrayed around the rim.

In a sea of black revelers, here was a white man dressed to fit in with the crowd. He wasn't wearing western garb under the robe. There were no trousers with cuffs, so it couldn't have been Bill Sandler, the professor I'd met from Louisiana.

I wasn't sure what to make of this, so I saved this one and continued my review. In the midst of the pictures I'd taken of the cargo transfer to Mr. Gund's Congo River barges, another picture caused me to stop scrolling.

The UN peacekeepers were a multinational group. As such, there were participants from several nations involved in the operation, almost all of whom were from African nations themselves. Seeing an occasional white face amongst them in itself wasn't surprising. However, on one of the barges in the background, a person not involved in the cargo transfer stood as a lone white figure atop the pilot house. The figure appeared in every one of a dozen photos and never moved from his vantage point. In two of the photos, his hands seemed to be cupped to his face.

I zoomed in. He was holding a pair of binoculars and watching the cargo transfer from *Marigold* to the UN barge. When I clicked to the next photo, the binoculars no

219

longer blocked his face and I recognized him. It was Dillon O'Connor, observing the proceedings in shorts and a short-sleeved native shirt. Clearly showing above a bare ankle was a tattoo—a black circle with a double FF in the middle, the symbol of Sinn Féin and the Irish Republican Army.

Why, that bastard. He was still up to his nefarious tricks of two decades ago, just as Grandfather had described at the Temple Swan. He'd double-crossed his own countrymen in IRA days just to put a few extra quid in his pocket. And now he appeared in the middle of Africa, overseeing my cargo transfer. Why, when I talked to him, did he not tell me?

Again, I reviewed all that seemed to link many of the events of *Marigold*'s voyage to O'Connor. He had contacted me to offer help in financing my trip; he had designated three crew members to Chamberlains to man my ship; his hand-picked crewmen had been up to something on board which ended up costing Tasmoon-Shamlyn his life; and the cargo he consigned was so overvalued its true nature caught the eye of the two opportunists in Luanda who ripped me off.

So what was he really doing in the Congo—checking on me to ensure the transfer of his contraband went well? I had assumed, talking to him via sat phone a few days before, that he was back in Ireland. But just because the phone number was listed in Ireland didn't mean that was where the phone actually was. And he had been at that Voodoo festival, too, because now I had a photo of the same tattoo he sported on the transfer barge on an ankle at the Voodoo festival in Cotonou. He was definitely following my progress.

That double-crossing son of a bitch. Maybe he had also put Dembo Johnson and Pendali Gangho up to their shenanigans, not only to spur their hopes for a big payoff, but also as a way to further harass me. And when I fired his onboard agents—Andjou, Wahral and Rajman—he had no choice but to come to the Congo to ensure the delivery of his cargo.

When I didn't put into Matadi to refuel, he knew I had to stop somewhere else soon. And when the Luanda bank manager had called Ótubé to verify our transaction, O'Connor was tipped off. He had his €5M and probably began working on a scheme to secure my cut, too. He had either had the Angolan brothers rob me as part of his revenge scheme, or they had acted on their own, as a chance of opportunity. Either way, I was out €2M euros.

Another horrible thought hit me. Had my grandfather once been in league with this snake in the grass? But how could I think poorly of my grandfather? He'd never suggested I deal with Dillon O'Connor. That had been my idea when Dillon had called me with his proposal of partnership. I had opened myself up for the ensuing trouble suffered at his hand.

Even after Grandfather warned me of O'Connor's sinister dealings with those he did business with, I didn't change tack. Had I simply taken *Marigold* to a Bristol breaking yard, I would at least have some money now and would be on my way to a sound future and have avoided my current dilemma. What a fool I'd been.

I put my camera down and lay back on my bunk to figure out what I should, or even could do.

As if Grandfather were listening to my thoughts, Daniru rang my cabin phone to inform me I had a radio message coming in. I went to the radio room off the bridge and found Grandfather's reply to my message sent just hours before.

Johnny

Told you D O'C was no good. He has his ways to reach long distances with contacts built over years in the business. He's after revenge for all that lost revenue from years ago. Be careful. Like the other skippers who had run-ins with him, I couldn't spend the money or he'd notice. So I hid the pilfered gold away where I knew D O'C would never look—aboard Marigold. *I told no one, not even you, for fear he'd have ways of turning heads.*

Couldn't put you through that. I wasn't going to tell you until you pulled into the breaking yards 'cause radio messages aren't secure. Call me when you reach the breaking yards and I'll tell you where to look.

GF

That's why Dillon O'Connor wanted to keep such close tabs on me. He's still looking for the gold, and until he found it, my entire crew and I were in serious danger. After I fired those three in Cotonou, he had only M'Nasi and Ótubé, men he'd specifically had me deal with, to keep tabs on me. Coming aboard *Marigold* to negotiate had given them access to the ship without raising any suspicions. Perhaps while I was tied up with them, they had managed to have a confidante search the ship. Maybe not a close inspection, but at least to check out some locations.

I folded the message, put it in my wallet between photos of Grandmother and our house in Dublin, and went back to my cabin with a new problem to solve. Where could gold be hidden on board a ship I knew every inch of? Certainly, I would have noticed even the most illogical place to hide bullion—a place strong enough to support the weight, but which still allowed access. I'd have to try harder.

If O'Connor was as determined as he had shown himself to be up to now to find the gold, how could I rule out the people I had assumed were loyal to me—my crew? After all, O'Connor had provided the entire crew for Chamberlains to place on my ship. Why should I assume the three I had sent off the ship in Cotonou were his only henchman? I had to be wary of almost everything and everyone from now on.

What the hell was I thinking? Miranda, Prankiop, Tengazy, Malik, and Patel had proven themselves in a gunfight leaving Benin. They wouldn't have done that if they were on O'Connor's side. Paranoia was getting the best of me.

A SOFT KNOCK on my cabin door awakened me from a deep sleep. I slowly opened my eyes only to see darkness beyond my porthole. It had been midafternoon when I had come to my cabin. Ocean swells were working *Marigold*'s hull, which told me *Marigold* was now well to sea and riding easily.

Shaking my head, I wondered what time it was. I had no recollection of how long I had brooded in my cabin or how long I had been asleep. The soft knock came again.

"Come in." I was alert enough to prop myself up on both elbows. I must have been a sight, fully dressed lying on an unturned down bed.

A red shaft of light from the darkened bridge came through the partially opened door.

"Capitáno," came a soft voice through the door crack. "Are you alright? You didn't come to dinner. It's 10:30 and no one has seen you since we left port."

My stomach grumbled. I cleared my throat and said, "Yes, yes, I am fine, Miranda. Thank you for checking. I must have missed dinner."

"Yes you did, Capitáno, but I saved something for you. I grilled steaks. I will put one on and it can be ready in no time. Medium rare?"

"No, that's quite all right, Miranda. I'm sure I'll be fine if I miss a meal."

She remained silent for a few heartbeats.

"You left the ship with the gendarmes and were gone for several hours in Luanda. When you returned, you never came down to say how it went. We were getting worried."

There was no question in her voice—no demand. If anything, it was a sincere concern. "Do you want to talk?"

I wasn't ready to share what had transpired: the banker incident, my conversation with O'Connor, or the message from Pop. I certainly wasn't going to mention anything about hidden gold, even to Miranda.

Pushing myself upright, I swung my feet to the floor. I must've been more exhausted than I realized because I was still wearing my brogues. I moved my cheeks against my teeth and then ran my tongue across them to work up some moisture in my mouth.

My eyes adjusted to the red light and could make out more than simply her dark shape in the door.

"I have to get some water."

I stood and poured tap water into a glass.

"Do you want coffee?"

I looked at her over the rim of the glass. She leaned against the open door, half filling the portal. Partially lit now, she had one shoulder outside of the door with the open edge pressed into her torso. One of her knees was part way in the room, as if trying to block as much of the intruding light as she could. She was lovely standing there in the half light.

I put the glass down. "No, that's okay. There's no need to bother."

"It is no bother, Capitáno. That is my job."

She eased past the door's edge and stepped into my cabin, silhouetted by the red glow from the bridge behind her. Her hair, normally pulled back in a ponytail, was loose and free. It fell just below her shoulders. She leaned back with both hands behind her and her shoulders against the door. One foot rested flat on the cabin deck with the other raised on its toes with the knee slightly bent.

She pushed the door slowly with her backside until the latch clicked softly shut. The red glow blinked out and the moon's albedo through the porthole bathed the room with soft colors and a dulled shadow white. A three day waxing crescent moon painted a diaphanous glow on her face.

"Do you want to tell me about it?"

My God, she was beautiful! I could say nothing as I drank in her beauty with every thirsty pore of my soul. She didn't move.

The air between us was still, redolent with the tropical heat. Suddenly I felt even warmer as sweat formed on my brow. I was charged with an invisible force—an attraction I struggled to keep in check. I didn't move.

"Capitáno Johnny, I know you are troubled. It's not good to keep troubles bottled up inside. At some point, you must trust someone. Otherwise, why is it good to be alive?"

I was electrified, as if thrown into a conscious world I'd denied myself for too many years. She had never spoken my first name. Her accent was spellbinding. I was as immobile as a statue. She released her grasp on the doorknob and took two slow steps to close the distance between us. Suddenly, the confines of my cabin were exactly that—confines.

"Capitáno Johnny." She pronounced it *Dzhonny*. "It's all right. You are with me. I will take care of everything."

She placed one hand on my shoulder and softly pressed until my knees bent and I sat on my bed. She knelt before me, unlaced my shoes, and pulled them off.

"See, is that not better?"

She pushed again gently until I lay back on the bed. My next sensation was her pushing her way next to me. One arm and one leg draped over my perfectly still body. She laced the fingers of one hand through my hair.

"Now, tell me all about it, Capitáno Johnny."

There was nothing formal in the way she said "Capitáno." It was intimate, the most seductive sound I'd ever heard.

"Are my troubles that obvious?" I muttered.

"Shhh," she whispered, putting her finger to my lips.

I AWOKE TO sun streaming through the porthole. I was under my sheets, completely undressed. Without moving anything but my head, I looked around the cabin. I was alone. I lay there and didn't want to move.

There was a soft double knock. The cabin door opened a hand's width, spilling more white light inside, as a brisk voice said, "Capitáno, are you decent? I have coffee for you."

Without waiting for a reply, and I wasn't sure I was capable of making one, Miranda pushed the door open with one foot. She placed a serving tray laden with a coffee urn, cup, and condiments on my desk. Gone was the more familiar greeting I vaguely remembered from last night. It was strictly Capitáno now.

"It is 7:30, Capitáno. Chenal Patel says to tell you we are on track and steaming well down the Skeleton Coast, whatever that is, and that everything is okay. If you would like, I'll be in the mess and can make breakfast when you come down."

"Thank you, Miranda. I'll be there in a few minutes. Give me time to awaken and get up properly."

"Very good, Capitáno. I will be waiting for you."

She shut the door as softly as she'd opened it. My privacy and the sanctity of the captain's cabin were restored.

I took a sponge bath and put on clean clothes. I felt refreshed, and not simply by my morning ritual. As I tied my shoes, I looked around my cabin, scrutinizing it for evidence of her presence. There wasn't a hint of the visitor I had last night. Or had I?

Chapter 15

FOR THE WEEK it took *Marigold* to reach Cape Town, I took walks around the ship, giving as my reason to the bridge watch that I was conducting my safety checks as captain. My real purpose was to search every hold, frame bay, storeroom, and cabinet, every conceivable place Pop could have hidden his gold.

I didn't know what form it was in or how it was stowed—bars or coins, in bags or by itself. For all I knew, he could have gold-plated something and painted it over. These possibilities came to me as I contemplated my frustrations standing at the railing on the fantail, idly picking at a flake of rust. I even drew a scornful eye from Miranda when I entered her pantry and wouldn't let her join me. Her irritation was short lived, though, and if any of the other crewmen were curious as to my actions, they never voiced their concern.

Though my reason for these shipboard meanderings was to find the gold, I came to doubt that Pop had actually hidden anything, since I knew *Marigold* inside and out and hadn't turned up an ounce. Maybe he was putting up a good show to frustrate Dillon O'Connor, perpetuating a myth to taunt the man. Regardless, by the last night at sea, I abandoned my search.

Late in the morning of the seventh day, the flat outline of Table Mountain, blanketed by the low-hanging clouds for which the landmark was known, came into view above the horizon. The harbor approach was routine, even for a first-timer like me. I tied *Marigold* up to the designated wharf and the crew set about doing what they knew best.

Tengazy and the new deckhand soon had the refueling truck at the pier filling our thirsty diesel tanks. Miranda and her galley helper, whom she had finally made peace with—forgiveness may be too strong of a word—were talking to the larder merchants for restock supplies for the galley pantry.

While I smoked a cigar on the bridge wing, I noticed a second floor shipping office three store fronts down the row of buildings opposite the pier. The name over the door was Van Rooyen Ltd. Having received no indication from O'Connor as to which freight forwarder to contact, I decided to try my luck and inquire about a cargo consignment. As Grandfather had told me on many occasions, fortune seeks not those who stand idly by.

Leaving Malik in charge of the ship, I ventured down the pier, puffing on my cigar and admiring the bustle of the waterfront. Shortly, I reached Van Rooyen's and entered. A bell above the inner door jingled to announce me. A slender man about my size looked up from a desk set well back from the front counter. "May I help you?" he asked in Afrikaans accented English.

"Yes, I am Johnny O'Scanlon, captain and owner of TC Miriam shipping." I pointed up the wharf. "That's my vessel, *Marigold*, at the berth over there."

He stopped his work and came to the counter. "Captain O'Scanlon, is it? How may I be of service?"

The change in his demeanor was a pleasant surprise. We shook hands.

"I'm from Dublin by way of Funchal and Cotonou, and I'm looking for a cargo bound for Calcutta, or anywhere on the east coast of India. I have three empty holds and the ability to carry a hundred tons of bulk cargo below decks, with containers on my main deck amidships."

His face lit up and he clapped his hands as if I had spoken some sort of magic code.

"Captain, this is a fortunate day for the both of us. As a matter of fact, I am in a tight spot with a cargo of forty-five tons consisting of cotton bales and seven con-boxes of machinery parts that must arrive in Mahajanga on the northwest coast of Madagascar within the next two weeks. The carrier I previously contracted informed me he was backing out of our deal. The receiving client has a strict time schedule to meet on his end, thus the urgent need for me to move this freight, or I'm liable for a penalty payment." He motioned for me to have a seat at his desk behind the counter.

Dillon O'Connor, you devil. "Well, Mr. ..." I hadn't gotten his name.

"Blaauw. Peter Blaauw. I am the proprietor of Van Rooyen Limited."

"Well, sir, it seems we may be able to resolve each other's difficulties. Please, give me the details."

"Good. My original contract gave me a thirty percent cancellation fee, which is pretty much standard. Since I own the contract, however, I am liable to the receiver for any incurred late fees on his end. And I don't know how hefty those would be. So you see, this lot of cotton and machine parts is costing me money sitting here, and a great deal more if I'm late."

He was in a bind. Apparently, he was oblivious to who had pulled the strings to put him in this precarious financial position. Having no instructions to guide me from O'Connor, I proceeded to haggle the consignment fee. We settled on a price that netted me €11,700, after crew and fuel expenses. Additionally, he agreed to pay me sixty percent up front; the rest would be COD in Madagascar. He was happy because he had preserved his cancellation bonus and avoided late fees. I was happy because, with the advance, I once again had working capital.

While his administrative assistant drew up the contract, Peter Blaauw asked, "Captain, it looks like we have some time while the paperwork is prepared. Why don't you join me for a pint to seal our deal?"

"That's most kind of you, sir. I think that's a splendid idea."

I surprised myself at how readily I accepted his offer. But I had reason to feel happy—my fortunes were turning around.

Over the next half hour, we traded stories. He told me his family got into the shipping, provisioning, and cargo consignment business when his great-grandfather, unable to scratch out a living farming in the interior, came to Cape Town and began work as an assistant to a ship's chandler. "By the time he retired, he was the owner and had turned it over to my grandfather, who subsequently passed it on to my father. Twelve years ago, I took over from him. How about you, Captain?"

Though a bit heady from the strong Dutch ale, I still had a clear enough mind to remain cautious and not give in to discussing the perils I'd endured in Benin and Luanda. But when I mentioned M'Nasi's name and described the Niger cargo broker, Peter's reaction surprised me.

"You don't mean Michael Nasir, do you?"

"No, his name was M'Nasi. I'm sure of it."

"A light-skinned Black man with a flair for fashion—well-tailored in the British style?"

He'd described Mr. M'Nasi to a tee. "Yes, dressed like a City of London banker. That surprised me when I met him, because I was under the impression he was a general—an advisor to the president of Niger." I told him about the internet news article I'd seen.

"General, ha! He's no general. I've seen him off and on when he's had dealings with shipments coming through here from or to almost every African port from Senegal to Somalia. If there's a revolution going on, he's got something to do with it.

"I'll not speculate on what he's vouching for in those shipments of his, mind you, but his manifests were always on the up and up. Since it was my reputation on the line, I made sure of that when I dealt with any of his cargos. But I'd bet my mother's corset that what he deals with has something to do with conflict. The declared value of those shipments of his were always high, if you know what I mean. If you ask me, he's in thick with those toffs in Europe's former Soviet Bloc, the ones who still have caches of old Soviet weapons for sale. And the way he talks and carries himself, he's not African—he's an Englishman."

I took a long draught of my ale, not wanting to show my sudden concern at hearing his revelation. I put my pint down and exhaled. I knew I should end the pleasantries and return to *Marigold* before I said something that would make this conversation too memorable in Peter's mind.

After all, I didn't know which side of M'Nasi, or Michael Nasir, Peter Blaauw was on. My impression was he was a legitimate businessman, but my business partner choices hadn't worked out too well recently. Though Dillon O'Connor hadn't specifically mentioned Van Rooyen Limited, he was at the least only once removed from this arrangement I had with Peter Blaauw, whether or not Peter knew it.

It was imperative that I gather as much information on Mr. M'Nasi as I could. After all, Dillon O'Connor had deliberately put me in touch with this man as the one I had to do business with if I were to get paid. Now I had to consider if both M'Nasi and Ótubé were every bit as much a part of O'Connor's plan to undermine me and TC Miriam as were Andjou and his two partners in crime. They had all been deliberately placed in my path by Dillon O'Connor. And now I learned that M'Nasi shipped goods to dangerous parts of the world where the likelihood of his consignments being contraband was high.

As much as I liked my conclusions, Peter had offered no proof, only speculation. In fact, he vouched for the veracity of M'Nasi's manifests. I wanted to believe his assessment, since it meant the cargo I'd carried from Cotonou to Congo was as benign as O'Connor had confessed to me. But, if M'Nasi were in league with the likes of Dillon O'Connor and Leonard Ótubé, then indeed, I'd been part and parcel to their subterfuge. Because I'd talked myself out of inspecting the Congo cargo while it was still in my holds, I wasn't a victim, but I was an unwitting participant. What I needed now was more information, and that perhaps Peter could provide.

"Did you know Mr. M'Nasi, or Michael Nasir, well enough to converse with him socially?"

"No, I only saw him when he was in the company of his clients, men I knew not to be, shall I say, perfectly honest in the goods they dealt in. That's why I did cargo verifications. To the best I could determine, those sales were the normal outfitting needs for the clients he was with."

"Outfitting? You make this sound like you were a holiday trekking guide. I got the impression from your earlier comments, the countries he serviced weren't garden spots."

I knew I was pressing him, but I was looking for confirmation as to the true character of the people with whom I'd done business. O'Connor's trying to do my business harm was one thing; that was revenge on his part against Grandfather. But to entangle me in shipping contraband would involve me in an ongoing crime. I couldn't do anything about what had already transpired, but perhaps I could find a way to tip off authorities, whoever that might be, once I returned home. To do that, I needed facts that Peter might be able to provide.

Peter fidgeted with his pint. I'd struck a nerve.

"Mind you, the last time he was in here, I only heard a bit of their private discussions, and only when they spoke in English. But it seems to me they were loading stores enough to resupply a sizable expedition bound for the Mozambique coast, somewhere near the outfall of the Zambezi River."

I debated whether I should push him harder. But with his mention of Mozambique, my interest was piqued. I was headed for the Mozambique Channel, albeit for

Madagascar to the east and not the adjacent continental nations. If there were bad people associated with M'Nasi still here in Cape Town, or possibly somewhere on the route I was about to take, I wasn't simply being curious, I was being cautious. And if M'Nasi were with them, I might be in jeopardy of his reporting my whereabouts to O'Connor. I'd already learned the hard way that Dillon O'Connor had a very long reach.

I pressed Peter further. "These men, were they Europeans—the ones with M'Nasi?"

"Two of them definitely were. Not only did they look like it, but they dressed that way, too. The rest of them were Middle Eastern, if I had to guess."

"Not African?"

"No, definitely not."

"And headed to—" I hesitated—"to Mozambique and not Somalia, Ethiopia, or Yemen?"

Peter was becoming frustrated. "Captain, these men weren't regular customers of mine. I only sold them galley provisions, canvas, and petrol tanks—fifty-liter cans to strap on trucks or Range Rovers."

I knew I'd reached Peter's limit of cooperation and available information. It would be best not to leave an impression which he'd recall if one of Dillon's or M'Nasi's cohorts came to ask. However, he added something unsolicited. "One thing about their transaction was a little unusual."

I leaned across the table towards him. "How's that?"

Peter leaned in, too, as if to join a conspiracy. "The one man in charge of the group, not Mr. Nasir, but a man in a well-tailored western suit, paid for the lot with a draft drawn on the Bank of Dubai."

"Hmm, an Arab bank." I leaned back. Using well-funded foreign banks wasn't uncommon in the shipping business. I certainly did it, but I used a bank from my country of origin. I wondered if Mr. M'Nasi's client had done so, too. Had Dillon O'Connor traded his IRA connections for dealing in Middle Eastern arms?

Before I could probe further, Peter said, "I'm thinking, Captain, that we should be getting back to make our arrangement official. We need to load your cargo and so can clear Cape Town. The sooner you can make delivery and get me off the hook for the late fees, the better I'll feel. Now let me go get the paperwork."

"Peter, mind if I borrow your computer to check my bank balance? You have a much better internet connection than I have on board with the satellite."

"Make yourself at home. I'll only be a minute."

After checking my balance, I scanned for specific articles in Cotonou and Luanda out of curiosity, or perhaps paranoia, to satisfy myself there were no new developments with my old nemeses. A Reuters account, datelined in Lagos, caught my eye. *Merchant seamen die in freak waterfront accident in Benin.* Buried in the story were the names Osaze Andjou, Pravesh Wahral, and Radeep Rajman.

I muttered to myself, "Why Dillon O'Connor, you bastard. You kept your word."

"Beg your pardon." Peter had come back and was holding our paperwork.

"Oh nothing. I was just reflecting on an article I read."

We signed the contract and I left Van Rooyen Ltd very relieved. I wasn't as flush with assets as I'd been on leaving the Congo, but this trip wouldn't be a complete bust in spite of, or in thanks to, Dillon O'Connor—I wasn't sure which. My lingering concern was how to digest the information Peter Blaauw had given me.

Arriving back on Marigold, I hollered up to the bridge where Daniru Malik was shouting directions to Kaamil Tengazy and Waajid Prankiop, who were working with the refuelers on the pier.

"Get some more hands from below decks, Mr. Malik. I have a paying cargo being delivered within the hour."

His smile was instantaneous. "A paying cargo?" He uttered something else in his native tongue, which I didn't understand, but got the meaning of just the same when Kaamil and Waajid gave a yell for joy. Daniru went back into the pilot house to call down for more help.

"Capitáno," a voice came from behind me. "This is wonderful news."

Miranda beamed. In spite of the sweat on her blouse from working with the ship chandlers, she was lovely.

"Ah, Miranda, have you finished resupplying the galley? I want to sail as soon as we have the fuel, cargo, and provisions on board."

"Yes, Capitáno, I just finished with the commissary chandler not twenty minutes ago. I was catching some fresh air while my helper organized the galley pantry."

"Very well. I'm glad you and your helper have made peace."

"Peace isn't such a good term. I'm accepting of it. He bakes at night and I cook in the day."

The grin on my face couldn't have been more telling. "Well, I guess that means your nights are free."

She angled her body away and said with downcast eyes and a hint of a smile, "That could be, Capitáno."

Chapter 16

FOR THE NEXT two hours, everyone one in the crew helped the stevedores load the netted cotton bales into the holds and secure them for the voyage. Once done, they set about lashing down the seven con-boxes between the hatch covers amidships. I inspected the deck hold-down turnbuckles with Tengazy and Patel. Satisfied that the machine parts would be safe in heavy seas, I told the men to prepare for getting underway as soon as possible. I wanted to be well clear of the harbor by sunset.

When I took my place on the pier-side bridge wing, I was strengthened by a wonderful sense of relief. I was captain of a legitimately working freighter, once again in control of my financial destiny, at least for the next few weeks, when I would reach the breaking yards of Bangladesh.

We rounded the Cape of Good Hope, a metaphor for exactly how I felt—full of good hope. And with my sights set on Madagascar, I was hoping for eight uneventful days. One thing was for certain, I wasn't going to take any chances at carrying a cargo I hadn't fully vetted. I'd done that once and it had cost me great mental anguish.

I'd been making rationalizations and drawing conclusions, sometimes at odds with my conscience, since leaving Cotonou. Now, I was fighting with my own common sense to not become paranoid. But sensing conspiracy seemed well within the realm of reality. O'Connor, M'Nasi, Johnson, Gangho, Ótubé, Andjou, the banker and his in-law cop in Luanda, all of them—at least some of them for sure—had conned me. Not all were in cahoots, but some certainly were.

Maybe I wasn't their target personally—just a target of opportunity, a roadblock between them and a great deal of money. The experience was like running into a spider web—intentional or not, I was caught in it. What I didn't know was, which spider had spun the web?

Daniru was on the bridge as we ran easily in the open sea. "Malik, who's on watch in the engineering spaces?"

"It is Waajid Prankiop, sir."

"Then ring around and have Kaamil Tengazy and the new deckhand, what's his name?"

"De Groot, sir. Dirk de Groot."

"Ring them up and have them come to the bridge. And round up Ms. Occhipinti, too. I need her as a recorder."

While he made calls from the bridge phone, I went to my cabin and retrieved a copy of my cargo manifest. Within a few minutes, I stood before my impromptu search party, clipboard in hand.

"Thank you for coming on short notice. I know you've had a long day, but I think it imperative we carefully examine our cargo to ensure it matches what's listed on this manifest. Waajid, you and Dirk enter the holds and inspect those cotton bales. Use a long metal rod to stick down into them to make sure no contraband is hidden within. I'd say check at least five bales in each bundle on a random basis. If you find something suspicious, then check every bale. Report back here when you're finished."

The two men gave me an "Aye, aye" and left the bridge.

"Miranda, you and I will go to the main deck and open each con-box and examine the contents. Here's a crowbar and a torch. I've got a torch and a hammer, so we can reclose the crates after we remove their lids."

"What do you expect to find, Capitáno?"

"I'm not sure, Miranda, but I'm not going to be blindsided again."

But I was on the lookout for something not on the manifest but which I had yet to find—gold bars and coins.

AFTER AN HOUR and a half of looking without finding anything out of the ordinary, Miranda and I went back to the bridge where Kaamil and Dirk were already waiting.

"Find anything?" I asked.

Dirk de Groot spoke up. "Nothing, Captain. It all checked out, freshly harvested, long fiber cotton ready for ginning."

I said, "Same with the con-boxes. Nothing but machine parts."

Pleased to discover the cargo was legitimate, I had to hide my frustration at not finding the gold Pop had confessed to hiding on board. He hadn't told me the value, but a standard gold bar weighing 10 kilos, at today's price, was worth about €300K. And if it was hidden on *Marigold*, it was beyond my ability to find.

"Thanks everyone, get some rest. I know you have watches coming up sooner than you would like. You can all use the down time. I know I can."

The men left, but Miranda trailed back. She turned to look at me.

"Capitáno, would you like a coffee? I still have some dessert left from dinner."

I didn't really want anything, but she sounded as if she were looking for an excuse to talk, so I agreed.

Miranda brought out a plate of cookies and two mugs of coffee. She poured, not quite filling the cups. "Do you want something stronger for your coffee?"

"No, no this is fine. I just want to rest before quitting for the day."

She stirred her coffee slowly, I guessed to gather her thoughts.

"Capitáno, I have been watching our new crewmen. You know, because of the problems we had with Andjou and those two *ladrános* we took on in Cotonou. The new men have been with us since Luanda, what, six days now? I think they are good men."

"What makes you say that?" I didn't doubt her; she'd been correct in assessments of crew members so far.

"They don't stay to themselves during meals, as did that group that left us in Cotonou. These men, I see them talking with Kaamil, Waajid, Daniru, and Chenal all the time. The young deckhand, Dirk, even tried to hit on me."

I gave her a concerned look.

"Don't worry about Dirk, Capitáno. He's a youngster who has been to sea with only other men. I'm the only woman." She glanced at me while she took a sip of coffee. I was sure she noticed my anticipation of her next statement.

"He's cute, no? But not my type. I told him he was just lonely and he should write his mother a letter to get his mind off things."

I laughed and the tension I'd been feeling relaxed.

"Tell me, Capitáno, do you feel better about what we're about to do? I mean, you have suffered a great deal, but it looks like you have finally caught a break from all those men you were dealing with before."

"You know, Miranda, I do feel good. I'm out a lot of money—money I surely could have used to take care of my grandfather for the rest of his days. But I'll get by. And thank you for your assessment of our new crewmen. You've obviously observed them much more closely than I could have. I think we're in pretty good shape now. Not the greatest of shape, but good shape.

"Now that I've gotten rid of those three crewmen who were O'Connor's snitches, I'm okay, although I wish I'd had the good sense to inspect the cargo we took to Congo like we just did here. As far as Gangho and Johnson, the best I've been able to figure out, they were simply lookouts for O'Connor. And being crooks at heart, they decided to take advantage of the situation, figuring *Marigold* as an easy prize that just happened to drop into their laps. Likewise, the two brothers in Luanda were opportunists who guessed right."

I took a sip of coffee, trying to decide if I should tell her of my new concerns about M'Nasi I'd learned from Peter Blaauw, and by my own inference, Leonard Ótubé. But I didn't want to remind her of her experience with Ótubé. They were O'Connor's men, since he'd specified I deal with them; and Blaauw was certain, though he couldn't prove it, that M'Nasi was at least collaterally involved with illegal arms dealings. But bringing up bad memories for her and conflating them with new suspicions about contraband were things she shouldn't have to deal with.

Similarly, I considered telling her of the gold my grandfather had stashed somewhere on board. I was frustrated, however, that none of my efforts had found it yet, and having two people with knowledge of the gold made me doubly vulnerable that the wrong person might learn of it. I trusted her completely, but this burden I had to bear alone.

Reaching across, I squeezed her hand, which she held longer than was necessary. This wasn't the time to pursue the situation.

"I think I'll get some rest. We're coming up on rough weather as we round the Cape. Who knows when I'll get a chance to sleep until we turn north again? Thanks again for everything tonight."

FOR THE NEXT twenty-four hours, *Marigold* sailed the most treacherous waters of the world, the Roaring Forties, as we rounded the Cape and entered the Indian Ocean heading northeast towards the east coast of Africa. But once we turned north and neared the Mozambique Channel, we'd have smooth sailing all the way to Madagascar. Nonetheless, I kept a weather eye on the seas and the barometer for foul weather as well as pirates. After what I'd been through, I trusted no one new.

IN ONE OF THOSE rambling story sessions I so enjoyed growing up with my grandfather was his mention that Madagascar was one of those places in the world you had to want to get to in order to reach. "You don't just run across it on the way to somewhere else." A huge island isolated in the Indian Ocean, it lay across no other trade routes—except to and from Mozambique.

Recalling those story times, I eased *Marigold* as close as possible, safety and maritime law permitting, to the island nation's western shore, ever mindful of African-based pirates, in the hopes of glimpsing some of the fabled Malagasy scenery. Though I had a wonderful view of the island's mountainous central spine, I couldn't make out much detail of the coastal features from six miles out, except for the green jungle canopy and occasional swaths of sugar cane fields.

Marigold entered the port of Mahajanga, which was nestled on the north side of an estuary that drained the central highlands into a partially protected natural harbor. The pilot brought her to within a hundred yards of the substantial container terminal and told me to anchor. He informed me the water depth next to the pier was too shallow to take any vessel over 350 tons. This was the first time I'd been in a port in which *Marigold* was considered to be deep draft.

I looked over the wharf's container staging area from the bridge wing. There was the scent of tropical flowers and fruits in the air, mixed with a salty sea breeze. Warehouses stood in the foreground, backdropped by a panoramic view of a good-sized port city, which receded inland towards a densely forested tropical interior. There were a few tall buildings, definitely not skyscrapers, demarcating a downtown.

Further back were steeples, or so I thought, sticking up in random isolation along the city's outskirts. I focused my binoculars on one out of curiosity. It wasn't a steeple, per se, though it was definitely religious in nature. These convex conical forms with large circular bases were *stupas,* or Buddhist monuments. I went to my cabin and retrieved my camera to record these unique gilded temples.

With the zoom lens, I peered past the rooftops into the jungle backdrop. As strange as the jungles of Benin had seemed to me, the tropical rainforest here didn't appear nearly as dark, mysterious, or foreboding. Travel magazines I'd read said Madagascar was home to animals found nowhere else on the planet, such as the fossa, a predator cross between a mongoose and a cat; fifty species of lemurs; the aye-aye, a nocturnal primate resembling a wingless bat; and the tomato frog, an amphibian with mildly toxic, orangish skin. But I'd have to take the magazines' word for it. I had work to do and no time to explore the hinterlands.

I made contact with my contracted shipping agent, who arranged for a lighter to come alongside *Marigold*. Within an hour of anchoring, I had cleared quarantine pratique and was off-loading my cargo to a smaller vessel. Conveniently, the shipper had sent out provisioning stocks for Miranda and a refueling barge for Tengazy and de Groot to oversee.

The agent was a pleasant man, a bit shorter than me, who sported a prodigious moustache and severely pointed goatee. His name was Edouard Philippe, a native Malagasy, whose European forbearers, he informed me, had originally emigrated as French merchants.

"Captain O'Scanlon, I am like many fourth and fifth generation descendants of my country's colonial past. I owe little to my European heritage except for my current existence. I'd love to show you around my island. Does your business allow you time to play tourist?"

"I'm afraid it doesn't. As soon as I finish off-loading and reprovisioning, I'll be on my way."

"That is too bad, sir. I am indebted to you for rescuing my consignment from Peter Blaauw of Van Rooyen's. When he notified me that the original transport company had cancelled, I had to fend off several angry customers.

Even though my company's losses would have been covered by insurance, I stood to lose a great deal of good will, which is much harder to earn back than money. So you see, your happening along proved of great benefit for me. At least let me buy you lunch while we wait for the cargo and fuel handlers to complete their work."

Impressed with his gratitude, I decided that accepting his hospitality wouldn't jeopardize my schedule. It would take an hour or two anyway for the crew and the stevedores to complete their work.

Getting the attention of my bridge watch, I said, "Chenal, I'll be ashore with Mr. Philippe should you need me. I expect to return in an hour or so."

On the water taxi ride to the quay, I couldn't help wondering if O'Connor's sudden arrangement of a consignment in Cape Town also extended to some clandestine arrangement with Edouard Philippe. O'Connor had already surprised me with the range of his business communications; to arrange something with a jobber, even in this remote section of the world, was not beyond my imagination.

The pace of commerce along the Mahajanga waterfront was impressive. The frontage street reverberated from the rumble of high-wheeled tractors pulling heavily laden, multi-dented wagons, and salvaged square-fendered stake trucks burdened with bales of dry goods.

The vehicles were vintage Vichy-era and German made, most likely abandoned after World War II on this remote island after their brief usefulness to an otherwise disinterested world, in a locale now bypassed by the more traditional trade routes of a modern era. Two blocks from the waterfront, Edouard pushed his way past swinging doors into a storefront restaurant with only six tables. We entered so quickly, I didn't catch the name.

"Have a seat, Johnny. I'll order for us. Do you have any preferences?"

"Based on the writing on the menu chalkboards we passed on the way to the table, I doubt I could tell you what anything is. This is all new, so surprise me."

"Good, I will order us a Malagasy smorgasbord. How about you try our national drink, *ranovola*, while we wait. It's made from burnt rice."

The robust iced beverage was refreshing in the heat of the day and helped set a convivial tone for our conversation. Within a few minutes, the waitress brought two appetizer plates. One looked like thin egg rolls, called *nem*, and the other plate held savory dough triangles stuffed with spiced meat she called *sambusa*.

"Eat up, my friend. I'm anxious for your reaction."

I bit into the *sambusa* and tasted a world of new flavors. "This is really good," I said through half a mouthful. The *nem* was equally enjoyable, but offered a wholly different taste sensation.

"Tell me, Johnny, where are you off to now? I'll have a cargo ready for consignment within a few days."

"I'm afraid unless they're destined for eastern India or Bangladesh, I'll have to pass on them."

"What's so important in Bangladesh that has you on such a tight schedule?" he said, taking a sip. "Are you picking up a hold full of athletic shoes or shirts and blouses?"

I chuckled as I took a drink of *ranovola*, which gave me the time to contemplate the reasons for his curiosity. With the hidden agendas I'd encountered to date in dealing with shipping agents, I wasn't sure if his was an honest inquiry or a scheme that was linked to Dillon O'Connor. I was about to answer when the waitress returned carrying a tray heaped with food.

"Oh my goodness," I said, looking at four serving dishes. "I can't eat all of that, Edouard."

He laughed. "Not to worry, Johnny, you only have to eat half of it."

As she spooned the food onto our plates, he gave me a running description of what he called *romazava*, a hearty meat stew. Then came fried rice, a seafood platter identified as *foza sy hena-kisoa*, and sliced vegetables called *lasary*. Everything was delicious.

After his first hurried mouthful, he said, "You were telling me about why you have to head to Bangladesh in such a rush."

I'd hoped he'd forgotten, because I still wasn't comfort-table confiding in someone I'd just met, hospitality not-withstanding. So I lied, or told a half-truth.

"Bangladesh does big business in buying old vessels and breaking them for scrap. I was hoping I might buy one that still has some life in her. It seems my parent company, TC Miriam, is looking to expand, what with all the lowered trade barriers brought on by the European Common Market."

"Mmm, good idea," he said, taking a mouthful of stew. "I would have never thought of checking with a broker in this part of the world. Most secondhand and older vessels for sale are normally brokered out of Europe and the Middle East. But now that I think about it, picking up a ship everyone else has given up on might bring a real bargain. I wish you luck."

He'd bought my story, so I decided to press my luck further. "Tell me, Edouard, have you ever run across consignment managers named M'Nasi or Leonard Ótubé?"

He chewed vigorously, obviously enjoying one of his favorite dishes, and swallowed. "I can't say that I have. Where do they operate from?" Watching his face, I didn't notice any recognition when I mentioned the names.

"I met one in Benin and one in Brazzaville, Congo. My business with them was profitable, and I was wondering if they had dealings along the Indian Ocean sea coast."

"Ah, so you are looking for cargo?" he said, taking another bite.

I laughed. "There's always the return trip, Edouard."

To my relief, he shifted the conversation to topics other than the shipping business. Edouard expounded on some of the island's unique attributes, their delicious food being only one of them. We had just started on some leaf-wrapped, honey-laced dessert called *koba* when Kaamil Tengazy entered the restaurant. He looked around from the doorway and I motioned him over.

"Is there anything wrong, Mr. Tengazy?"

"No, Captain, but Miranda sent me to find you and to let you know all the cargo is off. By the time you return to the ship, if you come with me now, we'll have everything ready to sail."

"Well, that's quite an efficient operation you have there, Johnny. I'm impressed."

And if I weren't too embarrassed to admit it, so was I. "I think I have my marching orders, Edouard. I hate to eat and run. Are you sure you won't let me pick up the bill for lunch?" I said, reaching for my wallet.

"Not on your life, my friend. This is my treat. It's the least I can do to thank you for saving me from having to face a legion of angry clients."

We shook hands and departed.

Tengazy and I had only gone a few yards down the main street when I thought I recognized a man emerging from a business establishment half a block in front of us. At first he was looking away from us, but as he turned towards us, I verified my suspicion. It was Leonard Ótubé and there could only be one reason for him to be here.

"Kaamil, continue on back to the ship. I'll be there shortly. Tell Daniru and Chenal to prepare for departure. As soon as I arrive, I'll want to get underway."

Tengazy didn't react to the urgency of my voice. I reiterated, "Go, go. I just left something in the restaurant. I'll be right along."

For certain Ótubé recognized me, because he started walking in our direction. Hoping that Tengazy would shield my movements, I proceeded at a brisk pace back towards the restaurant, turning at a delivery alley in the middle of the block. A few paces in I broke into a run past the back doors of businesses on either side. Refuse and waste cans clustered near back doors. I dodged around these to block Ótubé's view if he had followed me.

A rear door neater and cleaner than the rest came into view on my right and I ducked inside. I walked slowly to get my bearings and catch my breath. It was a furniture showroom, which meant it most likely had at least a second floor to display their goods.

I found the staircase and went up, not one flight, but two. I moved towards the balcony railing that overlooked the storefront entryway. A few minutes passed, which seemed like an eternity. My breathing eased, but my anxiety level was still high. I spent the interval trying to look like a casual customer perusing the bedroom furniture on display. A salesman came up to me, but when he realized I didn't speak French, he left, presumably to find an English-speaking clerk.

As I waited, I racked my brain to figure out why Ótubé would appear out of the blue. The only reason I could come up with was that O'Connor had sent him to follow me. He knew I'd be in Mahajanga because he'd set up the consignment in Cape Town and knew its destination. But why send Ótubé and not just query his shipping contacts by phone or cable?

Peering over the railing, I saw Ótubé enter the front of the store and approach a salesman. Too far away to hear them, I could tell from his expression he was agitated. Most likely, he was asking if I had been in. Fortunately, the salesman wasn't the one whom I had encountered. Evidently disappointed with the answer, Ótubé waved an arm in disgust and turned to scan the showroom.

Fearing he'd see me, I stepped away from the railing, but not quickly enough, because I heard him bellow, "Captain O'Scanlon."

Not waiting for a confrontation, I bolted for a hallway leading to the bathrooms. The corridor turned towards the back of the building where a set of narrow stairs led down. Taking the stairs two at a time, I reached the second floor landing.

Doors to the bathrooms were to the left, but to the right, the stairs kept descending to the ground floor. I didn't break stride. Reaching the ground floor, I pushed through a crash door into an attached warehouse, which held stored furniture. I looked for an exit sign, which I saw on the opposite side at the back.

In no time, I was across the warehouse floor, through the door, and once again in the connecting service alley. I turned right and ran for the next street. When I didn't hear anyone running behind me or calling my name, I slowed. At the corner I turned left, figuring that was the general direction back to the waterfront. I traversed two blocks before turning left again to head back to the frontage road where I walked at a determined pace towards the water taxi quay.

During my escape, it hit me that the only reason for Ótubé being here was to find a way on board *Marigold* to look for the gold. How he would do that, or what would happen to me or the crew in his attempt, I couldn't contemplate.

Tengazy was waiting for me aboard a water taxi. I jumped on board.

"Get us to that ship," I said to the boatman and pointed to *Marigold* riding at anchor. Tengazy gave me an inquisitive look but didn't ask. I couldn't tell any of the crew about Ótubé's presence in Mahajanga. And I especially couldn't tell Miranda after her experience with the man.

Daniru Malik greeted me on the bridge and reported all the paperwork had been signed, the bills paid, and we were cleared by customs to leave. As I took a quick look at the chart to refamiliarize myself with the track we'd follow, Miranda came to the bridge.

"Was your trip to the beach profitable, Capitáno?"

With great effort to hide concern from my expression I said, "Yes, it was, Miranda. I want to thank you for sending along Kaamil to find me before I ate and drank myself silly. The shipping agent's hospitality was superb, but a bit aggressive. I appreciated the excuse to leave."

"That's good. I just wanted to make sure you hadn't been kidnapped."

Her honest concern lifted my spirits. "Why, thank you, Miranda."

Then with a twinkle in her eye she said, "And who knows, maybe you were being held ransom in a house by some painted woman who would have demanded an outrageous sum to get you back."

"And you would have paid?"

"That, Capitáno, neither of us will ever know." She left with a twirl of her full skirt, a smirk, and a triumphant air.

Daniru Malik looked at me and smiled. "Captain, I think the woman has designs on you."

"Be that as it may, Mr. Malik, would you be so kind as to get my ship underway?"

Though my heart was still racing from my near disastrous encounter with Ótubé, the stop to top off fuel and off load cargo had been profitable. Edouard had paid me the remaining forty percent of my guaranteed payment, which I immediately forwarded to my home bank.

As we weighed anchor, I struggled to put thoughts of Leonard Ótubé and Dillon O'Connor behind me. My concerns about them were quickly displaced by the realization that I was on the last leg of my last voyage—three thousand miles to Chittagong.

For the first time in a long while, I felt optimistic about the future, gold or no gold. Back in my cabin, I decided to send a cable to update Grandfather.

On journey's last leg: Madagascar to Bangladesh. Some setbacks, but solvent now. Looked everywhere for item you mentioned—no luck. I expect to return three weeks hence after final sale of Marigold *in Chittagong.*

I wasn't sure how long it would take the maritime agent in Dublin to get the message to my grandfather at TC Miriam, but I was certain he would have it within 72 hours.

It had been a long day, and I was a few thousand euros to the good, finally on the positive side of the ledger. My bunk was more than inviting to me. My anxiety about finding the gold before O'Connor or his henchmen would have to wait.

Chapter 17

NEXT MORNING, MARIGOLD cleared Madagascar's north cape and struck an east-northeasterly course to pass well east of the African coast but south of the Seychelles. In the past few years, there had been reports of Somali pirates ranging as far to sea as the Seychelles to attack ships and kidnap their crews for ransom, ransoms ship owners willingly paid, thus making it exceedingly profitable for the roving bands of sea rogues.

In spite of a multinational, anti-pirate patrol made up of Russian and NATO navies, the pirates still ventured forth from the Horn of Africa in their high-risk, high-reward activities. Ship owners had sufficient kidnap insurance and the pirates knew this.

Though there was little personal danger and there had been only a few fatalities in the past several years, I could neither afford the money nor the time such an encounter would have entailed. TC Miriam, as well as *Marigold*, were on their last financial legs and I carried only the barest insurance to cover damage to the ship from natural elements, not total replacement.

The unresolved issue of not having found the gold gave me reason to take even more caution to avoid the pirates' hunting grounds. I'd suffer a double tragedy if *Marigold* were captured now. Besides, I'd had my fill of pirates and didn't want to be robbed a third time. My new course guaranteed more distance between me and where pirates roamed, but it also dictated I'd have to stop somewhere mid-ocean to take on fuel.

Ever since sailing from Luanda, when I had explained what the future held in store for *Marigold* and TC Miriam, the remaining crew from the original five had become more than my employees. They were partners in my enterprise now. Perhaps it was too much wishful thinking to classify them as friends, but I was certain that would come. As I discovered in conversations over the next few days with Daniru, Chenal, Waajid, and Kaamil, the crew members who had boarded in Luanda were working out well.

"They are professional merchant seamen, Captain," Daniru said without hesitation regarding the six new shipmates. I sensed by his body language that Kaamil was holding back on his endorsement, so I pressed him.

"Captain, I have sailed with men from all over the world. And these men are okay."

"What makes you so sure?" I urged.

"It is hard to say, Captain. When I ask one a question, he answers me straight out, but doesn't offer anything else. The five of us from Dublin enjoy…"

"Oh, you're Irishmen now, are you?"

"Captain, you know what I mean. They aren't being antisocial. It's just that they hang back. When we have time off, we five all play cards or smoke on the weather deck. But they're reluctant to ask to join in."

"Maybe they just don't like you, Kaamil," Daniru said with a big grin.

"Did you ever think to…"

Before I could probe further, Daniru interjected. "Is it my imagination, or are the seas picking up?"

I had to agree. "It does feel like the swells have grown larger since supper."

I looked at the barometer glass on the bulkhead. It was a few millibars lower than the last time I'd checked. "I'm going up to the bridge."

Oscar Djombe, the new navigation mate from Luanda, greeted me. "Good evening, Captain. Are you here to check the weather?"

"As a matter of fact, I am." The worsening sea state was obvious at first glance. The wind had picked up, wave troughs had deepened, and swells surged past eight feet.

"The most recent weather report says a low pressure system is heading our way on a northwesterly course. Right now it's located about 180 miles east southeast of us."

"You say it is heading northwest?"

"Yes, Captain."

I went to the chart table and examined the track. I still had plenty of good water to the south and east. If I altered course to track south of the storm, I'd avoid the storm's northwest quadrant, its most severe aspect. This small diversion would cost me fifty miles or so—maybe four hours at most. I wasn't on a tight schedule, but this course alteration would guarantee I'd have to make a refueling stop.

"Mr. Djombe, come right to course one five zero. Let's allow the storm to pass as far north of us as possible. Call down to the engine room and let them know the seas are going to pick up for the next six to ten hours. I'll let Miranda know in the galley."

By the time I reached the mess deck, everyone else had left, probably to batten down their gear. I stuck my head through the pantry door and saw Miranda finishing up from dinner. Behind her the Chinese cook was busy with a rolling pin, smoothing out dough.

"Hello, Capitáno. Are there storm clouds building on the horizon?" She wore a full length apron over a print T-shirt and jeans.

"I am afraid so, Miranda. You might want to adjust your menu plans for the next two meals. I wouldn't be making any soufflés."

"Now, when was the last time you saw me make a soufflé, Capitáno? Quiche maybe, but never soufflés. Anyway, I'm done with dinner. As you can see, I have turned it over to my night baker, Wong."

I was happy to see that she had struck a workable accommodation with Wong. I was more than glad I wouldn't have to weigh in on her turf to settle differences.

"Do you want something to drink? I'm going to have a little sherry."

"Sure, or if you want, I could get a bottle of something harder."

She eyed me for a long moment, debating whether or not to take me up on the offer. "I think I'm in the mood for sherry. It always lights a small fire in my heart."

Was she flirting with me? Ever since that evening when we left Luanda, there had been hints of familiarity in her voice and gestures, though never a confirmation that anything had happened.

Perhaps events had overwhelmed my subconscious and my dream stemmed from ruminations and fatigue. Maybe spending the night with her was only wishful thinking on my part. But propriety as captain, especially in full view of any crewman, kept me from offering even an allusion as to what had, or may not have, happened.

"That is a nice way of putting it, Miranda. I'd be glad to join you. Other than riding out this storm, there isn't much else to do. This is a pretty lonely part of the Indian Ocean." Wanting to test my observation of her galley working arrangement, I said, "I see you and Wong are getting along. How is he doing?"

"I made it very clear to him that his job was to bake at night and set up for whatever I put on the next day's menu. He is fine with that. I pretty much never see him. And that is also fine with me." She pulled a bottle from the cabinet. "What part of the ocean are we in, Capitáno?"

Her change of subject from the galley to our intended route was welcome. I'd come to enjoy our chats over the past few weeks, as long as they didn't involve her galley work, a volatile subject for her. We simply talked of things other than the galley and relaxed, just sharing time together. This was the first time I could remember ever being able to open up with someone.

"We are over a day out of Madagascar. I've been looking over the Indian Ocean charts for a convenient place to refuel and there aren't a whole lot of choices. We've diverted south to avoid any encounter with Somali pirates and now the storm. There's a British naval port in the Chagos Archipelago, British Indian Ocean Territory. We're only four days from there."

"I've been to a lot of places, Capitáno, but have never heard of this territory." She poured two fingers into each tumbler.

"What, no snifters? I'm insulted." I picked up the glass and offered a toast.

Miranda feigned rebuke and clinked my glass. "It is best to use a wide bottomed glass in this weather. I wouldn't want it to spill. But what I do care is that I'm not the one who has to clean up."

"Perhaps you've heard of Diego Garcia. It's a British possession in that island group." I paused before adding, "It will be the last refueling stop for *Marigold*."

"You look very wistful, Capitáno. Perhaps the nostalgia is giving you second thoughts."

She was right, of course. There was a lot about this woman that was right. I'd learned from sailing with her for over two months, she was uncanny in her instincts and her ability to read people.

"I think that may be some of it. On the one hand, I'm going to be giving up a big part of my life—actually, the biggest part of my life. This is all I've ever known. Ever since I was a boy of ten, I've been going to sea, first with my grandfather and now on my own."

"What about your father? Didn't you ever go with him?" But before I could say anything, she said, "I'm so sorry, Capitáno. I spoke too soon without thinking."

"That's all right, Miranda. In fact, everything I know about the sea, I learned from Pop."

"Are those your fondest memories—being at sea with your grandfather?"

"My best memory was of a fly fishing trip we made to Scotland when I was twelve years old. We took the *Marigold* over to Oban on the Scottish west coast, drove a truck into the highlands, and stayed for almost a week fishing and hunting. He taught me both."

"Did you catch anything?" she asked, pouring us more sherry.

"I caught lots of trout and bagged a six point buck on the third day."

"What did you do with the deer?"

"We skinned, dressed, and cooked it. We had so much, we shared it with the rest of the folks in the base camp lodge."

"You must have been a big hit. Venison is wonderful. I know how to make some very good meals with venison."

"Maybe you can pick up some at our next stop to demonstrate."

"Do you really think they have venison in Diego Garcia?" She said this with an impish grin. But then an empty stillness settled on her. "What are your plans going to be now? You have to start over after our problems in Angola, no?" I was struck by her use of "our" rather than "your" problems.

"I feel optimistic, really. I should clear a healthy enough amount when I sell *Marigold*." That is, less the amount I'd promised O'Connor. "It will give me enough to return to Ireland and satisfy my grandfather's nursing home bills for several years and pay off last year's taxes."

"But what will you do?"

"There's always work available at the water front."

"But can you do that—work for someone else after you've been the capitáno?"

"That's a good question. I guess I'll have to learn how. Or maybe I'll move to Scotland and hunt and fish the rest of my life."

She gave a small laugh and tried to pour more sherry, but there was only enough to wet the bottom of one glass. She held up the empty bottle.

"Well, if that little fire has started enough in your heart, maybe it's time to fuel it with some whisky. I've got a bottle of scotch?"

She nodded and I went to retrieve it from my cabin. In a way, I was glad she didn't follow me, although that wouldn't have been the worst circumstance I could face. While I certainly would have enjoyed the opportunity to confirm what I thought had occurred off West Africa, in the scheme of things, it wouldn't be my best course of action.

When I returned, Miranda brought out a fancy tin of Italian cookies, which prompted me to ask, "Did you make these?"

"No, I can't do the fancy things like the commercial bakers do. These I bought in Funchal. I was saving them for a special occasion." She winked.

"Oh? What are we celebrating?"

"We are celebrating being alive, surviving a storm—being with a beautiful woman—who cares, let's just celebrate. Now, if you please, Capitáno, my vessel is in need of refilling." She winked and held up her glass.

I swallowed as I considered her implication. I uncorked a bottle of Hebrides' finest and laced both glasses with an ample amber dash. "Cheers." This woman was getting the best of me—and I didn't even care.

She said, "*Salute*," and savored the first sip. "This is very good."

"It is quite smooth, isn't it?"

"So tell me honestly, Capitáno, what are you going to do after Chittagong?"

I took a sip. "I told you. I'll go back to Ireland and ensure my grandfather is set up. Then get a job."

"That plan won't last you forever. What will you do then? Is there anyone else in Ireland who is expecting your return?"

I looked at her over my glass, not knowing if I wanted to answer. I teetered between giving in to what my heart was saying or keeping up my stoic captain's front, the one wherein there was no room for relationships, other than professional, with a member of the crew.

"You definitely are straightforward, Miranda."

"Straightforward or not, it is a perfectly legitimate question. Have you really thought this through before you turn the ship into bits and pieces? That is the issue entirely. You seem to have couched your entire argument in terms of caring about your grandfather and haven't given one lick of thought to worrying about you or, for that matter, anyone who may be counting on you."

"Counting on me—who counts on me?"

"Me. Chenal Patel. Daniru Malik. Kaamil Tengazy. Waajid Prankiop—we all do."

"But you hired on with a contract. When you complete the terms, then you sign a new contract. That's the way it goes when you crew ships at sea. This life is your home. That's the way it's been ever since my grandfather taught me."

"So we are simply hired hands?"

I didn't reply. I could tell from her eyes she had me on that one, and she knew it.

"Let me ask you, Capitáno. Meaning no disrespect to your grandfather, but not every aspect of what he shared with you has turned out so well."

If only she knew, I thought. "Just exactly what are you saying, Miranda?"

"You showed me pictures that night, the night when we—you know, when you were so despondent. You told me the face you saw in the photos was of the man your grandfather mentioned to you one time—the man you went to visit, who involved your grandfather and parents in dangerous dealings, and who set you up with the cargo from Benin—the cargo that has brought you nothing but trouble."

Miranda's innocent reference to my grandfather's and Dillon O'Connor's dealing years ago forced another possibility to the fore—a possibility that could explain why O'Connor seemed to be going to such lengths to put an end to TC Miriam, my grandfather's pride and joy.

"You think my grandfather and Dillon O'Connor planned the operation that killed my parents? Pop would never have done that."

Deep down inside, however, I wondered if he had participated, not intending the consequence that resulted, but participating nonetheless in something that had gone terribly wrong. I couldn't imagine my grandfather's role in such an operation, but could easily see Dillon O'Connor being involved, implicitly or explicitly, in my parents' deaths.

My grandmother's unforgiving comments about the cause of their deaths and my grandfather's refusal to ever discuss the subject could have been the result of that tragedy and have added to the bad blood between Grandfather and O'Connor. Perhaps to such an extent that Pop had no compunction in filching gold from him, as a means not for late payments, but as a way to get back at him.

And the missing gold was probably the reason O'Connor had hidden any such rift from me. He realized he had a chance to get back at Grandfather for things said or done years ago and recover the stolen gold.

"No, no, I'm not saying that at all. But your grandfather did work with him at one point. Perhaps he was unwittingly duped by this O'Connor man in the same way you were. Did you ever consider that?"

"Of course I did. Grandfather spoke cavalierly about running contraband for the IRA in the day. But knowing him, that was just his way of showing bluster in a world where bravado gained acceptance among your peers. I think you're right. It was probably never his idea to endanger his daughter and son-in-law in an IRA scheme. Something must have backfired back then, something he's chosen never to divulge. But it was Dillon O'Connor who kept him and his fellow captains in poverty by paying them late in a time when every penny counted. Thank you, Miranda, I could just kiss you."

She was very still and didn't turn her head away or avert her eyes, as if expecting something.

But I was oblivious to her subtleties. The true picture now swirled through my mind. Dillon had probably tricked Pop, and after he was sucked into the conspiracy, Pop realized he was in too deep to get out. Then all he could do was to go along to get along. When a peace was struck between Great Britain and the IRA, he got out.

The more I rehashed it, the more certain I became. After all, it wasn't Pop's idea for me to go to Wexford to find Dillon O'Connor. It was O'Connor who used me, just like he used grandfather and undoubtedly everyone else he'd ever dealt with. He'd done it decades ago in Ireland and he was still doing it today. That son of a bitch!

"How could I have been so stupid?"

Miranda laid her hand on my wrist. "You shouldn't be so hard on yourself, Capitáno. You did nothing wrong."

"But I've put the entire company at risk."

"I'm part of your company, and I don't feel at risk. I am a big girl. I will survive, and so will you. Put it behind you. Now you must concentrate on getting the ship safely to Bangladesh and complete your plan. If that is right for you, then go ahead."

In that moment, I felt the deck press against my feet and I was pushed hard into my chair seat as the ship thrust upward on an up swell. Not two seconds later, my stomach fell away as the ship plunged down the other side of the crest. With a lurch, Miranda gripped my arm to hold herself steady.

I patted her hand and said, "Put the bottle back in the cabinet. I'm going to the bridge."

Oscar Djombe stood by the radar repeater with one hand on a grab rail for balance.

"Good evening, Captain. I think we're in the worst of it right now. In about an hour and a half the winds should lessen and the seas subside as we break through the storm's south wall. Ah, Miranda, you have brought me some coffee?"

Miranda held a carafe in one hand, firmly grasping a railing with the other. "It may not be as good as what we were just drinking, but it will help keep you awake." She placed the carafe into a secure holder by the chart table. "Now where is he going?"

I barely heard her exchange with Oscar Djombe as I opened the bridge wing door, letting in a spray of wind-driven water. I stepped onto the starboard bridge wing and was immediately pelted with rain driven by a sixty-knot wind. I'd no sooner dogged the watertight door behind me when it opened and Miranda stepped out.

"You'll get soaked—" But by the time I'd said it, she was drenched. She had left her apron in the galley and her T-shirt was plastered to her by wind and rain. It wasn't an altogether unpleasant sight. I grinned and added, "But I guess you knew that coming out here."

By now, her shoulder length hair was molded to her head. She looked like a drowned rat, caught in the red glow of the bridge's night lights, which highlighted her beautiful face.

Miranda reached one hand for the rail running the top length of the bulwark. She snaked the other hand around my back and waist, gripping a belt loop to hold tight.

She raised her voice to be heard over the wind. "Do you like exposing yourself to the elements for punishment, or are you daft?"

I simply stood there soaking in both the storm and her warmth. Finally, I made a small confession.

"Whenever I get down in spirit, I like to look at the sea. When it's angry like this, I'm humbled by it all. The storm grounds me and reminds me there are things I can't control and really shouldn't worry about. It's almost like being in church."

I released the handrail with my hand that was closest to her and pointed to the mounting waves. "If Mother Nature wanted to, she could swallow us up, ship and all, in a heartbeat. But she doesn't."

With the same arm now around Miranda, and knowing I was hidden from view from anyone inside the bridge, I pulled her close. She turned into me and snuggled, lifting her face to mine. I bent down and kissed her, softly at first, and then with passion.

"Tell me, Capitáno, are you down in spirit now?"

We held each other for a while, soaking wet but feeling warm in the tropical storm. Then she turned and went back into the bridge enclosure. I followed and stamped my feet on the scupper grating just inside the door.

Oscar Djombe looked at me and smiled. "I guess I don't need a firsthand weather report, Captain."

I started to respond when I saw Miranda head, not down to the mess deck, but towards my sea cabin door at the after end of the bridge. She opened it and went inside.

Oscar, ever the steadfast mariner, kept his eyes forward, staring at the incessant spray and the rain battering the bridge windscreen. Tactfully he said, "I will call you if I need any help, Captain."

When I opened my cabin door, Miranda's sopping wet clothes were draped over the shower curtain rod and she was toweling off her hair.

"Don't just stand there, Capitáno Johnny. You need to get out of those wet things."

I PULLED MARIGOLD in for a refueling stop in Diego Garcia, referred to by the only internet site I could find on my satellite feed as the "Flower of the Indian Ocean." No more than a speed bump in the ocean, the island's maximum elevation was only twenty-two feet. From the outfitting pier, I could see across most of the width of the sand and coral island.

There were few buildings other than utility structures built to house replenishment supplies. The Union Jack fluttered in the fierce heat of a tropical sun as it struggled to catch some wind. Even at midmorning, the sun was brilliant against a blue sky dotted with high, wispy clouds. Sea gulls squawked in their desperate attempts to roust one another from scraps on the nearby beach. Despite the heat, my British hosts went about the refueling operation with professional efficiency.

My admiration for their excellent portage service was eclipsed by a twinge of nostalgia as I realized I was refueling *Marigold* for the last time. Once at the breaking yard, any fuel remaining in the fuel tanks would be salvaged for a fraction of its value. But the mariner in me said it was best to top off and be safe, rather than sorry.

I backed *Marigold* clear from the wharf at 3:00 p.m. Within twenty minutes, I had struck a course to the northeast that would take me the remaining 1,750 miles to Chittagong—the end of the line.

Six more days and I could put the old girl to rest for good. Surprisingly, I was feeling good about my decision to put an end to her. It was time. Since leaving Dublin, the last three months at sea had produced rust streaks training down her hull from the deck scuppers and a transom nameplate which was missing letters. But she was watertight and mechanically sound.

The diesel engines still had years of life left in them. If I had the time and the means, I would dismount them and auction them separately. I might make a few thousand pounds that way. But I didn't want to spend any more time in Bangladesh than I had to. I was getting there right at the end of the dry season and this was one country I didn't want to remain in when the monsoon began.

NEXT DAY, MIRANDA treated the crew to gourmet meals: breakfast, lunch, and dinner. And to Wong's credit, though she would never admit it, the breads and desserts were the best I'd eaten in a long time. Miranda, in her own way, was helping me celebrate the end of the line for *Marigold*.

I shared more than a few wistful thoughts with her during our intimate times, which occurred with welcome regularity during this last week at sea, not that she displayed any overt public familiarity when in front of other crewmen. It was always Capitáno, never Johnny.

Only a fool, however, would think that on such a small vessel the crew might not have guessed what was going on. From what they could see, she still used her own stateroom in the crew's living quarters. Only the bridge watch ever saw her slip into or out of my sea cabin.

However, they never let on that they noticed or cared. And why should they? They were being well fed, the journey was almost over, and they were in line for a good bonus on top of their contracted pay for their loyalty and understanding. For each of them, this had been a good gig. I was thankful I'd set aside their money before that majordomo and his brother-in-law in Luanda robbed me.

But I wasn't home free yet. I still had to find an honest businessman in Chittagong with whom to do business. My dealings with port officials so far cautioned me that such a trait wasn't always a given. Also, there was the matter of the gold. I still hadn't found it and I had no way of knowing if Dillon O'Connor had abandoned his search for it. His behavior to date would suggest otherwise.

I doubted he would come to Bangladesh, but it wasn't beyond his past patterns to have his trusted agent in the only port in this part of the world with breaking yards. If he had such an agent in Chittagong, I had no idea how I would recognize him or his intent until it was too late. All I could do was keep up my guard.

Chapter 18

As I CLOSED the coast for my final time as captain, I was amazed at the sight of the river delta called the Mouths of the Ganges. Whereas the Congo River hit the Atlantic with a ferocity and a flood of mud that surged over a hundred miles out to sea, the Ganges filtered its way innocuously into the Bay of Bengal through a maze of mangroves and hundreds of islands after its long journey from the Himalayan highlands.

The river branched again and again into dozens of channels, all big rivers in their own right, to deliver the outflow across a two-hundred-mile front astride the northern limits of the Bay of Bengal.

It was through this massive mixture of brackish water that I sailed *Marigold* to the Burmese peninsula to reach Chittagong. The specific tributary that washed through Chittagong was called the Karnafuli River. Not as impressive as Mother Ganges with her many mouths just up the coast to the northwest, she was as big and as muddy as any major river I'd ever seen.

I tied up to the quay of the Port Cargo Station and went ashore to find a breaking yard broker along the Strand Road. Wanting company more than anything else, I coerced Tengazy to join me under the pretext that I might need him to translate.

"I am Pakistani, not Bengali," he complained. "There is a great difference in our cultures."

"But you joined the merchant marine fleets out of Calcutta," I countered.

"That doesn't mean I understand this business of cutting up ships. Not to mention that Calcutta is in India, over a hundred miles away, and not in Bangladesh, Captain. And neither is Pakistan."

Both Daniru and Miranda laughed out loud on the mess deck when they overheard me trying to convince him. They weren't helping my cause.

"But Kaamil, if they start that singsong local dialect when speaking English, you'll understand it so much better than I will. You must remember," I shifted my voice to a lower pitch and a heavily accented Irish brogue. "I speak an entirely different Ainglish, donae, laddie."

With a big grin, Kaamil reluctantly agreed to accompany me. "But don't blame me, Sahib," he said mimicking a native of the old British Empire, "when they best you properly in the deal."

Our first stop was in the Office of the Port Authority of Chittagong. The front counter had a bank of teller windows for conducting business. Behind were arrayed several cubicle desks, each with an industrious civil servant, bent on being busy on administrative tasks.

I rang the front desk bell and a slender man dressed in local garb, most suitable for the heat of this tropical delta, looked up, stopped his work, and came to my assistance.

I presented him with my ship's papers, my passport, and captain's license for his perusal.

"Do you have a manifest or bill of lading to declare, Captain?"

"No, not this time. I'm afraid it's off to the breaking yard. That will be my next stop."

"Aye, not an uncommon occurrence here in Chittagong." Then, reading my name again on my documents, he said, "Ah, you will wait just a minute. I have a cable for you, Captain O'Scanlon."

He disappeared behind a tall hutch with dozens of compartments, where I could see him concentrating on matching something written on a clipboard with the pigeon hole numbers.

"Yes, yes, here it is," he said, handing me an envelope.

I slid my finger along the closure flap and removed a sheet of foolscap with characteristic teletype print. It was dated two days ago and was from my grandfather.

Aye, laddie, good to hear from you. I'm doing fine, but the food here is worse than on a Russian fishing scow. I should have told you Dillon never did anyone a favor. You did what you could, but some things are beyond repair. Be sure and walk Marigold *stem to stern before you sign her over. And don't forget to look up.*

What did he mean, 'look up'?

I thanked the clerk and motioned for Tengazy to follow me. The next stop was at Sepoy Import Export, two blocks up from the quay. A dark faced man in a business suit emerged from behind a grand partner desk to greet the two of us. He listened to my business proposition for scrapping *Marigold* and then offered a suggestion.

"Captain O'Scanlon, if I might? Instead of selling her for scrap, I would be glad to broker her as 'lease as-is'. I have clients looking for vessels which still have life left in them, for making deliveries to Southeast Asian port cities with their interior connecting estuaries. I feel fairly certain I could realize a €60,000 profit per consignment, which of course I would share with you."

275

I hadn't considered this possibility. It was different from the straight partnership I had tried unsuccessfully to arrange in Dublin.

"It sounds interesting. But who would these clients be that want to lease a ship rather than simply hire a freight forwarder?"

From the look on his face, he was expecting me to be impressed with the possibility of a large return on successive leases rather than pressing him for the nature of the business being done.

"Well sir, there are people who would rather carry cargos in a vessel they control, not necessarily own, than having to consign the cargo to a middle man. The arrangement I'm offering cuts down on paperwork and expedites handling."

As attractive as the money sounded, the business plan he described bothered me. Technically I would be a blind partner, not privy to the actual nature of the ship's transactions. I'd had enough dealings wherein I didn't have full knowledge of what was in my holds.

"I thank you, sir for the suggestion, but I'm sure I want to carry on with my plan to sell her for scrap."

"Certainly, then could I give you the names of brokers who deal more directly with that?"

He gave me the names of representatives of breaking yards in the area and assured me they would be more than happy to do business with me.

The breaking yard broker I visited next was only too happy to entertain my business. The sign on his office window read Cox's Bazar Breakerage. Inside, I explained what I needed. After the agent examined my paperwork, however, I was disappointed with his proposal.

"Captain, I can offer you £150 per ton, but can only rate *Marigold* at 650 tons. You see historically, ship owners overstate the displacements of their vessels, hoping to make more money. Since I have no dry dock in which to make a more accurate estimate of your ship, this is all I can offer."

I looked at Kaamil who gave me the slightest shake of his head, which reinforced my reaction to the agent's offer. Turning to the agent, I said, "Sir, you are asking me to spot you forty tons at only fifty-five percent of the scrap iron commodity value listed in today's *International Herald Tribune*. I think that if you can't make a better offer, I'll have to go elsewhere."

"I understand, Captain, but that is the best I can do."

"In that case, come on Kaamil, we must keep looking. Good day, sir."

As we walked out, I turned to Kaamil and said in a stage whisper, "That man is clearly a cheat."

"See, Captain, you didn't need me to figure that out."

At Maritime Recycling, I received a similar runaround. This time the agent offered me credit for Marigold's full 690 displacement tons, but he'd only allow £145 per ton. I quickly came to the conclusion the only recycling he was doing was everyone else's money through his pockets. I couldn't drag Kaamil out of there quickly enough. I was sensing a clear industry conspiracy here and was starting to worry.

By the time Kaamil and I entered the fourth broker's establishment of the day, I had dozens of uncomfortable thoughts running through my head. What if the brokers were all colluding to undercut the true value of the client who had to sell? What if that rascal from Luanda, or even

Benin, had called ahead to tell them how desperate I was? Worst of all, what if Dillon O'Connor had found me out and was extracting my last pound of flesh for his benefit? I had no factual basis for my sudden worries. Nevertheless, my thoughts sent a shudder through me I was certain Kaamil could see.

Sundarbans Breakerage was in appearance much like the other agents' offices. But the people who greeted me there were dressed in traditional local style, rather than in western clothing. Noticing the receptionist's broad smile, I asked to speak with the commercial purchasing agent. She stepped behind a beaded curtain while Kaamil and I waited.

I was still peeved from my discussions with the proprietors of the previous breakerage houses and had the growing suspicion that Chittagong was a den of thieves, not too different from Cotonou, Benin.

As I drummed my fingers on the counter, a DHL delivery driver wheeled in a trolley holding boxes. He loaded them on a shelf along the wall and scanned a barcode. He loaded outgoing parcels, printed a receipt, and wheeled the trolley out to his truck.

The beaded curtain parted, drawing my interest back inside, and a middle-aged man warmly greeted me. He wore the traditional dhoti kurta with an embroidered linen shirt, which made more sense to me in Bangladesh's tropical humidity and heat than did a coat and tie.

I listened half-heartedly to what he was saying, since out of the corner of my eye, I saw what I recognized as a familiar face talking to the DHL driver in front of the shop. It was Leonard Ótubé, that two-faced scoundrel who used Miranda to best me in negotiations in the

Congo—the consignment exchange overseen not so inconspicuously by Dillon O'Connor—and who chased me on the waterfront streets of Mahajanga.

What possible explanation could there be for this scalawag to be in the same port at the same time as me unless he was still in league with Dillon O'Connor? And that could only mean O'Connor was still trying to completely ruin TC Miriam, my grandfather, and me.

My disastrous train of thought was interrupted by someone calling my name. "Captain O'Scanlon, can I help you?"

I turned my attention to the agent who was politely addressing me. "Uh, sorry, sir. I thought I saw someone." I glanced out the window again. Ótubé was gone and the DHL driver was driving off.

"Captain, O'Scanlon, is everything all right?"

"Oh, yes, I'm sorry. For the life of me, I thought I recognized someone out your window. But how could that be, this is my first visit to Chittagong? Uh, yes, sorry for the momentary lapse, I'm looking for..."

He listened attentively to my proposal and then examined the *Marigold*'s docking plans I produced for him. All the time he was looking at the blueprints, he took notes in a small ledger. His interest was more than casual. After several minutes and many notations in his little book, he said, "Do you mind if I come to the wharf and look at your *Marigold*, Mr. O'Scanlon?"

I didn't bridle at his use of "Mr." instead of "Captain." I was only too glad that he had interest enough to come look at *Marigold* firsthand. When we reached the wharf, he paced off the distance from stem to stern and annotated his findings accordingly.

"Now, if you don't mind, can you take me aboard to examine a centerline hold? I don't like to rely on Plimsoll markings for an accurate draft reference, even though your insurer uses them."

Kaamil took him aboard for his inspection while I lit up a cigar on the wharf proper. Twenty minutes later, a pleasantly animated broker and my crewman returned to the pier. Kaamil gave me an it's-okay-to-trust-this-guy look. I was impressed with the broker now. He was all business and knew exactly what he was doing.

I puffed on my cigar. "Well, how did she do, sir?"

"Captain O'Scanlon," he started. This was a good sign. He had dropped the "Mr." and reverted to "Captain."

"Everything seems to be in order. I am prepared to offer you a net of £252 per ton on 690 tons, and that is after the cost of breaking. Plus, it just so happens I have a ready client for your two main diesel engines for which I am prepared to offer an additional £17,000. That would be £181,880 contingent on your delivering her to my breaking yard, which is situated 21.6 miles up the coast on the mudflats. I would need you to arrive within five days of this agreement. I will provide you with a pilot to assist. Do we have a deal, sir?"

I stopped puffing on my cigar. I hadn't expected such an immediate, nor such a precise offer. This man's style appealed to me. Furthermore, he was piecing out the sale of my marine diesels. My good fortune was so great I almost wanted him to repeat it to make sure I'd heard him correctly. What he was offering was well more than I could have realized in a Bristol or Turkish breaking yard.

Too good to be true or not, my spirit was buoyed by a gut-feel that this man was a legitimate businessman—

somewhat of a rarity, I'd come to realize of late. Clearly, he knew that the current scrap metal quote was readily available on the daily benchmark commodities exchange listings in the international newspapers. And he certainly knew his way around vessels. Yet he didn't offer any hesitancies about *Marigold*'s dimensions. He'd done the calculations himself.

Thus reassured, I offered him my hand, which he gripped firmly and smiled.

"Yes, indeed we do have a deal. Let me get the registration papers and certifications from my cabin."

"Why don't you bring them to my office at 1:30 this afternoon? I shall be prepared to present you with a banker's draft at that time."

I was ecstatic. After being fleeced by port services in Cotonou, losing over €2M to the crooks in Luanda, and burning through much of my ready cash on the transit around the Cape, I was now more than solvent. Quickly, I ran through some mental calculations.

I would have to pay off the crew this afternoon, retaining only the original five mates to make the transit up the coast. Within seventy-two hours of saying my goodbyes, I could be back in Dublin, hoisting pints at the Temple Swan, ready to make good on the rest of my life, whatever that happened to be. At last, the dark clouds that had plagued me of late cleared.

"Before you go, sir. Would you tell me if there's a DHL office near here? I've got a package to send."

What I had in mind was to give a peek around the DHL office to see if it had really been Leonard Ótubé I had seen earlier.

"Certainly."

He gave me directions and assured me it was only a five-minute walk. I thanked him and headed out. The office was situated four blocks up from the waterfront and a few blocks over. Seeing the familiar DHL logo above the door and no sign of Leonard Ótubé, I entered.

I rang the bell only to receive the surprise of my life when the other O'Connor ne'er-do-well, Mr. M'Nasi, came from the back office.

Before I could recover from my surprise, he said in a very educated British accent, "Hello, Captain O'Scanlon. I see you've made it to Chittagong."

I'm sure my mouth stood open and made me look foolish, but I wasn't expecting this. Gathering my wits and what confidence I could muster, I replied.

"Are you following me Mr. M'Nasi, or should I say General M'Nasi, or is it Michael Nasir?"

He let out a horse laugh and held up both hands, confessing. "Guilty as charged, Johnny."

Now I was even more confused. If this man were working for O'Connor and meant me harm, or worse, he had me fooled. "But I thought..."

"I'm sure you did, Johnny. But I guess some explanation is in order."

"That would be most welcome. Just who the hell are you and what are you doing here?"

"I've been tracking that shipment you delivered to Brazzaville, Congo, and what resulted from it."

"And that has to do with Leonard Ótubé, I gather?"

"Precisely. I can't tell you why I'm looking for Leonard Ótubé, but it's important. There was something hidden in that consignment of UN supplies of yours which hasn't come to light yet."

"You mean like guns?"

"Mmm, something as dangerous, but not guns, or hardware for that matter."

O'Connor's explanation to me on the phone was ringing true. Whatever Ótubé was supposed to have gotten in that shipment wasn't there, and that's why he and O'Connor were still following me. Plus, there was the gold. M'Nasi continued. "Ótubé works for a man called Dillon O'Connor."

"I'm all too familiar with him, I'm afraid."

"When O'Connor's shipment arrived in Brazzaville, the items he was expecting weren't there. He suspects you may have them."

"But I don't have anything of his. I thought about breaking the container seals, but never had the chance."

"Johnny, it's not about anything you did or didn't do. It's about what O'Connor thinks you did. He sent Ótubé to keep tabs on you, one way or another, and to find what he's looking for."

I thought out loud. "Then that was Ótubé I saw at the Sundarbans office."

"You saw him? When?"

"Today when I was at the Sundarbans Breakerage to make arrangements to scrap *Marigold*."

"Are you sure it was him? Did he see you?"

"Of course it was him. I'll never forget his face. And I saw him in Mahajanga, too, when he chased after me. But I was able to get back aboard and leave the harbor before he caught up. He saw me just after I'd delivered another consignment arranged by Dillon O'Connor."

M'Nasi looked down and thought out loud. "Ha, that's where I lost him."

Then looking at me, he said, "Okay, here's what we'll do."

"We," I protested. "Who's 'we'? I'm sitting out here in the cold and you're saying 'we'?"

"I know it's confusing, but trust me, Johnny, I'm not with the bad guys. We've got to stop these men and you're our only connection."

My head reeled with dozens of questions, but M'Nasi was very convincing. "What do I have to do?"

"Continue with your plan to scrap the ship. That way, Ótubé won't suspect that either I or you are on to him."

"You mean, you want me to act as bait?"

"Don't worry, he won't do anything until after you scrap the ship. He knows you don't have what he's looking for. It's probably still somewhere on board. Once you transfer ownership, he has no need for you and can scour the ship on his own time."

"But he won't find the guns. I've been everywhere on that ship, and believe me, they're not there."

"Guns? Who said anything about guns?"

"Then what the hell is he after?"

"Blood diamonds, Johnny. That's how arms dealers make their payments today. They're worth ten times more than gold and are lighter and easier to conceal."

I looked at him. "But I'm telling you, even if they were postage stamps, they're not there."

"I know, but he doesn't, and neither does O'Connor. They were concealed in one of the storage bladders you delivered. I had my men pull them out while they were on the UN barge being transferred to Brazzaville."

"Your men. You have them. Who the hell are you, James Bond?"

"I told you, Johnny, I'm not one of the bad guys. That's all you need to know. Once we catch him inside the ship, tearing it apart for the diamonds, we'll take him. The last thing we need to find are his connections in this part of the world that link him to Dillon O'Connor. Once we have that, we'll take in the whole lot of them."

I looked at him. As incredulous as his story sounded, it was plausible, and he seemed to be on the up and up. He'd said nothing about Pop's gold and I wasn't going to mention it. I'd play along with his scenario and then be rid of the lot of them: O'Connor, Ótubé, and M'Nasi, whoever the hell he was.

MIRANDA GLADLY WORKED with our recent crewmen to book flights home or to a destination that promised employment, their choice. She lay on a big farewell dinner that night as we tried unsuccessfully to empty the pantry. After dinner, I had her move the rest of her personal possessions to my cabin. There was no sense in making a pretense to any other arrangements at this point.

I awoke the next morning at first light. Miranda was still sound asleep next to me. Seeing no need to rouse her, I dressed and slipped silently from the cabin and went to the seaside bridge wing to take in the sea air. Though greeted by the unpleasant smells of an overcrowded, overused port city, I was exhilarated. The crew's celebration last night, the extraordinary love making with Miranda, and the prospects of a financially sound future offset my bittersweet decision to scrap *Marigold*. And one of the three villains, Mr. M'Nasi, who had haunted me for the last two months, was now no longer a concern. Things were looking up. It was time to make a change in my life.

285

WITH DANIRU ON the bridge, Kaamil in the engine room, and Chanel and Waajid on the main deck to handle lines, I welcomed aboard the Sundarbans pilot to the bridge. I backed *Marigold*, for the last time, clear of the wharf. Once fair in the Karnafuli River, I headed south and then northwest, following the coastline a scant few miles offshore. The pilot pointed out the charted landmarks as we made our way up the shallow coastal stretch.

With two hours left before I judged we'd reach the mudflats where the breaking yard was situated, I decided to make one last nostalgic tour of my home for the past two decades. The warning in my grandfather's telegram, "Be sure and walk her stem to stern before you sign her over... and don't forget to look up," rang in my head. He was telling me something...of course! He was telling me where the gold was hidden. That had to be it.

I strode the weather deck and stared down through the open hatches into each hold. There was no need to drop down to inspect them. The brilliant overhead sun shone into every crevice. They were empty.

The large engine room ventilation exhaust funnel beckoned to me from just forward of the fantail. Right beside the funnel was the watertight door that led down to the throbbing bowels of the engine room.

This was a part of the ship I hadn't visited since the night of the engine repairs in the storm after leaving Funchal. When I stepped through that door, I was greeted by the comforting, familiar sound of diesel engine pistons straining to produce power and the pervasive odor of diesel vapors.

I descended three stories, past the cargo hoist, to the lower engine platform. The diesels continued throaty noises in their last efforts of service to me and *Marigold*. At the very least, these engines would have a little more life. I wondered what adventures they would take another vessel on, and for how long.

I shook my head at the distraction; I needed to check every conceivable place Grandfather might have stashed the gold.

In the forward corner of the engineering work space, right beside the foul smelling water closet, was a small berthing space. It had once been the auxiliary sleeping cubicle for the engineer officer to use when workload required his constant presence.

I placed my hand on the doorknob and hesitated. I was reluctant to intrude on the memories that might lay on the other side, reminders of Grandfather's tales of working in these spaces when he first started TC Miriam. Then, remembering my purpose, I shook off my reluctance and entered. I stood there to let my eyes adjust.

My first impression was that it was obvious from the layered dust that this bunk room hadn't been used for years. I couldn't make out the interior, so I reached along the wall and found the light switch. I took a few steps over to the bunk bed frames and sat on the lower bunk, the same one Grandfather probably used many years before. How many times had he worked down here and then laid his head down for a nap before returning to his demanding duties?

I leaned back and laid my head at one end of the bare mattress, disregarding the exposed ticking along the seams. I looked up at the interlaced network of springs on the underside of the bunk above. There, on the end cross brace, where someone's head would have rested, an L and an S were etched in the rusting support. Larry Shaughnessy. My grandfather's initials could be seen only if one were lying fully flat on his back. I let my eyes wander, scanning what my grandfather had looked at for so many years.

At the foot of the bunk, on the underside support frame of the bunk above, were a series of dull metal tubes about an inch in diameter. Most were about six inches long, a few others nearer to a foot in length, and three were half again as long. The tubes were tack welded to the underside structure of the metal frame, well out of sight from anyone except for the lower bunk's occupant.

Look up.

Fumbling to open one, I realized each tube had a threaded closure cap on one end. It took me a couple of minutes, but I finally managed to loosen one corroded cap, hard fast after years of disuse. Inside the tube I saw something shiny. I worked with my finger, pried at it, and finally extracted a gold coin.

A Krugerrand.

Using the small torch I always carried, I could see something else shiny in the tube. Another Krugerrand?

From an old engineer's toolbox, I grabbed a crowbar. A few hard jerks easily broke the spot welds and I pried the tube from the structure. Working feverishly now, I jimmied the other tubes from their hiding place. When all was said and done, I dislodged 1,279 one-ounce coins, just shy of eighty pounds. Having read the newspaper for commodity values in preparation for dealing with the ship breakers, I knew gold was valued at $1,650 an ounce. This translated to a cache worth around $2,110,350.

Holy shit.

This was Grandfather's stash that O'Connor had been so desperate to find that he financed my trip and put his loyal crewmen on board to look for it. But the incident with Tasmoon-Shamlyn brought their dealings to light. My exiling them from the ship left me with only O'Connor's other personally placed agent provocateurs to deal with, M'Nasi and Ótubé. Since Mr. M'Nasi revealed himself to be on my side, Leonard Ótubé was the only remaining hurdle for me to clear to secure my grandfather's legacy, rightfully obtained or not.

One thing for sure, O'Connor didn't know I now had the gold. He still thought it was hidden aboard *Marigold*. I had to keep him thinking that to keep him out of my way. With M'Nasi's information, I had the goods on Dillon, for a change. When I got back, I'd go to the authorities with what I knew about the blood diamonds and the names of O'Connor's cronies.

But what if something happened to me and I didn't get back? I couldn't let him get away with it.

I thought for a minute and hit on an idea to write a letter to my solicitor in Dublin, telling him what I knew. I'd mail it sealed in an envelope to be opened in the event of my demise. That way, Pop would be protected regardless of what might happen to me.

But right now, I had a more pressing matter. I looked at the pile of coins on the mattress and wondered how was I going to get them off the ship. I couldn't let their existence be known. Gold attracted unwanted attention, especially with the likes of Ótubé lurking in the area. One thing was for certain, I had to avoid him at all costs.

I heard the ship's engines slow. *Marigold* was approaching the breaking yard. I had to get these coins off the ship without O'Connor's agent finding out. I started to put the coins into two leather satchels I'd found on a workbench, but they were too flimsy. Then I saw a metal transport case used to carry precision tools.

It was lined with cushioning foam to prevent damage to the delicate instruments it was designed for. This was perfect to keep the coin tubes from rattling and drawing attention. I snugged the coin-laden tubes into the foam and shut the lid. Lying on the workbench were some lock-wire pliers and a roll of wire used to securely fasten valve hand wheels. Quickly I lock-wired the clasps on the case shut and crimped the wire ends with lead seals.

The transfer case was heavy. A firefighting crash cart in one corner of the engine room was what I needed to get the gold-laden case to the electric equipment hoist and up to the weather deck. Once there, I wheeled it forward to the bridge. I stowed the crash cart in my sea cabin and returned to the bridge wing.

Imagining several sets of eyes looking at me as if to wonder what I'd been up to, I stood behind the Sundarbans pilot and Daniru and tried to calm my breathing. The last thing I wanted was to answer any question as to where I'd been. A fortune in gold lay not thirty feet away, and I fought to keep my anxiety in check.

More pressing questions popped into my head. How was I going to get the gold out of here without tipping off Dillon O'Connor, whom I suspected would know of my presence as soon as Leonard Ótubé saw me again? How was I going to lug an eighty-pound tool chest off the ship, out of Chittagong, and onto a plane for home?

As I pondered, I noticed the Sundarbans logo on the pilot's shirt. It dawned on me that we all—crew, pilot, and the gold—had to somehow get back to the breakerage office with our personal baggage before we could leave the city. However, that's where I'd seen Leonard Ótubé talking with the DHL driver.

If Ótubé saw me lugging a heavy chest, then O'Connor would know I had the gold. Plus, O'Connor could easily find out how much I'd sold *Marigold* for, which gave him reason enough to find me, and now the gold.

The entire process took me only an instant to imagine. I began to sweat, unable to determine my next course of action. By process of elimination, O'Connor had to know the gold was on board and he no longer needed me or Grandfather. He'd let the breaking yard tear apart *Marigold* piece by piece and have his agent on hand to retrieve his prize.

Marigold slowed as she rode up the shallow bank of the breaking yard's mudflats. Eighty yards onto the mudflats, her keel scraped her to a stop, fast aground. She was high and dry from her stem to her stern. The trusty diesel engines rumbled to a halt for the last time. My journey was over, but not my travail.

I stood in my private quandary, waiting. Finally, I said, "Daniru, tell Kaamil, Waajid, and Chenal to meet me and Miranda at the head of the mudflats in ten minutes."

"Aye, aye, Captain."

Captain. It would be hard not being called that again.

"Mr. O'Scanlon…"

I was aware the Sundarbans pilot was saying something to me. It was "Mr." now, and in a few days, *Marigold* would no longer resemble a ship. She would be a disintegrated scrap heap, just like the other hulks that lay abeam of her on the mudflats, all in various stages of disarticulation from their recognizable features as ocean-going vessels.

The sudden stillness from the cessation of ship's machinery was replaced by sounds outside the pilot house. I heard the sing-song chants of the work force's labored songs, men going about the business of torch cutting, power sawing, jack hammering, and banging to turn the vessels rowed up along miles of mudflats into skeletal shells, shadows of their former glory.

I couldn't bring myself to feel sad at imagining what would befall *Marigold*. Instead I was happy. In the strong box in my sea cabin was the real epitaph for TC Miriam, for me, and for Miranda.

For too long I'd kept anything except being captain of my vessel at bay, rationalizing that I didn't have the financial independence I thought I'd need to consider anyone else. But now it was time to openly express to her, and demonstrate to others, the feelings I had for too long kept locked up inside. First, however, I had to get us and the gold off the ship and out of Bangladesh.

"Mr. O'Scanlon."

"Uh, yes, I'm sorry. Go ahead."

"Mr. O'Scanlon, in about four months you will receive a final letter from Sundarbans. By then, we will have broken down most of the large pieces of metal from the vessel and the final weight will be known. Any overage we obtain from that will require us to compensate you at the same rate as we agreed in our contract. We will send you a bank draft for any such overage. Would you confirm the address where we can reach you?"

"Thank you, sir. That is most fair. I will give you that address back at your office."

"Of course, sir."

Miranda joined us on the bridge. I turned to her.

"Miranda, we need to meet up with Chenal, Waajid, and Kaamil. We had best depart before the cutting torch gets too close. Daniru, could you help me get the cart in my cabin down to the mudflats? Be careful, it's heavy."

Turning to the pilot I said, "You don't mind, do you? It's just personal mementos I found on my last walk through of the ship."

"Of course, sir, no problem."

The remaining three members of the crew waited for us on the main deck. Seeing my struggle with the weight, Waajid helped Daniru lower the crash cart and its sealed tool chest to the mudflats below.

As we walked on the plywood planks laid down on the flats for our convenience, Miranda said, "For being so nostalgic about this old girl, you seem to be in a hurry to get off of her. Why the rush?"

I put my finger to my lips. For the moment, that seemed to mollify her curiosity. As I walked astern of *Marigold* for the last time and looked up at the transom nameplate, I saw again where bullet strikes had chipped away at the letters. Her name now read *Mar go*.

I smiled and said, "Let's go, Miranda. We have a plane to catch."

THE PILOT GAVE us a ride back down the coast—the five of us, our luggage, and the strong box—to the Sundarbans office. All during the fifty-minute drive, I wondered how I'd avoid Leonard Ótubé.

I feared such an encounter for two reasons. First, Miranda hadn't seen him yesterday when I saw him outside the office, and I didn't want her to have to relive the unpleasantness of her experience in the Congo. Just as importantly, if he were there again, this was beyond coincidence. He could only be here for one thing: to extract the proceeds from the scrap sale of *Marigold* and recover the missing gold that O'Connor was more than certain Grandfather had hidden on board. This final act of revenge would completely ruin Pop's as well as my ' future.

As we rounded the road onto the street fronting the office, there was a black Land Rover closing us from the opposite direction. Through its windshield I could see that Leonard Ótubé was in the passenger seat. Driving the car, and thus closer to me, was Mr. M'Nasi.

But as soon as the faces registered, the SUV passed by, driver's side to our van. M'Nasi looked directly at me, smiled, and put one finger to his lips as if to say, "Shhh."

The Land Rover continued on and was quickly gone in the direction from which we had just come. From the way he suddenly increased speed, he was spiriting Leonard Ótubé away from the Sundarbans office.

Relieved at not having to face Ótubé again, I ushered my crew from the van and into Sunderbans. I couldn't sign the final paperwork with the agent quickly enough.

Miranda gave Daniru, Kaamil, and Waajid hugs and I shook their hands saying goodbye. I gave each of them an envelope containing their final salaries and bonuses, plus a little extra. Taped on the inside of each envelope was a Krugerrand, which I was certain would warm their hearts when they found it later. I wished them Godspeed. The men disappeared up the street, suitcases in hand, for the travel agency.

I told Miranda I had something to finish with the agent and asked her to ring us up a cab. While she busied herself with this, I set about taking care of the strong box. I hurriedly plastered a customs declaration and a Handle with Care sticker on it, then strapped it with metal bands in both directions for strength as well as security.

My experience with parcel freight express delivery was that if the shipper's business—in this case TC Miriam— were legitimate and the declared contents—machine tools—seemed plausible for the container and fit the sender's business profile, no suspicions would be raised by customs. I had never received or sent a package this way to later discover customs officials had bothered to inspect the contents. As long as there was nothing for the drug/explosive dog to alert on, hiding the gold in plain sight seemed the best course of action.

I asked the Sundarbans proprietor to personally see to it that it was sent via secure air freight, signature receipt required, via three-day delivery service to the TC Miriam office in Dublin. That would give Miranda and me plenty of time to make it back to accept delivery.

The agent happily agreed. When he lifted the case, he asked, "What's in here, keel ballast?"

I laughed and replied. "No, they're sentimental mementoes of my grandfather's, tools and instruments he used during his sea-going career."

Letting this out of my sight was a big risk, but I had no choice. The bulk would slow me down. And I wasn't sure Ótubé wouldn't reappear. At least this way, all he'd find was an old strong box labeled machine parts.

Besides, he wouldn't be looking for what I might be carrying. It was me and access to my bank account they'd be after, like the Luanda bank manager and his crooked cop brother-in-law.

BY LATE EVENING, Miranda and I were at the airport hotel in Delhi. The next day we'd fly nonstop to London.

"Will you now tell me why you wanted to get out of Chittagong so quickly and why you felt it necessary to buy first class tickets? And for heaven's sake, what was so important to lug off the ship and send home via sealed courier?"

I pulled her to me and took a single Krugerrand from my pocket. I laced it through my fingers the way magicians did, letting the overhead light glint off the coin.

She gasped. "Where'd you get that?"

"It was in tubes welded into the engineer's bunk in the number one engine room for all these years."

"How did it get there?"

I took small bottles of scotch from the suite's minibar and poured us a drink. I told her the stories my grandfather had related—stories about running contraband for the IRA in the 60s and 70s.

"How many are there?"

"Let's just say, my dear, you, me and my grandfather won't have to worry about money for a long while."

"Explain this to me. If your grandfather knew the gold was there, why didn't he tell you about it sooner? It was foolish of him to leave a fortune like that hidden aboard *Marigold* all this time."

Her question was a valid one, and I knew that only a full explanation would satisfy her.

"You see dear, there was a side to my Grandfather I haven't told you. It seems in his early days, when I was too young to sail with him, times were lean. To make ends meet, he and some of the other sea captains were approached by Dillon O'Connor to run shipments, some of which were, shall I say, of a dubious nature. It turns out the IRA was using those skippers through Dillon O'Connor as a front to move contraband. The transactions were paid for in Krugerrands, since gold wasn't traceable.

"It turned out that O'Connor wasn't that timely in paying his skippers. So several of them started skimming Krugerrands, holding back what they figured was rightfully theirs.

"O'Connor was never able to determine exactly who or how much he was losing, other than his profits weren't what they should have been. And sometime during one of these IRA episodes, my parents became involved and were killed up on the border with Northern Ireland. Grandfather never talked about it, and from what little I remember, it was near my fifth birthday. Grandmother was more than upset with him. The reasons were never explained to me. Grandfather simply never brought it up, most likely out of deep-seated guilt.

"By the time Grandmother passed away three years ago, for reasons known only to Pop, he chose not to mention it or the gold, that is, until he sent that message saying that he'd hidden the gold somewhere on board *Marigold* because Dillon O'Connor would never have thought to look for it there.

"A few months ago, as I was trying to figure out a way to save TC Miriam and provide a sound financial future for Grandfather, I advertised for partners to invest in the company. O'Connor read the ad and invited me to Wexford to discuss a partnership. But when I told him I was determined to sell *Marigold* instead, he offered to pay for the trip by consigning me the shipment from Benin to Congo, Brazzaville."

Miranda looked up at me. I wasn't able to tell if she believed all or any part of the story, but she knew she wasn't going to get any further from me.

"I think we need to call your grandfather. If nothing else to tell him we're safe and that you've found his pot of gold."

"I don't think…"

"Eh, don't give me excuses, Johnny O'Scanlon. If you've a decent bone in your body, that's what you'll do."

I knew by now not to argue with Miranda when she got strong-headed. And while I dialed the number, she kept poking my arm to tell me to get a move on.

"Shh, stop it, it's ringing. Hello." It was the receptionist at the nursing home. I gave her my name and asked her to bring Pop to the phone. With my hand over the receiver I said to Miranda, "They're at lunch. She's getting him."

"Pop, yeah it's me, Johnny."

"Where are you, laddie? You're not in trouble, are you?"

"No, Pop, I'm on my way home. I'll be there by this time tomorrow. Just wanted to let you know we're fine."

"Who's we?"

"Me and Miranda, I'll explain tomorrow. Anyway, that stuff you told me to look for? Well, I found it."

"And you got it all? O'Connor didn't get his thievin' mitts on it?"

"Yep, I got it all."

"I'm sorry I put you through all that, Johnny. I probably should have brought you in on it sooner, but I didn't want to give O'Connor a chance to get hold of it. He'd already taken too much from me with his half-baked scheme that got your mom and dad killed thirty years ago."

"What are you saying, Pop? I've never heard you speak of this before."

"Flaherty and his wife were supposed to be the couriers that night. But O'Connor said they had to back out. He asked if your folks could substitute. All they had to do was cross into Belfast, retrieve an envelope, and come back across the border. But the British got wind of the scheme, I don't know how, and as they were making a run for it in the car, they opened fire. O'Connor said there wasn't anything he could do from our side."

"Why wasn't he using someone else with more experience?"

"O'Connor said they needed two faces who'd not be recognized. Your folks had never been there and he had dummied up the proper passports and visas. O'Connor told me later that the British had a spy on our side that tipped them off."

I was quiet; I needed time to process this.

"Johnny, I know it's hard news to take, but keeping it from you was for your own good. I didn't want to raise you with all the heartache and rancor Miriam and I had to face. You came out okay, laddie. I just thought I needed to tell you, that's all."

I wasn't mad, or hurt, or disillusioned. After all, I had never really known my parents, so I felt no grief. Pop was still my Pop. In a way, I was relieved to have filled in the missing pieces of my life.

"That's okay, Pop. I understand. Well, we'll be there

soon enough in person, so I'll let you get back to your lunch."

"That's fine, laddie."

"Love you, Pop." I hung up the phone.

THE NEXT MORNING, I woke Miranda with a hug and a kiss. "Let's go Miranda, get a shake on."

"Where are we going?" she mumbled, trying to wake.

"Someplace where I have a fireplace to tend and salmon to catch, my dear."

Epilogue

ONE HUNDRED AND thirty-two days later, I received two letters forwarded from my Dublin Bank to me at the Scottish Highlands Lodge where Miranda and I had set up temporary residence. One letter had the address I left behind with Sundarbans:

Johnny O'Scanlon
c/o TC Miriam
138 Bayswater Rd
London, UK
W2 4HP

It contained a check and a short note written on Sundarbans Breakerage letterhead.

"Mr. O'Scanlon. Per our agreement, final dispensation has been made in the matter of break and scrap of MV *Marigold*. An additional sum of £10,291 has resulted from the disposition of an additional 41 tons. Respectfully, R.D. Binjonni."

"Well, what do you know? It's from Sundarbans, Miranda. It seems *Marigold* fetched an additional forty-one tons. I guess there are a few honest men left in the world."

"What are we going to do with it?" Miranda asked.

"I guess I'll deposit it. We don't need it at the moment."

She snuggled closer. "At least not for a little while. Why don't you send it to Rajip Tasmoon-Shamlyn's family? That would be a good gesture, seeing as how he didn't sign up for nor deserve what happened to him."

I kissed her. "I'll do it. I'll send a note to my solicitor this afternoon."

While I held her, happier than I had any right to be, I reflected on what had happened only six months earlier. All of the loose ends were coming together—except one. "Miranda, dear."

"Mmm," she purred.

"What did you say, or rather, what did you do with Leonard Ótubé when we offloaded that UN consignment in the Congo River? Remember, you insisted I go topside and leave the two of you alone."

She unslung her arm from across my chest and pushed herself upright on the sofa. She reached for her highball glass and took a sip. "If you must know, Johnny…"

"Of course I must know. I've been worried sick ever since then. I've had to walk on eggshells to avoid the topic. I think it's time you tell me. Whatever it is, I can handle it. I won't think less of you."

She cocked her head and scowled. "You think I had sex with him, don't you?"

"Well, the thought has been on my mind."

"Just so you know, I didn't."

"So what did you tell him that made him agree to my terms in the negotiation?"

"Remember one time I told you about the men in my village where I grew up, how they were in an organization, L'Azendia?"

"Yeah, and I also remember your telling me all the things the women had to do to get along in your village."

"I grew up watching the village women become puppets to the men. They did it because they were afraid of them and needed them for money, for protection, and

302

for their own survival. I vowed when I left there, I'd never be afraid of men like them. So, I became very strong-willed. I watched my brothers, uncles, and the neighbor-hood men, and I learned from them how to intimidate."

"You intimidated Leonard Ótubé? How the hell'd you do that?"

"I told him my uncle was the head of L'Azendia and if he didn't do exactly as you wanted, I'd have my uncle find him and make him wish he, and his entire organi-zation, had never been born. My uncle would destroy his business and divest all of his assets to charities around the world so they could never use them again."

I looked at her with amazement. "You said all that? Could you even do any of what you said?"

She looked at me and smiled.

"It matters not whether I could or couldn't carry out any of those threats. What matters is that Leonard Ótubé thought I could."

"Humph. Well, thank goodness you did." I squeezed her tightly and kissed her. "Oh, and remind me to never get on your bad side."

"One good thing, Johnny. I won't ever have to see the likes of Leonard Ótubé again."

Her saying his name reminded me, she'd never seen Ótubé at the Sundarbans office in Chittagong and I hadn't told her. I debated whether or not to tell her now. If I did, she'd worry about his suddenly reappearing again.

More importantly, she'd worry that I hadn't told her everything. I couldn't live with myself if I started our marriage off withholding something as important as this.

"Miranda ..." I confessed to having seen Ótubé when he chased after me in Madagascar, again when I first set foot in the Sundarbans office in Chittagong, and finally as we were arriving at the Sundarbans office the next day. I also mentioned the signal M'Nasi gave me as he drove past us with Ótubé as his passenger outside the Sundarbans office after leaving *Marigold*.

Miranda cleared her throat to collect herself. "Johnny, what did M'Nasi mean by that?"

"Honestly, I think Mr. M'Nasi—or Michael Nasir, as Peter Blaauw knew him—I think he was cautioning me not to draw attention to them. Right now, I think I've had M'Nasi all wrong."

"How could that be? He's the one Dillon O'Connor had sell you that bogus cargo in Cotonou."

She had me again. In not telling her about Ótubé, I had omitted telling her of my first Chittagong encounter with M'Nasi. I started with my first impressions from meeting him in Cotonou, the discovery of the internet article with him dressed as a military man advising the president of Niger, and then running into him in the DHL office in Chittagong.

"Initially, I thought O'Connor had forced me to deal with M'Nasi and Ótubé as part of the consignment deal so he could keep tabs on his investment. When I questioned why building supplies were so valuable, I thought these two were part of a network involved in contraband headed by O'Connor. When Peter Blaauw in Cape Town started telling me about rumors he'd heard of M'Nasi's arms dealings, I thought my suspicions were confirmed.

"But Peter never found any discrepancies between M'Nasi's declared manifests and the inspected goods he shipped through Cape Town. I thought I had carried contraband from Cotonou to Congo, but I had no proof."

"So, what was M'Nasi's, or Nasir's role?"

"I don't know, Miranda. I'm not sure I'll ever know for certain. But M'Nasi did tell me he's been tracking O'Connor's and Ótubé's contraband activities all over Africa for a long time."

"You mean we were carrying guns?"

I thought about revealing M'Nasi's story about the blood diamonds, but I was already stretching her sense of the believable.

"No, quite to the contrary. I'm not sure who M'Nasi works for, but evidently he was telling me the truth when he said he was tracking down people like O'Connor and Ótubé to get to the heart of their finances. Once he finds who's behind it all, he'll shut them all down and send them to jail."

"Does he work for the police?"

"I don't think so. If he were with the police or Interpol, he would have told me. More than likely, he works for a government agency such as France's DGSE or Israel's Mossad, organizations who prosecute international terrorists, arms dealers, and their financiers."

She gasped. "And these men were on *Marigold*! In my galley!" Her hand trembled as she brought it to her mouth.

I put my arm around her and held her close. "It's okay, Miranda. It's over now. Whoever these bad men are, M'Nasi assured me they'd never be able to harm us. Besides, we always have your uncle to go after them if M'Nasi was lying."

Her sniffles sputtered as she tried to laugh.

I reached for my drink and noticed the other letter still lay there, unopened on the table. It was addressed to me from my bank. It contained a sheet of bank letterhead and a newspaper clipping from a ten-day old *International Herald Tribune* article. I read the clipping headline and the short announcement.

"Wexford Man Found Dead—Police Investigate. Long time Wexford resident, Mr. Dillon H. O'Connor, was found dead under what police said were suspicious circumstances. His body was discovered in his home by DS Scarborough of the Wexford police at...."

I put the clipping aside, curious as to why my bank would be forwarding me such a story, though I wasn't displeased with the report. The other sheet in the envelope was also on bank letterhead, but the handwriting was scratchy, similar to Pop's.

I thought you might be interested in this newspaper article that happened to catch my eye. Dillon told me a fortnight ago that he owed you this.

Taped to the bottom of the letter was a bank deposit slip to my account for the amount of €1,917,539.

"Well, Miranda my love, will you look at this?"

Author's Note

Having always been an avid reader, I felt the urge to try my hand at writing when I retired. My initial impulse was, "How hard can it be?" The good engineer that I am, I studied. I reread classics of modern literature, Crane, Fitzgerald, Hemingway, Twain, and King and read librarian-suggested literary novels that I normally wouldn't have bothered with. Last, I studied how-to-write books recommended by the Bettendorf Library staff.

I wish to thank my colleagues at the Midwest Writing Center (MWC) in Rock Island and Writers on the Avenue (WOTA) in Muscatine who offered me feedback during biweekly sessions with fledgling and established local writers. They were encouraging, indulgent, and sometimes daunting in their critiques of my flash pieces, short stories, poetry, and excerpts of longer works.

I particularly want to thank my beta readers who patiently read drafts: Mary Davidsaver, Jen Wieland, Terry Giglio Voss, Dan Eigenberg, Carly Dawson, Wayne Sapp, and above all my wife, Kathy. Their honest criticism provided me a thick skin and a willingness to work harder at getting my literary message across to the reader.

I especially give thanks to Misty Urban, Managing Editor of Pearl City Press, who taught me that the real work in writing only starts with typing 'The End.' Her editing improved this novel immensely.

About the Author

Dan Moore is a graduate of Duke University and a retired US Navy captain. He has published nonfiction in the *Naval War College Review*, award-winning short stories with the Midwest Writing Center, short stories and poetry in anthologies for Writers on the Avenue, and poetry in Iowa Poetry Association's *Lyrical Iowa*. His submarine novel *Westpac* was featured on the WVIK 90.3 FM radio program "Scribbles." He lives with his wife in Davenport, Iowa. *The Last Voyage of the Marigold* is his first published novel.

Made in the USA
Monee, IL
28 March 2022

93668550R00177